Wishing You Harm

A Brooke Roberts Mystery

Nancy Labs

PARAMETER
PUBLISHING
Doylestown, PA

Library of Congress Control Number: 2021907425

ISBN: 978-1-944280-02-4
ISBN (ebook): 978-1-944280-03-1

Printed in the United States of America

 Doylestown, PA   2021

Cover notes:

Ouroboros: From *Snake Mix* font, a freeware font from Jordi Manero Pascual (*Woodcutter,* www.woodcutter.es) 2016

Background map (section): Ortelius World Map—*Typvs Orbis Terrarvm,* 1570, Public Domain in the U.S.; (This work is in the public domain in the United States because it was published (or registered with the U.S. Copyright Office) before January 1, 1926.) Library of Congress, Geography and Map Division.

Photo: Fall Sunset, Photo by Wayne Labs

Wishing You Harm

Prologue

Early Spring

S he'd stolen before. Plenty of times. She was an elite operative who served her clients well.

This theft had seemed no different than the others. The medallion was beautiful. Priceless. And deadly, as she'd come to realize.

She'd seen firsthand the harm done by the madman who'd possessed it, and she could attest to the power the object bestowed. The rituals she'd witnessed in that Long Island mansion had frightened her in ways she'd never been frightened before, and now, all she wanted was to be rid of the thing. Just a few more miles and it would be out of her life forever.

She approached the drop-off site—a strip mall parking lot where her client's lackey waited. She was about to put on her turn signals when her well-honed instincts shrieked a warning. She'd deliver the medallion, and then what? The muzzle of a gun to her back? Orders to keep her mouth shut as she got into a waiting SUV? And after that?

She glanced in the rearview mirror. No one appeared to be trailing her.

She continued past the strip mall. There was a Salvation Army drop box at the edge of town. A quick stop and the medallion passed through the slot. Soon it would have a new owner.

Someone who knew nothing of its storied past. Someone who regarded it as a cheap trinket to be tossed in a jewelry box and forgotten.

She got back on the road and headed south. No one had seen her, so why did she feel afraid?

One

Mid September – Six Months Later

Brooke stared at the shards of glass strewn across the basement floor. She'd spent the day at a retrospective celebrating her late husband's life and work. She'd returned home from the art gallery, overwhelmed and drained and desperately sad, only to find all this waiting for her.

The young cop nodded toward the broken window. "This is how the intruder broke in. If you've got some plywood, I'll board it up for you. It's getting dark and you'll want to keep the critters out."

She nodded her thanks and followed Detective Jason Radley up the stairs to the living room where a female officer snapped pictures and a third person dusted for prints. The room was in chaos as was the rest of the house. Closets torn apart. Drawers emptied. Upholstery slashed.

"My husband died two months ago," Brooke stammered. "A hiking accident. Today was a retrospective to honor him." She looked around in dismay. "His name was Karl Erikson. I kept my last name—Roberts—for professional reasons."

"Thanks for clarifying. Is there somewhere we can talk?"

She led Detective Radley to the kitchen. It was a mess, but at least the chairs were intact, unlike some of the furniture in the living room. She glanced at the bottles and cans littering the counters. The silverware dumped on the floor. The broken dishes and shattered bowls. Why would a thief create all this chaos?

Radley got a notepad from his pocket. "I'll start with a routine question. Is there anyone who wishes you harm?"

The question struck her as odd. "Someone did this, so of course someone wished me harm."

"What I'm trying to determine is if the perpetrator is someone you know. More specifically, someone who knew you'd be away this afternoon."

She turned the question over in her mind. Until today, she hadn't left the house since Karl died. Not since her world fell apart. Not since pain and grief and loneliness moved in to take his place.

"I can't imagine anyone I know doing this."

"Did you notice anything missing?"

She shook her head.

"How about jewelry?"

She thought of the pieces Karl had given her. Amber, turquoise, and amethyst set in silver. Diamonds, rubies, and sapphires that belonged to his mother. "I saw better pieces mixed in with the costume junk on the bedroom floor," she said. "It's odd that the thief left them behind."

"Odd indeed. And your computers? Anything amiss?"

"I haven't checked, but I back up all my work."

"And what kind of work do you do?"

"Editing. Desktop publishing. In the afternoons I paint in the studio above the barn."

At the mention of the studio, a fresh wave of grief washed over her. "What I mean is I used to paint. I haven't since Karl died. We're both artists. That is to say, he was. I am."

"And the studio? I assume it was vandalized as well?"

She glanced toward the barn across the driveway. If any spot on earth could be considered a sanctuary—a place of peace in a world gone mad—it was the second-floor studio she and Karl had shared. She thought of the paintings he'd left unfinished: *River in Winter. Sailboats at Dusk. Farmhouse in the Mist.*

Each in Karl's unique style. Enough reality to let you recognize the subject. Enough abstraction to make you see it in a whole new way.

"I haven't been up there since his death. I unlocked the door when students stopped by to pick up their work, but I didn't join them."

"I know this is difficult," the detective said, "but when we're finished here, we'll need to check it out."

"I understand. Just don't ask me to go up there with you."

He shifted in his seat and nodded in the direction of the living room. "The slashed upholstery suggests that the thief was searching for something he or she knew was hidden in the house. Gold. Cash. Thumb drives. That sort of thing."

"I've got nothing to hide."

"And your late husband? Might he have had something to hide?"

The question stopped her. Karl hadn't been himself in the months leading up to the hiking accident that took his life. He'd been silent. Moody. And oddly religious. What had come over him? Was he hiding something? A secret life separate from the one they shared? It was a question that had kept her awake at night.

"If my husband had something to hide, I was unaware of it."

"Fair enough. Have you contacted your insurance company?"

She shook her head.

"You'll want to do that right away. But keep in mind that this is a crime scene and we can't have people tromping around the place touching the evidence."

"For how long?"

"We should have things wrapped up by tomorrow afternoon."

He got to his feet and tucked the notepad into a pocket. "You'll need to stay somewhere overnight. Same reason—we don't want the evidence disturbed. Your insurance company will most likely reimburse you for a hotel room."

"My uncle offered to let me stay with him."

"Terrific. Nice to have family nearby." Detective Radley walked over to the counter and glanced out the window. "It sure is lonely back here in these woods. I'll bet it gets spooky at night."

"I'm used to it. Or at least I was until…"

Her voice trailed off. It was mid-September. The days were getting shorter. The nights longer. Karl was gone and now this. Would she ever feel safe again?

"I'll need a phone number where we can reach you," the detective said. "And the keys to the studio."

She gave him the keys and waited while he entered her cell number into his phone. That completed, Jason Radley left her at the table and went off to inspect the studio above the barn.

▼ ▼ ▼

Elena Voss glanced out the window. At 30,000 feet the flight was smooth with little in the way of turbulence. So what could explain this odd feeling? It wasn't a premonition exactly. More of a nagging sensation that something important had been left undone.

But what?

She'd sent the contracts to the network honchos. Tomorrow they'd firm up the details and in the evening she'd join her colleagues for a cocktail party to celebrate the upcoming season of *The Unveiling*, her highly successful cable documentary series.

Her audience was eagerly awaiting the next revelations. Esoteric doctrines. Hidden knowledge. Ancient wisdom simplified and packaged for mass consumption. Everything was going as planned. The timing. The pacing. The drip, drip, drip of challenges to accepted orthodoxy. The public mind bending to her will.

So why was every nerve in her body set on edge? Every muscle tense? Why was she—Elena Voss—so afraid?

Upon landing, she checked her messages. Yes! Her lackeys had reported in. She returned the call, anxious to hear news of their success.

She pressed through the crowds in LAX, her carry-on bag bumping against her hip as she hurried toward baggage claim. And then the world seemed to go dark, and she stopped, barely able to breathe let alone speak. "What do you mean, you didn't get there in time?" She listened to their answer. "Someone else was at the house ahead of you? Who?"

The explanations began, but she cut them off. "How could you let this happen? You're professionals."

A wave of nausea swept over her. "Fools!" she shrieked into the phone. "I'll make you pay for this!"

She hung up, her head reeling.

Six months earlier the object had slipped through Elena's fingers, and the operative who'd dared to betray her trust had paid for her duplicity with her life. And now, just when Elena was sure the medallion was hers for the taking, it had slipped through her fingers yet again.

Two

Brooke's Uncle Nelson pointed at the scrambled eggs and toast on her plate. "You've barely eaten, my dear. You need to keep up your strength."

She obliged him by taking a small bite and washing it down with lukewarm coffee.

Her phone rang and when she saw that the caller was Detective Radley, she excused herself and went out to the living room. Radley informed her that there'd been no sign of a break-in at the studio above the barn, and then he asked her to meet him and another detective at the house at 9:30 to wrap things up.

The call concluded, she returned to the table and resumed picking at her food.

Her 82-year-old uncle put down his crossword puzzle and removed his reading glasses, an indication that whatever he was about to say was important. "You need a home security system," he announced. "Get estimates, and when you've made a selection, we'll have it installed. Don't hold back. I want you to have the best protection money can buy."

"Why bother?" she asked. "The house will be on the market soon. And besides, the best protection money can buy sounds expensive."

"No problem. I intend to take care of it."

Brooke frowned at the thought. "I can't ask you to spend that kind of money."

"You're not asking. I'm offering, Or should I say *insisting*?" His expression softened and his rheumy blue eyes gazed at her pleadingly. "Please allow me to do this. I feel so helpless otherwise."

She saw the love written on his face and knew that this was no time to be stubborn. "You are the dearest, kindest thing that ever lived. You know that, don't you?"

"I know nothing of the sort. I just know I'll sleep better knowing you're safe. And until the system's installed, you'll be staying here in the guest room. I won't take no for an answer."

She smiled at him. "I guess that settles it then."

At 9:30 Brooke guided her SUV down the tree-lined driveway toward the rustic home she and Karl had shared. It wasn't as rustic as it appeared. It had been designed to suggest a life of primitive self-reliance while offering the latest in modern conveniences.

A white sedan waited in the drive, but before addressing its occupants, she checked her appearance in the rearview mirror. Her chin-length chestnut hair was neatly combed, but her blue-green eyes showed the aftereffects of last night's crying jag, and a touch of lipstick and blush had done little to disguise her misery and fatigue. But it hardly mattered. She was sure the police had seen much worse.

Jason Radley emerged from the passenger side of the sedan, and a stocky man in a gray suit got out on the driver's side. He appeared to be in his mid-fifties with a wide nose and jowly cheeks, and his dark eyes studied her from beneath a pair of bushy gray eyebrows. Without waiting for an introduction, he offered his card: *Homicide Investigator, Detective James Burleigh.*

Brooke felt her hands trembling. Why was a homicide detective being assigned to a burglary investigation? She looked at him, confused. "Homicide?"

"Don't be alarmed," he said. "The timing of the break-in so soon after your husband's death has raised a few questions. Our goal is to answer those questions so we can determine whether or not there's a connection between the two incidents."

She turned her face away, torn between grief and anger. Two months earlier she'd told the police that Karl's death was suspicious, but they'd brushed her remarks aside. Hysterical wife. Distraught widow. Her concerns hadn't been given any credence, and they'd been dismissed out of hand.

But nothing about Karl's death had made sense. Although he was 24 years Brooke's senior, he'd been in superb physical shape. He was hale and hearty at 60 and a robust outdoorsman who wasn't likely to tumble down an embankment. Especially not there. Not at the familiar spot he'd loved since childhood.

She thought back to that bright Sunday in mid-July. Other summers she and Karl would have set off like gypsies to sell their paintings at outdoor art festivals. But since finding God, Karl had taken to going to church on Sunday mornings, leaving her to work the festivals alone.

She'd returned that evening, expecting to find him at the stove whipping up something wonderful as penance for sending her off by herself. He hadn't been there, so she went to the studio, and when he wasn't there either, she'd noticed, belatedly, that his truck wasn't in the drive.

She'd called his cell. Not once but a dozen times. Finally she called the police and fifteen minutes later an officer stopped by the house. Karl hadn't been gone long enough to be considered *missing*, but the officer promised they'd stay on top of the situation and she should let them know if he turned up.

And then he'd asked a question: "You two having marital problems?"

Marital problems? Did disagreeing about God count as a marital problem?

"We love each other deeply," was all she'd said.

But it wasn't the police who'd found him. Early the next

morning a walker along a wooded path reported seeing a body in a ravine. An *accident*, the investigating officer told her later. Karl must have fallen, struck his head on a rock, and drowned in the shallow stream at the foot of the embankment.

"I'm sorry for your loss," the officer had said, shaking his head sadly as her world fell apart.

Four days later she'd stood at the graveside and placed a rose on Karl's casket, her grief on display for all to see. And yesterday at the retrospective, it was like she'd buried him all over again.

She invited the detectives inside, and like yesterday, she offered seats at the kitchen table. The homicide investigator took the lead and began by asking for the names of those who knew Brooke would be away from the house the previous day, starting with immediate family.

She told him that Karl's kids—28-year-old Stephanie and 30-year-old Brett—were aware that she'd be at the retrospective all afternoon. They'd been at the event as well; Brooke had seen Stephi several times throughout the afternoon but Brett just at the beginning.

The detective asked about her relationship with her stepchildren. *Strained*, she told him. They hadn't approved of their father marrying someone so much younger—Brooke was only eight years older than Stephi and six years older than Brett and could have been their sister rather than their stepmother. Beyond that, they'd resented her presence in the house that Karl had built with their mother.

"Your husband's ex-wife. Did she attend the exhibition?"

"Janine? No. She felt it might make things awkward."

"Did she know the house would be unattended while you were at the art show?"

"Of course."

"Anyone associated with her who might also have known?"

An image of Janine's second husband popped into Brooke's mind. She'd never liked the guy. Never trusted his glib manner and his flattering tongue.

"Janine's second husband knew I'd be away."

"And he is...?"

"A psychologist named Greg Greenwood."

"Would the two of then have known if something was hidden here?"

"Possibly. Janine lived here a lot of years before I came along."

That was it for family and so they moved on to friends. Gallery owner Madeleine Hewitt had taught in the art department at the same university where Brooke's late husband had taught. She'd retired early to open Hewitt Fine Arts Gallery about the same time Karl retired to paint and take private students. Madeleine's husband. Sidney, had been Karl's childhood friend, and he'd taken Karl's death quite hard.

"Sidney Hewitt was at the retrospective?" the detective asked.

Brooke shook her head. "He had a touch of something and stayed home. He sent his regrets."

Burleigh asked about Karl's students, of which there'd been too many to recall. Brooke suggested that there might be a list of names and contact information in the study. She'd avoided the room since Karl's death because it reminded her of him and that's why she'd closed the door and hadn't stepped inside. She had no problem with Jason Radley looking there for a list of students, and Detective Burleigh excused him to do so.

"Who stood to gain by your husband's death?" he asked as his partner left the kitchen.

Brooke frowned at the question. Things always came around to money. Not love and loss and a future left in ruin, but cold, hard cash in people's grasping hands.

"His kids each get a third of the estate. Not a fortune, but a nice sum for young people saddled with debt."

"And you? What did you stand to gain?"

"Heartache. Loneliness. Soul-crushing grief. Shall I go on?"

The detective frowned. This was clearly not the response he was seeking. "I meant materially."

She explained that she'd receive a third of the major assets which included the house. Stephi and Brett had grown up there, and it seemed only right to let them have a third of its value. They were anxious to sell and it would be only a matter of days before it was on the market. Beyond that, Brooke was the beneficiary of two life insurance policies and she'd be keeping the items she and Karl had purchased and the investments they'd made together. She offered to supply the detective with the paperwork that was currently in the hands of their attorney.

He thanked her and took a moment to refer to items on his tablet. "According to the notes from your interview last July, you said you and your late husband were having differences of opinion. What was that about?"

"Karl started going to church. I didn't. We'd both been skeptics and suddenly he wasn't. The change was difficult to get used to."

He asked about the church Karl had attended and he wrote down the name when Brooke supplied it. After that he placed the notepad in his pocket and rose to his feet.

"That's it for now, Ms. Roberts. As soon as Detective Radley finishes up in the study, you can start putting things back in order."

He was about to leave but turned back. "One other thing," he said. "Did your husband have acquaintances at church?"

"We didn't talk about church. At least I didn't, and I didn't pay much attention when he brought it up."

"Then you wouldn't know if he might have been meeting a lady friend there?"

Brooke drew in her breath. "A lady friend? I have no idea."

She watched from the kitchen window as the men left the

house and got into the white sedan.

A lady friend?

Why had she never thought of that?

▼ ▼ ▼

Janine Greenwood carried the groceries into the kitchen. Carrots, asparagus, spinach, tomatoes, grapes and strawberries. Fresh, organic, and brimming with nutrients. Later she'd make a salad, and as the darkness settled over the river, she and Greg would put on sweaters and share a candlelit dinner on the deck. She'd open a bottle of wine, and after two or three glasses, maybe he'd open up and tell her about the meeting he attended over the weekend.

Or maybe not.

She fumed at the thought. After fifteen years of marriage, it was unacceptable that Greg still kept secrets from her. They were soul mates as well as business partners. Secrets had no place in a relationship like theirs. And yet, there it was. At least once a year he disappeared for two days. She suspected that these meetings were elite gatherings of advanced lodge members with important business to attend to. But Greg remained secretive, and all she knew for certain was that this year's meeting started Friday night and ended sometime Sunday afternoon.

On the way home, Greg claimed to have visited a nature center to indulge his passion for bird-watching. *There's something magical about birds*, he always said. *The way they take to the sky without a care in the world.*

Janine envied the birds for not having a care in the world. At the moment she had a number of cares. Among them was her deep regret at having missed her ex's retrospective.

"It'll be awkward," her daughter Stephi had said. "Everyone will be looking at you and then at Brooke to see who cries first."

And so she didn't go, even though she of all people deserved to see Karl's paintings one last time. She'd watched hundreds make the journey from first brush stroke to final creation. Some came together in a day—*a la prima*—quick, confident strokes that erupted in color. Other paintings took months to unfold, sometimes in oil; sometimes acrylic. But never water color. Transparency, in art as in life, was not Karl's forte.

She'd consoled herself by going to Philadelphia to visit the places she and Karl used to frequent in their student days. She'd eaten coffee and a Danish at their favorite diner and wandered through Old City, soaking up the history around Independence Hall. After that, she'd turned her steps toward Mordecai's Antiques and Oddities, the quirky little shop where she and Karl had worked in their undergrad days.

The store was still quirky. Still filled to the rafters with the bizarre, the grotesque, and the arcane. Mardi Gras memorabilia. Carvings of angels, saints, and devils. Antique crystal balls and vintage Ouija boards. Not much had changed over the years except for the owner.

The Mordecai Simmons she remembered had been a shrewd businessman with an animated personality and a keen sense of humor. But the Mordecai Simmons she found in the office at the back of the store was a feeble and confused senior citizen—old or older than much of his merchandise. It took a while for him to place her, but when he did, he mumbled something about her ex-husband having stopped by months earlier with a medallion he wanted appraised—a piece he'd acquired at a Salvation Army Thrift Shop.

At that point, Mordecai had leaned across the desk as though about to reveal a secret. "If I didn't know better, my dear," he'd said in confidential tones, "I'd have told your ex that he possessed a rare and highly desirable occult ritual object. But after a lifetime in this business, I'm not so easily fooled. I can spot a reproduction when I see one."

When she informed him of Karl's recent death, the tenor

of the conversation changed. The old man became agitated and began wondering aloud if the medallion had been authentic after all. It brought with it a curse—surely she could see that. When she expressed confusion, he became angry, not just at her but at himself for having dismissed the item so lightly.

Alarmed, Janine got to her feet and excused herself, but the owner's son stopped her before she could leave the building.

"I couldn't help but overhear my dad's outburst," Ezra Simmons said apologetically. "His memory's failing. He may have seen your ex-husband a few months ago or it could have been years ago. Or it could have been someone else entirely who brought an item in to be appraised."

So that explained it. Mordecai was senile. Then why was Janine troubled by the things he'd said?

She finished putting the produce in the fridge and glanced at the clock. She had to hurry. A client was due in fifteen minutes and she needed to get ready.

She left the non-perishables on the counter and headed for the Reiki studio at the back of the house. She lit some candles and a stick of incense and sank to the floor in the lotus position, her spine erect as she focused on her breathing. This was how she prepared herself for her sessions. Her clients deserved a practitioner who was centered and focused.

But she was having trouble centering and focusing because her thoughts kept drifting back to Karl. They'd been high school sweethearts, and while there'd been moments of teenage angst and some particularly challenging experiences she'd prefer not to recall, they'd managed to put the past behind them and move into what Janine had hoped would be a blissful future. They'd married at Christmas in their junior year of college and lived in a tiny apartment in Philadelphia while they finished their degrees. There was Janine's first teaching job at a Quaker school and Karl's MFA that led to a position in a university Fine Arts department. Eventually they'd built the house in the woods and passed pleasant years raising their children to be wild and free.

And then as often happens, they began to grow apart. Janine felt drawn to the exotic and the mystical while Karl remained earth-bound. As the differences between them became more marked, Janine fell under the spell of a handsome psychologist named Greg Greenwood. He wasn't just a psychologist; he was a motivational speaker, a life coach and a hypnotherapist. He was sensitive. Funny. Gentle. In short, he was everything and more that she could have wished for in a life partner.

The divorce was swift. The re-marriage even swifter. Within a year, she and Greg had expanded their home to include space for their business: *The Center for the Mystic Healing Arts.* Soon they were sharing their wisdom with others.

Meanwhile, Karl had remained in a rut. Skeptical. Disparaging. Arrogant. Tormented, at times, by regrets from years gone by. And then one day he found Jesus. How was that possible? Jesus, of all things?

And now Karl was dead, released to wherever his karma—or his faith—had taken him.

Janine reined in her wandering thoughts. It was time to set her intentions for the upcoming Reiki session. "Peace," she murmured, as the air slowly escaped her lungs. "My next client is seeking peace."

She inhaled again and let it out. Slowly in. Slowly out. A minute went by. Two. Three. The silence deepened. And then a ringtone jangled from her pocket.

Not another cancellation! She'd had three this week with no indication that her clients intended to reschedule.

But it wasn't her Reiki client calling to cancel. It was her daughter, Stephanie.

"I can only talk a minute, Steph. What's up?"

"You won't believe this! The police were just here! In my apartment! On my day off!"

Janine felt her blood run cold. "Is everything all right? It's not your brother, is it?"

"Of course it's not my brother. They don't arrest people for being hopeless idiots. Daddy's house was broken into yesterday. The police stopped by to ask questions."

"Your father's house was broken into? Was anything taken?"

"Beats me. But the thief ripped up a bunch of furniture and the cops figured he was trying to find something hidden in the upholstery. And get this," Stephi continued. "The cops are reopening their investigation into Daddy's death. They're calling it suspicious instead of accidental."

Goose bumps prickled up and down Janine's arms. "Your father tripped and fell. It was a tragic accident. There was nothing suspicious about it."

"Try telling that to the homicide guy and his sad-eyed side kick. And FYI, they want to talk to you and Greg. And Brett as well."

"To us? What do we have to do with this?"

"You knew Brooke would be out of the house yesterday. You and Greg weren't at the retrospective. And Brett left after only a few minutes."

"Are you saying we're suspects?" Janine's voice was shrill. "For the break-in or for…?" She felt suddenly faint and found herself gripping the edge of her Reiki table.

The doorbell chimed at the rear entrance.

She glanced at her watch. Her client was early!

There was no time to calm herself. With her thoughts spinning in her head, she said a hasty goodbye and went to open the door.

Three

Thanks to those cops, Stephi's day was ruined. Totally. She'd racked up comp-time by working extra hours, and at the very least she deserved to enjoy her day off. But the cops had barged in, stealing the day from her and leaving her upset and miserable.

She went to the kitchen and poured a glass of wine. Normally she didn't touch the stuff this early in the day, but if she didn't calm down, she might start screaming and there was no one to listen to her screams except the neighbors who'd complain about the racket.

She'd worked her butt off becoming an art therapist so she could help troubled teens. All those hours of study. All those seminars and internships. For what? Her job was important, and she deserved decent pay. No—she deserved a fabulous salary, not the lousy pittance the county paid her every month. And she deserved a better place to live than this tiny, rat-trap of an apartment. There wasn't even space for a roommate to move in and split the rent. But why should she need a roommate at this point in her life? She had a master's degree, and she deserved a penthouse for what she put up with every day.

Just a week ago, she'd told her tale of woe to her mom and Greg. Not enough money. Not enough space. But instead of reaching for her purse, her mom gave her a book called *Feng*

Shui Made Easy. She told Stephi to study the section about creating a money corner and said that if she followed the directions, cash would start pouring in.

Greg's advice was no better. Instead of writing a check, he told her to practice creative visualization: *Picture a well filled with money. Imagine yourself lowering a bucket into that well and bringing up bundles of cash. Picture yourself touching it. Spending it. Investing it. Before you know it, prosperity and abundance will be yours.*

Her brother Brett's remarks had been more to the point. Which didn't mean he'd helped her out—far from it.

"What numbskull told you there was money to be made in helping losers quit being losers?" he'd asked. "At the end of the day, they'll still be losers, you'll still be broke, and all those years of school will have been money down the drain."

She hadn't hesitated to tell him what she thought of him. "You're obnoxious, you know that? I can't believe I'm related to a thoughtless jerk like you."

"Ooooh, my feelings are hurt," he'd mocked. "I think I'll cry." But he didn't cry. He just kept laughing. And then he'd stopped long enough to remind her: *Once Dad's estate settles, you'll have plenty of money.*

She'd put her hands over her ears and turned away. Their father was dead and only a scumbag would dream of profiting from this enormous tragedy.

And yet...

"The house shows extremely well," the real estate agent had told Brooke, Stephi and Brett when they'd met together a week earlier. "It should go quickly and for an amount close to the price the three of you are asking."

It was true. The place was a charmer. Not huge, but roomy enough at 2,500 square feet. A one-story timber frame with a vaulted ceiling and two fireplaces: one in the living room and one in the master bedroom. A hot tub on the rear deck. Enormous windows with views of the surrounding forest—views that were especially stunning in the fall and in the snows of winter.

Stephi adored that house. All her memories were inside those timber-framed walls and outside in the surrounding woods. A pang of grief shot through her at the thought of selling it and she realized then what a foolish idea it was.

She made up her mind in an instant. She'd refuse to sign the listing papers, and since she was one-third owner, the sale would be off. She'd tell her brother and Brooke that selling it was out of the question, and then she'd give up her crummy apartment and move in with Brooke—as difficult as that would be. She'd reclaim her childhood room and lie in bed at night looking up at the stars through the skylight like she did when she was little. In the winter she'd wrap herself in a furry blanket and sit by the fireplace breathing in the fragrance of burning logs and sipping hot chocolate, just like she and her dad used to do on those deep, dark evenings when the snow draped the trees in white.

And not just any white. *Titanium white.* A brilliant white with a high refractive index as her father had explained on several occasions. Only an artist would care about a detail like that, and that's what her dad had been. She regretted now that she hadn't listened more carefully when she'd had the chance because now he was dead and she'd never get to talk to him again. She wanted to talk to him and she wanted to sit next to him and she wanted to hear him laugh and call her Sweetie, and she wanted to hear him describe the new-fallen snow as titanium white.

Daddy she sobbed into the emptiness. *I love you. And I'd rather have you here with me than all the money in the world.*

She closed her eyes and tried to picture his face. But it was no use. She was too upset and everything was a blur.

And now the cops were calling her dad's death suspicious instead of accidental. She knew what that meant, but she could barely bring herself to think of the word. Her father, the kindest man in the world—murdered? Who would do such a thing? It made no sense.

The detectives hadn't said the word either, but she could tell what they'd been thinking. The older one especially. He'd kept studying her from beneath his bushy eyebrows, his questions like bulldozers plowing through her anguish.

Every now and then the younger one looked up from his notepad. His eyes had this gentle look, like he knew what she was suffering. What was his name again? She glanced at his card.

That's right. Detective Jason Radley. He was cute, in a long-faced, Basset hound kind of way. Out of curiosity, she'd looked at his left hand. No wedding ring. Sweet.

In a way, she and this young detective had a lot in common: they both wanted to make the world a better place. Once the case was closed, perhaps they'd get together for a drink. She pictured them at her favorite bar, swapping stories about their daring exploits. Jason Radley cornering vicious killers. Stephi rescuing troubled kids from lives of hopeless despair. Eventually the conversation would drift to lighter topics. Music. Movies. The beach. There were endless subjects to draw upon.

Too bad the older cop had kept butting in with an endless stream of nosy questions. Like what Stephi's brother had been up to the day of the retrospective. She probably shouldn't have said the things she'd said about Brett, but anger and disappointment had driven her to it. Instead of being supportive at the retrospective, he'd made a brief appearance and disappeared, leaving her to cope with her father's colleagues and students while dealing with her own heartache and grief. What kind of a brother would desert his sister at a moment like that?

Even so, she wondered if she'd gone too far with the things she'd said about Brett. What if she'd inadvertently implicated him in something terrible? And then she laughed at the thought. It would serve him right. He was a jerk and a self-absorbed imbecile who couldn't wait to spend their father's money.

She glanced at the phone lying next to her. Had the police

gotten in touch with him yet? If not, he might appreciate a heads-up.

She called his number and when the call went to voice mail, she left a message. "Call me right away. And by right away, I mean immediately. Not five days from now."

She tossed the phone down and sat staring at the floor.

Her father was dead. The house would be sold. The estate settled.

And then she'd have money—a lot of it—or so it seemed from her perspective.

But a big part of her life was gone forever, and there was no one in the world who cared.

▾ ▾ ▾

Brett slid onto the leather upholstery. He couldn't afford this monolithic assortment of nuts, bolts, and microchips, but in his line of work, appearance was everything.

He'd just gotten off the phone with his sister. And now, here in the safety of his car, it was all he could do to stay calm.

His dad's house had been broken into. His death upgraded from 'accidental' to 'suspicious.' And now the police wanted to talk to him about what had gone down on Sunday afternoon.

He took a minute to review his recent messages. None from the cops.

And then he wondered if cops actually called ahead to schedule appointments. It's not like a suspect got to say: *Sorry, my schedule's full. I can't work you in until late next week.* And that meant the men in blue would probably be waiting for him at home.

Mr. Erikson, they'd say. *We'd like a word with you.* Once inside his condo, their eyes would dart to and fro as they added up the cost of his deluxe living quarters, and they'd wonder how a recent hire with a beginner's list of clients managed to pay the mortgage. They'd tuck that thought away and open with a more generic question. An icebreaker, like *Where were you yesterday between the hours of whatever and whatever?*

He'd give them an answer. But would they believe him?

He'd gone to the retrospective, expecting to stay for the duration. Not for sentimental reasons or because he was a huge art lover, but because he'd offered to act as emotional support for his kid sister who was all teary-eyed at the prospect of seeing their father's work assembled in one place.

As the date approached, he'd actually found himself looking forward to the occasion. He had fond memories of kibitzing with his dad's colleagues, and the retrospective offered an opportunity to do some serious networking. He'd shake hands, accept condolences, and pass out business cards, all the while assuring his dad's compatriots that their assets would be well-managed in his capable hands.

Once he'd impressed the gray hairs, he'd turn his attention to the art groupies. College girls. Grad students. Young professionals. Each one sporting a wine glass in one hand and a brie-topped cracker in the other while artsy lingo dripped like rain from their lips. He'd mention a famous artist or two—he was pretty sure abstract expressionists were back in vogue—and before you knew it, a pretty face would accept his invitation for a drink—and maybe more—after the exhibit.

He'd arrived at the gallery at a little after one and swaggered through the door, his stride announcing, or so he hoped, that he was the son of the artist whose memory was being celebrated. The heir to his father's fame and fortune. The man everyone wanted to talk to. The hand everyone wanted to shake.

He'd stopped to look at the first painting and then something seized hold of him, and he felt like he'd stepped on an improvised explosive device.

He recognized the place. A secluded spot where his dad used to take him every April—just the two of them—for the opening of trout season. The last time they'd cast their lines into those chilly waters Brett had been thirteen and not exactly pleasant company, having arrived at the age where he'd rather spend his weekend with friends than with dear, old dad.

And yet there it was. *Fisherman's Cove in Spring.* Just as he remembered it.

He'd tried to force back the tears, but a few escaped, so he'd swiped at his face with his sleeve and moved away from the painting, chastising himself for acting like an idiot.

The next painting kicked him dead center in the gut.

He and Stephi had gone hiking at Ricketts Glen with their parents before the divorce—back in the days when life was fun, before the fighting started. He'd forgotten about that afternoon, but in an instant it came flaming back. The blue sky. The cascading water. The trees reaching for the heavens. His mom and dad holding hands as they walked through autumn leaves. Both of them laughing like being together was the most wonderful thing in the world.

The next series brought back even more memories.

Mountain Laurel near Milford.

Bushkill Falls in Early Autumn.

Elk in Cameron County.

His dad loved the outdoors and especially loved the grand and beautiful state of Pennsylvania. How many trails had his family hiked together? How many places had they fished and camped? How many fires had they built, and how many marshmallows had they toasted until they were gooey and melt-y and dripping off the stick?

Again his eyes filled with tears. "*Dad!*" he'd wanted to cry out right there in the gallery. "*I forgot how much I loved you.*"

He spotted his sister in the crowd. Overcome by grief, he'd murmured a hasty goodbye and fled the gallery, leaving her with a glass of wine in one hand and a stupid little French pickle in the other. He made it to his Lexus, and once inside the luxurious interior, he let the tears flow.

If flow was the right word. Mostly it was a spastic kind of snorting and sniffling with his chest heaving as he fought for control. Gradually the tears subsided. Gradually a numbness set in. Unable to return to the gallery, he blew his nose a couple of times, started the engine, and pulled away from the curb.

Where had that outburst come from?

It's not like he and his dad had been close of late. In fact, there'd been plenty of times when Brett could sense his father studying him, his eyes probing as though searching for hidden depths that, frankly, didn't exist. Years ago Karl Erikson used to throw out prompts designed to awaken his son's inner philosopher. At other times he'd toss out a phrase crafted to call forth the budding scholar or poet. But Brett wasn't any of those things and eventually his dad abandoned the quest without taking time to discover Brett's true strengths. And Brett had strengths. Plenty of them. He was the practical one of the family. The one with his feet on the ground and his eyes fixed on the bottom line. He was a man who steered clear of primrose paths and one who wouldn't be caught dead wearing rose-colored glasses.

That's why investment banking suited him. He liked money. Liked playing with it and watching it grow. He liked balance sheets, financial reports, and long columns of numbers attached to dollar signs.

And while he wasn't exactly rolling in the green stuff, he was on his way up. In fact, he'd recently made a brilliant move, one that was already beginning to pay off.

He'd had a moment of doubt at the initiation ceremony. It wasn't the spiritual mumbo-jumbo or the spooky ritual with the blindfold that bugged him. It was the oath at the end. An oath pledging unwavering loyalty upon penalty of death. "An ancient tradition," his sponsor assured him afterward. "Scripted in a different time and a different culture, but fraught with symbolic meaning for today."

The chilling ceremony was soon forgotten once he'd been welcomed into their midst. Lodge members looked out for each other. Negotiated deals on one another's behalf. Helped each other out of a tight spot, even if it meant placing a discreet thumb on the scales of justice. From that moment forward, he was one of them. His brothers had his back and he had theirs.

Like today, for instance. A VP from the sixth floor had taken him aside for a brief chat. "I'm hearing good things about you," he'd said as he shook Brett's hand. It wasn't just any handshake, but a secret one known only to brothers. "Keep up the good work," he'd smiled.

The thought still gave Brett a thrill. *Hello world,* he grinned. *Brett Erikson is on his way up.*

He pulled into his parking space in the garage beneath his luxury condo. Sure enough, a few spaces away a white car sat idling.

Cops.

It had to be.

Now all he needed was an alibi for Sunday afternoon.

▾ ▾ ▾

"Slow down," Greg Greenwood told his wife. "You're talking a mile a minute."

"I can't help it," Janine said, her voice all fluttery. "We both knew Brooke would be at the retrospective yesterday afternoon, and we both knew the house would be empty."

"And so the police will assume we broke in? Is that what you're saying?"

Janine rolled her eyes like she always did when her patience was wearing thin. "I'm saying it looks bad. They'll want to know where you were yesterday, and that means you'll have to tell them about the meeting you attended, whether you like it or not."

"Don't be absurd. You know that's impossible so there's no need to dwell on it."

But Janine kept at it. And she had a point. The police would insist on knowing where the weekend session had been held, who'd been there, and who could vouch for Greg's presence.

Frustrated, he got up from the table and walked over to the deck railing. The candles on the table sent his shadow sprawling across the lawn, making him appear huge, like a giant. Which is how he wanted his wife to see him. As a giant. A titan. A force to be reckoned with.

"I'm not at liberty to talk about the meeting," he said with his back to her. "Our sessions are secret. You know that."

"Tell that to the police," she shot back.

She reminded him that without coming clean about where he'd spent the weekend, he had no alibi for Sunday afternoon. She, on the other hand, could attest to her whereabouts. She'd arrived at Mordecai's Antiques and Oddities shortly after eleven. When Greg called her at noon, she was on her way to lunch at Reading Terminal Market, and she had the receipt to prove she'd been there. After that she visited some stores and caught a three-fifteen train home. Greg, on the other hand, had promised to be back by four, but he didn't show up until six because he'd supposedly stopped to do some bird watching.

"Did anyone see you out there watching birds?" she demanded. "The police will want to know."

He assured her that plenty of people had seen him, but he didn't know any of them, and they didn't know him, and it was unlikely that anyone paid attention to just another guy with binoculars.

He could feel his frustration deepening, so he took a deep breath and then another, hoping to clear his thoughts. He and Janine needed to be of one mind when they spoke to the police. To make that happen, he'd have to try a softer approach.

He came back to the table, sat down next to her and gazed into her eyes. "Listen, Sweetie," he said, his tone soothing, or so he hoped. "There's no way I can discuss the meeting or the identities of those who were there, so let's not even mention it. We'll tell the police you took a trip to the city while I went out for an afternoon in the great outdoors."

She drew back, and there was a long pause as her eyes probed his face. "You're asking me to lie? You know how that will turn out. Lying destroys the soul. I've seen it happen plenty of times, and so have you."

He reached for her hand and stroked it gently, his index finger outlining the bones beneath the skin. "I agree with you one-hundred percent. And I won't be lying exactly. Just omitting the part about the meeting and exaggerating the time I spent outdoors on Sunday afternoon. A few tweaks to avoid complications."

"It sounds like a lie to me."

He left it at that and moved on. He had other matters to settle before the cops put in an appearance. Like the medallion Mordecai Simmons had made such a fuss over. "I don't think you need to tell the police about the medallion," he said matter-of-factly.

She yanked her hand away from his. "What do you mean? The medallion could be the detail that breaks the case."

"And it could be the detail that points a finger of suspicion in our direction. The police might conclude that once you learned about the medallion, you raced out of the store and headed home so you could go to the house to search for it. It's not like you're not familiar with the place. You and Karl built it together, in case you've forgotten."

He watched her face. Yes, the argument had hit home.

"But it's more complicated than just that," he continued. "The police might decide that you and I colluded on the matter. That when we spoke on the phone on Sunday, you told me about this medallion thing and I dashed off to meet you at the house so we could search for it together."

Janine let out a sigh. "What are we supposed to do? I have to tell the police about my visit to Mordecai's so that they can verify my whereabouts. When they contact the store to confirm my visit, Mordecai will probably tell them about the medallion."

"So call the son—Ezra or whatever his name is. Tell him

the police will be contacting him to verify your alibi and that you've chosen not to mention the medallion because his father's mental state makes it impossible to know if the thing even exists. Why implicate the store or its customers over something so uncertain?"

"And if Ezra doesn't see that as a problem?"

Greg looked at her sternly. "You'll have to *make* him see it as a problem. Unless you prefer the two of us being considered suspects in a break-in and a robbery. And perhaps a murder, depending on how the investigation proceeds."

He studied her face, trying to gauge the effects of his argument. Her jaw had lost its defiant tilt and the fire in her eyes had been reduced to embers. With a bit more coaxing, she'd come around to his way of thinking.

He rose to his feet and looked down at her. "Can you imagine what could happen if we're accused of these crimes? You and I are energy workers, Janine. With criminal allegations hanging over our heads, the practice we've spent years building will collapse under the weight of suspicion, fear, and doubt. Is that what you want for our future?"

She sat in silence, her eyes downcast.

He smiled inwardly. He knew he'd won. Not a resounding victory, but a victory by default. Janine had run out of arguments.

She gazed at the flickering candle. "I'm so confused," she said. "Ever since Stephi called this afternoon I've been a wreck. My Reiki session was a mess, and now..."

A sound worked its way from the front of the house to the rear deck.

The doorbell.

The fear on Janine's face was easy to read. "The police," she whispered. "They're here."

He glanced warily in the direction of the noise. "Stay calm. And by all means, keep quiet and let me do the talking."

Four

Elena caught a late flight out of LA and was back East before dawn on Tuesday. She'd booked the limo and notified the housekeeper who'd promised to ready the sprawling Lehigh Valley Victorian, her retreat from the chaos of Manhattan. The woman would see to it that the refrigerator and pantry were well stocked. That there were fresh flowers in the living room, dining room and second-floor office. Paper in the printer. Wood and kindling for fires on chilly evenings.

She leaned against the leather upholstery, her eyes fixed on the passing headlights. Yesterday had been a success—as far as most people measured success. The enthusiasm for the upcoming season was sky-high, and the cocktail party following a day of meetings had been attended by some of the best and brightest in the industry. As far as documentary series were concerned, *The Unveiling* was well on its way to capturing top ratings.

But at the moment, her West Coast triumphs meant nothing and neither did the ceremonies, rites, and rituals she'd been forced to cancel in order to rush back East. All she could think about was the root of her current malaise: a duplicitous little snake named Ezra Simmons.

She'd paid the manager of Mordecai's Antiques and Oddities an astronomical sum for what she'd believed to be exclusive information. There'd been no contract. No handshakes. Just a pledge she expected him to honor given their previous dealings.

In exchange for a fee, Ezra Simmons had given her a name and a phone number. From there she'd arranged an appointment, allegedly to discuss art classes in a private studio but really to inquire about an object known to be in the instructor's possession, an object he'd brought into the store to show Ezra's father. When she'd approached the artist, he'd refused to sell the piece. Within a few days of that refusal, he was dead. And now that her most recent plan had failed, another had yet to be developed.

But first there were a some details to attend to. She had no doubt that Ezra Simmons had sold the artist's contact information to someone else. Someone who desired the object as much as she did. How else to explain the fact that someone got to the house before Elena's operatives?

She wondered how much money Ezra had raked in from his double dealing. But at this point it hardly mattered. She'd exposed his duplicity and now he'd have to pay. But first she'd toy with him and watch him squirm.

In the meantime, she had more important matters to contend with. Like formulating a plan. With that in mind, she closed her eyes, summoned her spirit guides, and awaited their arrival.

▼ ▼ ▼

Gallery owner Madeleine Hewitt sat in her well-lit breakfast nook scrolling through the comments about Sunday's retrospective. A huge crowd had gathered to honor her dear friend, the late Karl Erikson, and to celebrate his life. Rarely was an opening so successful.

She heard the doorbell ring from the front of the house. That was odd. Who would be stopping by so early on a Tuesday morning? A moment later her husband Sid appeared in the kitchen, his expression grave. "A couple of cops are here to talk to us," he announced.

Puzzled, she followed Sid to the living room and found two detectives waiting. Their news took her breath away. Brooke Roberts' house had been broken into on Sunday during the retrospective at Madeleine's gallery. Not just broken into, but ransacked.

The detectives followed this announcement with a series of questions. Did Karl Erikson mention having something hidden in his house? And at the gallery on Sunday—did Madeleine notice anyone leaving early? Was there anyone who was expected to attend, but never showed?

When it came to alibi's Madeleine was indisputable. She'd been at the gallery from noon when she let the caterers in, to nearly six when she turned off the lights. Everyone saw her, and there were no shortages of witnesses to attest to the fact.

▾ ▾ ▾

After that the focus shifted to Sid. He'd been Karl Erikson's closest friend, so why hadn't he attended the retrospective? The question led to a lot of fancy footwork as Sid groped for the right terminology. He'd been indisposed. Under the weather. Out of sorts. Eventually he hit upon the correct wording. He'd been hung over. That was it. His clarification led to a discussion of Saturday night's fiasco at Antoine's, complete with the names of those who'd been with Sid and Madeleine at the bar and who could speak to his impressive level of intoxication.

Madeleine sat through that portion of the interview with zero feelings of sympathy for her stammering husband. In fact, it was a pleasure to watch him squirm. She'd told him to knock off the drinking and he'd insisted on doing the opposite and now he was being called to task.

Eventually the interview ground to a conclusion and

Madeleine hurried off to open the gallery. She got there at 10:30, half-an-hour past her usual opening time. Not that it mattered. It wasn't like art enthusiasts were lined up on the sidewalk waiting breathlessly to get inside. Tuesdays were notoriously slow. As were Wednesdays and Thursdays. Weekends were a different story when visitors thronged Bethlehem's vibrant commercial district. With its boutiques, award-winning restaurants, and bustling casino on the site of the former Bethlehem Steel Works, the city was a popular destination for day-trippers.

She cruised through the gallery, turning on lights in each of three darkened rooms. The sudden brilliance caused the canvases to leap from the shadows, vibrant and colorful, and—unlike their creator—throbbing with life.

She shook her head at the thought. *Rest in peace, old friend.*

She entered her office at the back of the gallery and switched on the computer. While waiting for it to start, she picked up the guest registry from Sunday's retrospective and rifled through the pages. The book was nearly full, and no wonder. Karl had been a popular instructor at the university and a noted local artist. On Sunday, dozens of former students, colleagues, and friends had crowded through the door to share memories and pay tribute to his life and career.

She scanned the names, trying to match them with the young faces she remembered from the days when she'd taught art history. She'd been able to reacquaint herself with several at the retrospective, but had found their remarks disheartening. "*My parents were right*," a talented former student had told her. "*You can't feed your family by creating art.*" His words were echoed over and over again by former art majors working in fields unrelated to their studies. She sighed at the thought. Reality could be a tough pill to swallow.

Which brought her back to the reality of the morning's police interview and the subject of alibis. Sid's alibi, not hers. She'd been counting on him to be there at the retrospective, filling champagne glasses, ringing up sales, and amusing their guests with clever conversation. In other words, she'd wanted him to play the congenial host while she kept a watchful eye on Brooke. But after hanging over the toilet bowl in the wee hours of Sunday morning, Sid had begged off to spend the day at home, slopping around in pajamas and slippers and feeling sorry for himself.

They'd gone to Antoine's on Saturday night, and as usual, Sid had been the life of the party. With Karl's retrospective uppermost in his mind, his anecdotes that evening had a common theme: his glory days with his lifetime pal. At first his stories had garnered lots of laughs, but after he'd downed a few, folks at the bar began exchanging sideways glances as the stories grew depressing and the party morphed into something closer to a wake. Bit by bit, the crowd thinned out, and around eleven Madeleine was finally able to coax her woe-be-gone husband out to the parking lot where he staggered to the car, barely able to walk.

And that's why she'd felt no sympathy for him this morning as he'd wriggled and squirmed beneath the detective's daunting stares. And that's why she didn't particularly care that no one could vouch for his whereabouts on Sunday. She supposed she could have told the cops that Sid had been in no shape to slither through a basement window and ransack a house. Instead, she'd bit her tongue, watching with amusement as the miserable so-and-so struggled to defend himself.

The buzzer rang from the front of the gallery. Amazing. An actual customer.

Her heart sank when she glanced at the monitor above her desk.

It was David Price, the director of the Tri-County Historical Conservancy. Madeleine sat on the board of that stellar organization, and up until Sunday, she'd held the new director in high regard. But now, next to Sid, David Price was the last person she wanted to see.

She watched on the monitor as he made his way through the gallery, looking perfectly respectable in what she presumed was a moderately priced dark suit with a bit of custom tailoring to ensure a good fit. His crisp white shirt was accented with a conservative tie, and she could find no fault with his impeccably groomed, wavy brown hair. He looked young at nearly forty and there was nothing to suggest that a raving lunatic lurked just beneath the surface of his flawless appearance.

He entered the second of three rooms and stopped before a huge painting of Brooke seated in a canoe. Her hand dangled in the water while all around her the soft summer light spilled through the trees, painting her white dress in shadows of lilac, teal and rose and streaking gold through her chestnut hair. The effect was stunning, and there'd been a lot of interest in the piece on Sunday. But no takers. The work was so personal, so intimate, so much a story of Karl's love for his wife, that purchasing it would have felt like an intrusion into the world they'd once shared.

Not that David Price could appreciate such things.

Madeleine rose from her seat and steeled herself for the confrontation that was about to ensue. She was above all a woman of principle, and there were times when women of principle had to speak their minds.

She emerged from her office and made her way noiselessly to the middle room.

"So," she began "I see you've returned to the scene of the crime."

Price lurched and spun around. "Madeleine," he said, a weak smile on his lips. "There you are. I was just admiring the painting."

"Of course you were admiring it. It's lovely. Would you like to buy it?"

"No. What I mean is that while I'd like to—who wouldn't?— that's not why…"

His words trailed off, and she waited for him to continue.

"I'm not here to buy paintings. I'm here to talk. There's a story behind Sunday's disaster."

"I should hope so." She gestured toward the rear of the gallery. "We'll talk in my office."

She sat behind her desk and waited with hands folded while Price settled into a chair. He looked up at her, meek and embarrassed and seemingly tongue-tied, like a wayward child who'd been sent to the principal.

"Let's hear it," she began. "How do you explain the appalling things that came out of your mouth at Karl's retrospective?"

When he failed to respond, Madeleine took it upon herself to refresh his memory.

"You barged into the gallery Sunday afternoon, marched over to Brooke, and demanded to know why her husband wasn't with her. You then stated that he'd have to be a sanctimonious ass to prefer God's company to hers. You added insult to injury by informing her that only a hardhearted cad would abandon his wife on such a beautiful day."

She shot him a look known to intimidate everyone except Sid. "Karl Erikson is dead and there was nothing sanctimonious or hardhearted about his absence on Sunday. It was impossible for him to be here, because he was at the time and is at present six-feet beneath the ground. We were gathered in the gallery on Sunday to celebrate his life and his art. What in the world were you thinking?"

It took a while for the younger man to gather his thoughts. "I didn't barge in," he stammered. "I walked calmly through the door. And I didn't march over to Brooke. I saw her out of the corner of my eye and made a point of going over to speak to her."

"Thank you for clarifying. Now explain yourself."

He shifted in his seat. "It's a long story."

"It would have to be. Proceed. I haven't got all day."

And so he told his tale. He'd met Brooke once before at an outdoor arts festival on a Sunday in mid-July. Her paintings had struck his fancy, and so he'd stopped to talk to her. In the course of the conversation he'd asked what was involved in doing outdoor shows. She said her husband usually helped with setting up and taking down, but lately he'd been going to church on Sundays.

"I could tell she was bothered by his absence," he explained. "She said her husband had always been skeptical about religion. That he saw it as a crutch and something insecure people turned to out of fear. Then all of a sudden he'd started going to church. I sensed that she felt betrayed."

Madeleine nodded. That much of the story was true. Karl's sudden conversion had been a matter of concern, not just for Brooke, but for Karl's friends as well. In fact, on several occasions, Madeleine herself had been the subject of his ominous calls to repentance. The memories of those moments weren't pleasant.

"Brooke tried to make a joke that day at the festival," Price continued. "Something about having to do all the work herself now that her husband preferred God's company to hers. She laughingly called him a sanctimonious ass and in the spirit of fun, I added that only a hardhearted cad would abandon his wife on such a beautiful afternoon. When I used those words in the gallery on Sunday, I was only quoting what she herself had said two months earlier and what I'd said in response."

He looked at Madeleine, his eyes heavy with remorse. "I had no idea she was Karl Erikson's widow. They have different last names, and Erikson was a lot older than she. She obviously didn't remember me or remember what we'd said that day at the art festival, and so the whole thing fell flat. More than flat. It crashed and burned."

He gave a slight shudder. "Everyone within earshot stopped talking and stood there gaping at me with their mouths hanging open. Before I could guess what happened, a group of women clustered around Brooke and steered her away from me like I was a monster. When I realized what I'd said, it was too late to call it back."

Madeleine gazed at the desolate creature seated across from her. The whole horrific incident had been an innocent blunder.

She surprised herself by laughing. David Price wasn't a lunatic after all. Just a moron who'd put his foot in it in front of an unforgiving audience, and it was clear that he'd suffered long enough.

"I'm glad you came here to sort things out," she said, once she'd stopped laughing. "Having said that, I believe you owe Brooke an explanation. And an apology."

Price sat up straighter, his expression eager. "I'd like to apologize. Preferably in person. But I'm not sure how to make that happen."

"I'll be glad to help you with that. I'll give her a call and tell her to expect a visitor."

"Would you do that? Really?"

Madeleine paused to jot down Brooke's address on a scrap of paper that she handed to him. "There are times when it's best to confess our sins, even when they're unintended."

Five

Brooke stared at the house from the safety of her car. The sun glistened through the trees, blanketing the property in a crazy quilt of shadow and light. Storms were due in the afternoon, but for now, nothing but azure skies and billowing clouds.

Her phone rang. Brett.

"I stopped by the house last night," he bellowed into the phone. "And no one was there."

"That's right. I'm staying with my uncle until a home security system is installed."

"Somebody needs to be there. If the thief didn't find what he was looking for, he'll be back. And next time he might do more than break a window and throw stuff around."

Brooke found his remarks infuriating. "So you're suggesting that if this person returns in the middle of the night, I should be there to single-handedly fight him off?"

There was silence for a moment. "Okay, I see what you're saying, but if you're not willing to keep an eye on things, then I'll have to step up to the plate. I'm one-third owner, after all, and I want the place protected."

Brett was right, of course, and so she'd agreed to let him stay there overnight. She cringed at the thought of him rummaging through the house, searching for treasures the thief might have missed. She had contacted three companies that handled security systems and the sooner one was installed, the better.

The sound of tires in the driveway pulled her out of her thoughts. She looked in the rearview mirror. The insurance company rep was right on time.

After a brief inspection, he informed her that her policy covered a thorough cleaning. It did not include picking things up and putting them away—she'd have to do that herself. He gave her a figure for replacing the slashed furniture and broken lamps and for repairing the basement window. After promising to have a check in her hand within two days, he excused himself and left.

The second appointment, the one with the real estate agent, didn't go nearly as well.

"You need to see this from a buyer's perspective," the woman said as they walked from room to room. "Before the break-in this was a charming timber-frame dwelling in a park-like setting. Now it's an isolated cabin in a dark, lonely forest."

The agent's eyes swept the room. Broken lamps. Slashed sofa cushions. Items ripped from shelves and strewn across the floor.

"Buyers are spooked by a house's history," she continued. "If you list now, families will stay away, and you'll attract only bargain hunters and landlords, neither of whom will approach your asking price. Come spring when buds are on the trees and birds are chirping, it'll be a different story."

Five minutes later, Brooke watched the woman drive away. Feeling fearful, she locked the door, both the deadbolt and the chain lock, and stared at the mess in the living room. Sooner or later she had to pick everything up, but she didn't know where to start, not with her thoughts in a quandary.

She'd spent a sleepless night thinking of the question the detective had asked her—the one about Karl meeting a lady friend at church. She'd lain awake, combing through her memories to see if there was something she'd missed. Other than the religious differences that had cropped up in the final months, Karl had seemed content in their marriage. No—he'd been more than content. He'd been passionate and thoughtful and devoted at times, or so it had seemed. Wouldn't she have noticed if he'd fallen out of love with her?

She wondered if their age difference had become a problem. Had he sought out someone with greater knowledge and life experience than what Brooke could offer? A companion to walk alongside him toward a shared sunset?

"You're dating your father," her friends had taunted her years ago. "Your dad walked out when you were ten, so you're compensating by dating this older guy. Not that he's not hot," they'd quickly added. "But that doesn't change the fact that he's too old for you."

The parallels were obvious. Brooke's dad was 24 when she was born. Karl was 24 years her senior. According to her friends, she'd replaced a missing father with a surrogate.

For just a moment her father's face flickered through her mind. She could almost see his smile and his dark hair that curled against the nape of his neck and his eyes that sparkled when he laughed.

She shut down that line of thinking. One heartache at a time was all she could handle.

She turned her attention to the clutter in the living room and at the same time, she noticed that the real estate agent had left the door to Karl's study open. Brooke was about to close it but paused to glance inside. The room was a scene of chaos as was every room in the house, but a leather-bound book stood out among the items strewn across the Persian rug. Karl's Bible.

Brooke wondered if he'd tucked something inside, knowing it was the last place on earth Brooke would think to look. And if she did look, what would she find? A church bulletin with a woman's phone number scribbled on it? A business card with contact information? A clue, a hint, anything to suggest there'd been someone else in Karl's life?

She'd avoided the study, fearful of the memories it contained, but a stronger impulse drew her through the door. She crossed the room and picked up the Bible from the mess on the floor. She stared at the leather bound volume. Karl had asked her on several occasions to read passages he'd hoped to share with her, but until this moment, she'd never so much as touched it. She opened it now, but the moment was anticlimactic. No thunderclaps from heaven. Just pages and lots of them.

Brooke flipped through the contents from Genesis to Revelation and back again. No church bulletins or business cards. Only sticky notes. Dozens or them along with verses highlighted in yellow.

She read a passage that told of a man possessed by an unclean spirit. *My name is Legion,* the demon said, *for we are many.* That was strange. Why would Karl have highlighted those words?

She flipped to another sticky note: *...in latter times some shall depart from the faith, giving heed to seducing spirits and doctrines of devils.*

And then a passage from Ephesians: *For we wrestle not against flesh and blood, but against principalities, against powers, against the rulers of the darkness of this world, against spiritual wickedness in high places.*

What was this about? Seducing spirits? Rulers of darkness? Spiritual wickedness in high places?

Brooke flipped to other sticky notes and discovered a similar theme. No—more than a theme. An obsession.

Pictures flooded her mind.

Hieronymus Bosch's *Last Judgment.*

Michelangelo's *Torment of St. Anthony.*

Rodin's *Gates of Hell.*

What had been going on in Karl's mind as he read these words? He'd always been rational and at times cynical when it came to religion. He'd had no time for superstition and no patience with those who held to such beliefs. What could explain his interest in these verses?

Brooke took a deep breath and forced herself to calm down. The logical place to seek answers was Karl's church. She could make an appointment to speak to the pastor, but what would she say?

My husband was obsessed with demons. Can you tell me if he was going mad?

That was the crux of it, but she wouldn't word it that way. Instead she'd ask if the pastor had known Karl, and she'd try to find out if he'd had friends or acquaintances at church and perhaps those acquaintances would help her understand what he'd been thinking in the weeks before he died.

Brooke took her phone out of her pocket and stared at it.

Should she really do this? Would the pastor be able to help or would he scoff at her concerns? Or worse, would he exploit her fears by coercing her to attend church on Sunday mornings? It didn't matter if he did. There didn't seem to be any other viable course of action, so she looked up the number and placed the call.

"Birch Hill Fellowship," a woman's voice answered.

"I need to make an appointment to speak to your pastor."

"Of course. May I ask what this is in regard to?"

"A personal matter. And please, I'd like to speak to him as soon as possible."

The voice went silent but returned after a few moments. "Pastor Ingram has some time Thursday morning at nine. Would that work for you?"

She agreed to the time and gave the woman her name.

"Very good," she said. "We'll see you then."

Brooke disconnected and put the phone in her pocket.

What had she just done? Was she being disloyal? Betraying Karl's memory? Making a laughing stock of him?

She looked at the books littering the floor. Some were texts Karl had used in his classes at the university. Some were glossy tomes collected over decades. A few were catalogues from exhibits they'd attended together. She picked up the catalogue from the Cezanne exhibit at the Louvre. Suddenly she was there with Karl, standing in front of *Chateau Noir* with its blotches of blue and green foliage and the house emerging on top of a hill.

Another took her eye. An exhibit at the Guggenheim and another at the Metropolitan. And there were others, each one a trove of memories. The Tate. The Uffizi. MOMA. The Prado.

Brooke leaned against the desk, her thoughts swirling in her head.

For we wrestle not against flesh and blood...

If not flesh and blood—then what? What had Karl been wrestling with in this study late at night?

A powerful gust shook the house followed by a low rumble in the distance. The predicted storm was approaching.

Suddenly terrified, she rushed from the room and slammed the door behind her.

▼ ▼ ▼

David Price glanced out the window of his Miata. A storm was brewing, but it didn't darken his mood. Things had gone better at the gallery than he'd anticipated. He was back in Madeleine's good graces and she'd soon be doing damage control by explaining his behavior on Sunday to the other members of the Tri-County Historical Conservancy's board of directors. He definitely owed her a favor, not just for today but for the many ways she'd offered assistance in the months since he'd returned to his home turf in the Lehigh Valley. She'd even helped him find a house, a two-hundred, fifty-year-old beauty on the Delaware River. With its tasteful blend of period details and contemporary upgrades, the house was the perfect residence for the director of an agency committed to historic preservation.

He turned down a long, wooded lane leading to Brooke's

house. He had pleasant memories of the day he'd met her. Temperatures in the mid-seventies. A breeze out of the west. Bees buzzing. Butterflies fluttering. Birds soaring through a tranquil sky. He'd stopped to admire the paintings and had lingered to admire the artist, a thirty-something woman whose chestnut hair escaped from beneath a floppy hat with flowers on the brim. She'd reminded him of a painting by Itzchak Tarkay with one exception: she didn't seem world-weary like the women Tarkay liked to paint.

David came to a stop in front of the house just as lightning brightened the sky followed by distant thunder. He glanced warily at his surroundings. This house had been plopped down in the middle of a forest. What if a branch broke loose and came crashing down on his car?

Well, he was here now and that was a chance he'd have to take. He got out and climbed the stairs to the porch. Before he could knock, the door flew open. And there she was, staring at him through the screen.

He tried to read her expression. Anger? No. More like fear. A definite case of bad nerves.

And who could blame her for that? She was a recent widow whose house had just been ransacked. She lived all alone in the woods and was probably spooked out of her wits.

"You startled me," she said. "I wasn't expecting anyone."

"I'm sorry. I came here to apologize for my blunder at the retrospective on Sunday. I'd like to make things right."

Her face gave no indication as to whether or not the apology was accepted or whether she even remembered the incident, for that matter.

"I made a mess of things," he continued. "I came here to tell you again how sorry I am."

A spark of recognition flickered across her face. Yes, he could tell she remembered him, and the memory wasn't pleasant.

"Fine," she said abruptly. "You've apologized. So, if that's all…" She started to close the door.

"Wait! I didn't know the situation. I didn't know your husband was…if I'd realized…I mean, I never dreamed, but if I'd known, I wouldn't have said what I said."

Her expression hardened. "How did you get my address?"

"From Madeleine Hewitt. She promised to phone to say I was stopping by." He hesitated. "Don't tell me she didn't call."

"She may have. I haven't checked my messages."

"That explains it." He attempted a smile. "When I saw you at the gallery on Sunday, I remembered that we'd met at an art festival last summer. I didn't know you were Karl Erikson's wife, and I figured you were just one of many guests at the retrospective. If I'd known he was your husband I wouldn't have said the things I said."

She eyed him thoughtfully as though something he'd said had been bothered her. "When was this art festival where we supposedly met?"

"A Sunday in mid-July."

A look of distress darkened her lovely features. "That was the day…"

She didn't need to finish. The look on her face told him all he needed to know. That was the day her husband died.

He struggled to find words. "I'm sorry," he said. "For your loss, first and foremost, and secondly for the way I poured salt in the wounds. Let me know if there's any way I can make it up to you."

She shook her head. "It was kind of you to straighten things out. Now if you'll excuse me I have things I need to do."

He reached into his pocket, brought out a business card, and thrust it at her.

She took it and read aloud. *"David Price, Director. Tri-County Historical Conservancy."* She eyed him curiously.

"We're a non-profit agency that preserves forests, farmland, and historic properties. We serve this county and two adjacent counties. In addition, we act as consultants to museums, schools and universities regarding all aspects of historic preservation."

"I know all about your organization," she said. "My uncle sits on the board. And on several others as well."

"And your uncle is…?"

"Dr. Nelson Roberts."

David felt his spirits lifting. He knew the man. Dr. Roberts was a retired professor whose keen mind and youthful enthusiasm made him a highly valued member of the conservancy's board of directors.

Brooke stood a moment gazing at the card. "Historic properties," she mused. "Do you know anything about antiques?"

"Some. But I generally rely on appraisers and curators to authenticate an item."

"Then perhaps you can help me after all." She explained that she was in the process of settling her husband's estate and she need to know the value some pieces from his side of the family. Could he recommend an appraiser?

David couldn't believe his luck. In a matter of minutes, the conversation had shifted from his idiotic blunder to something he was actually quite competent to discuss. "I know just the person," he said. "Julie Franklin."

"And her rates? Not that it matters. I'm just curious."

"Don't worry about her rates. Consider it taken care of— an act of contrition for the mess I created on Sunday."

"I can't allow a stranger to pay for something like that."

"I won't be paying for anything. Julie owes me a favor. Lots of them, considering all the A-list clients I've pointed in her direction. I'll speak to her tonight and tell her to be in touch." He paused to consider his offer. "I'll need a number where she can reach you."

"I'll get my card."

When Brooke returned, he put the card in his pocket, and after saying goodbye, he darted through the rain that was just beginning to fall.

That went well, he told himself as he guided his Miata down the drive. He'd gotten a load off his chest, but more importantly, he'd established a connection with someone he found interesting.

More than interesting.

She was talented.

Lovely.

And no longer married.

And he wasn't either. Thanks to divorce, not death.

Don't rush things, he told himself as he turned his car toward home. Her husband's only been gone a couple of months and she's still grieving.

He'd wait and follow up on Julie's appraisal with a friendly phone call. *Did the appraisal go smoothly? Was Julie helpful? Did Brooke have any more questions? Was there anything further he could help her with?* That sort of thing.

Later he'd suggest conversation over coffee. Perhaps a walk by the canal.

Nothing too obvious.

Not for a while anyway.

▾ ▾ ▾

Detective Burleigh watched the chief head down the hall. Chief Matt Feldman supported the coroner's original conclusion about Karl Erikson's death: an accident, end of story. Feldman had stopped by Burleigh's office to inform him that the investigation would be short and sweet—a brief review that was expected to verify the coroner's original verdict. In other words, Burleigh was to let sleeping dogs lie and move on to other matters.

He knew better than to raise a ruckus. It wasn't the first time strained budgets, limited resources, and personnel shortages stood in the way of justice. And it wasn't the first time he'd had to dig in his heels and buck the system to get to the truth.

The sheer coincidence of the two events—Erikson's fatal accident followed two months later by the break-in—hinted at a connection. If there was one, he was determined to find it.

He scrolled through the details of the original report. Erikson's body had been discovered in a shallow stream, and the coroner had made a ruling of accidental death: the artist had tripped over something and plummeted down an embankment descending at a 65-degree angle to the water. The impact had knocked him unconscious; the water finished the job. There was nothing at the scene to suggest a struggle, and in the absence of evidence to the contrary, the death had been ruled accidental.

The place had been a favorite spot where the artist often went to commune with nature and think about whatever it was he typically thought about. Burleigh wondered who else knew of this spot, and he wondered if someone might have joined Erikson there that day.

Sounds of laughter spilled out of the break room down the hall. Something was going on today—that's right—the chief's birthday; there'd been a reminder in yesterday's email. Burleigh supposed he'd have to put in an appearance, but at the moment this seemed more important.

He scanned the notes of his various interviews. Stephanie Erikson's alibi was sound and her grief seemed genuine, both at the present time and in the days immediately following her father's death.

The same couldn't be said for Erikson's son. Back in July the interviewing officer had noted Brett Erikson's lack of emotion. It had seemed odd, but grief affects different people in different ways—delayed reactions are not unusual. During the interview this past Monday, Brett claimed to have become emotionally distraught at the sight of his father's paintings. He'd left the gallery in a hurry and said he spent the afternoon visiting outdoor spots he and his dad used to frequent. There were no witnesses to confirm or deny his statement.

Erikson's ex-wife Janine had avoided the retrospective, choosing instead to make a sentimental journey to spots in Philadelphia that had meant something to her and the deceased during their college days. One of the places was an antique store where they used to work. Burleigh checked the story later and verified Janine's account of the matter.

She'd reported eating lunch at the Reading Terminal Market and had provided a receipt to that effect. After some shopping, she took the train home and drove 45 minutes from the station to her residence—not enough time for a detour to ransack Brooke's house and clear out by the time she returned.

Greg Greenwood's alibi was extremely weak. Bird watching? Seriously? He insisted it was a hobby he'd pursued for years, and he'd shown the detectives his binoculars, cameras, photo albums, and books about birds to prove it. But he'd taken no photos of birds that day, and no one could vouch for his whereabouts at the time of the break-in.

Again Burleigh heard laughter from the break room. He recalled opening the fridge that morning and seeing a sheet cake with the words: *Happy Birthday, Chief,* in blue icing. He should be there, kissing up to the boss, but the clock was ticking on the Erikson case and birthday cake would have to wait.

Gallery owner Madeleine Hewitt had a stellar alibi. She'd arrived early at the gallery on Sunday to admit the caterers and get things ready for the retrospective. She'd been there the entire time and had stayed until six to clean up.

Sidney Hewitt was another story. He said he'd had a hangover and had spent the day in bed, getting up only to visit the bathroom or to eat tea and toast. There wasn't a soul to corroborate his story.

None of the people interviewed claimed to have known anything about an object Erikson might have hidden in the house, although several mentioned that he'd been known to pick up odds and ends at flea markets and thrift stores.

The fingerprints at the house were those one might expect,

but there was nothing surprising about that. Thieves knew enough to wear gloves. As far as footprints were concerned—nothing—and the only other evidence was some black threads taken from the broken window.

And that brought Burleigh back to the day of Erikson's fall two months earlier. In the off chance that he'd been murdered, was the killer the same person who'd broken into the house or were the two incidents unrelated?

He leaned back in his chair and closed his eyes. The chances of linking an unnamed object to an unknown burglar and tying it all to a murder that might have been an accident seemed much more difficult than he'd originally thought.

So where to go from here?

He'd pay another visit to the people he'd already interviewed. After that he'd visit the pastor of the church Erikson attended.

And after that? After that the investigation would fizzle out, the boss would have his way, and Burleigh would be left with his doubts.

Which reminded him—he'd better put in an appearance at the party. Best to keep things cozy with the chief.

Six

The worst of the previous night's rain had subsided, leaving behind a chilly mist and a landscape painted in shades of moss and mud. Brooke would have preferred to linger at her uncle's apartment, sipping coffee and reading the paper while Uncle Nelson fussed with his crossword puzzle. But there were things she needed in the house. A change of clothes for one. And Karl's Bible so she could show the highlighted passages to the pastor when they met on Thursday morning.

She drove down the driveway, her thoughts still tangled up in the words Karl had highlighted. They were the stuff of madness, of nightmares and irrational fears. Not that Brooke's fears were all that irrational—just the opposite. The knowledge that something might still be hidden in the house—something that would tempt the intruder to return for another search—weighed heavily on her mind.

Brooke stopped in front of the house and stared at the door. Tomorrow the home security system would be installed. After that she'd feel more secure, or so she hoped.

Today's errand wouldn't take long. Five minutes or so and she'd be back behind the wheel and headed to the safety of her uncle's apartment. Even so, it was difficult to coax herself out of the car and up to the porch. Once inside, she locked the door behind her and stood there, listening for she didn't know what.

The silence was undisturbed and so she continued into the living room. There was a duffle bag on the floor, and on the coffee table, an empty McDonald's bag—witness to the fact that Brett had stayed there the night before, presumably to guard the place, but more likely to snoop around for hidden treasure. In the bathroom she found further evidence of Brett's visit. His shaving kit on the sink and gobs of toothpaste he hadn't bothered to wipe up.

Brooke went into the master bedroom and surveyed her clothes, jewelry, books, make-up, and assorted stuff strewn across the floor. How much of this mess had Brett snooped through? She could picture him inspecting pockets for forgotten dollar bills. Rummaging through jewelry and wondering about its value. Touching her lingerie with vile thoughts stirring in his mind.

Disgusted, she dug through the scattered clothing and found a pair of black capris and a top to wear to her appointment the next day. She stuffed them and a few other items in a tote bag she'd brought with her and returned to the living room.

The door to Karl's study was closed, just as she'd left it yesterday. She started toward it but stopped. Was something waiting on the other side of the door?

Brooke shook off the thought. She'd experienced irrational thoughts years ago after her mother's suicide. Trauma, the therapist had explained. Trauma distorts reality and makes us imagine things that aren't real.

Steeling herself, she went to the door and reached for the knob, but quickly pulled her hand away. She couldn't go back in the study. It was haunted—how else to explain those passages. The Bible would stay on Karl's desk, and tomorrow she'd do her best to tell the pastor what she'd seen without presenting the evidence.

And then reason called out to her and told her to open

the door. There was nothing lurking inside the study. Just memories, and they followed her everywhere.

Brooke opened the door, grabbed the Bible from the desk and stuffed it in her tote bag. Within seconds was she back outside and racing for the car. She dove inside, locked the door, and closed her eyes, surprised at the rapid pounding of her heart.

Once she'd calmed down, she opened her eyes and glanced in the rearview mirror. An unfamiliar black SUV was making its way down the drive. Who did it belong to and why were they there? She wasn't expecting anyone.

Was it the intruder?

Was he returning to finish the job he'd begun?

She looked back at the house. Should she run inside and bolt the door? Too risky. The driver of the SUV would see her and realize she was in there, all alone and frightened. Her only hope was to crouch down in the car and wait for an opportunity to start the engine and escape.

She heard tires crunching on the gravel. The noise ceased and then a car door opened and—bam!—slammed shut. Trembling, she raised herself just enough to see over the edge of the window. A tallish guy in jeans and a black hooded sweatshirt stood with his back to her. He seemed to be removing something from the vehicle, and a moment later she saw what it was. A long-handled axe that he hoisted over his shoulder.

She ducked down again, her heart racing as his footsteps drew closer. She braced herself for the sight of wild eyes staring down at her through the windshield, but the footsteps continued on. Seconds later the crunch of the intruder's boots on the gravel gave way to the clomp, clomp, clomp of his boots on the porch steps, followed by the sound of his fist pounding on the door.

She waited to hear the axe blade shatter the front door as he stormed inside, prepared to smash through drywall and rip up floorboards in a mad desire to find whatever lay hidden there. She listened and waited, but all was strangely silent. Curious, she inched her way up to the window and saw the intruder on the porch looking through the kitchen window.

He turned and she ducked back down. Had he seen her?

Brooke froze as his footsteps clomped down the stairs, but once again he bypassed the car and again there was silence. She peeked out the window and saw him looking into Karl's study. After that, he walked around the house and disappeared from sight.

This was her opportunity. Now that he was out of earshot, she dialed 9-1-1 and listened as the dispatcher told her she was in luck—there was a police car in the area. But she wasn't about to wait for the cops to arrive. She started the engine, backed around, and sped down the driveway in a spray of gravel. A glance in the rearview mirror revealed the intruder bolting from around the house, his axe raised as he shouted for her to stop.

But she didn't stop. Instead she accelerated, her eyes fixed on the rearview mirror. A blast from a horn startled her and there in front of her was the promised police vehicle The driver swerved to avoid a crash, and at the same time she yanked the wheel to the right, lurched off the driveway and bounced to a stop inches from a towering Norway maple. Within seconds a cop was looking at her through the window.

"You all right, ma'am?"

"I'm fine. But the guy at the house has an axe." The officer didn't linger to chat. Instead he turned and raced in that direction on foot.

Brooke collapsed against the steering wheel. *It's okay*, she told herself. *The police are here. I'm safe. Soon the intruder will be in custody and everything will be fine.*

Another vehicle pulled into the driveway—a white sedan with Detective Burleigh at the wheel and his partner in the seat next to him. They continued toward the house, and ten minutes later, Burleigh approached Brooke's car on foot.

"You okay?" he asked as she lowered the window.

"A little shook up, but otherwise fine."

He eyed her with concern. "Sounds like things got a bit scary back there."

She nodded. "Has he admitted to the break-in on Sunday?"

He shook his head. "The guy claims to know nothing about a break-in. He says he's a family friend. Does the name Rob Tate ring a bell?"

"Rob Tate?" Brooke fell silent. Rob was one of Karl's students. Karl's favorite student, if the truth be known. And a decent guy, or so she'd always assumed. Rob hadn't been at the retrospective on Sunday. Had he been here ransacking the place? It didn't seem possible.

"Tate says he stopped by to return an axe your late husband loaned him," Burleigh explained. "He saw your car in the drive and figured you were home. When you didn't answer, he looked through the kitchen window, saw the mess and decided to check it out. He says he was worried something happened to you."

Brooke reran the scene in her mind. "That kind of makes sense," she acknowledged.

She followed the detective down the drive on foot. When they arrived at the police SUV, she immediately recognized the person in the backseat.

"Hey," she said to Rob.

"Hey, yourself," he responded.

She turned to Burleigh and nodded. "Yes. It's definitely Rob."

"Fine then," the detective said. "I need to hear your version of events. After that, you can decide if you want to press charges."

Twenty minutes later Brooke poured a mug of coffee for Rob and another for herself. It seemed like old times having him here in the kitchen, and she could almost imagine Karl coming through the door, pulling up a chair and joining them.

She thought back to the first time Rob had shown up for

classes, his arms laden with sketchpads and drawing materials. He'd emerged from his truck wearing what she'd soon recognized as his standard uniform: jeans, a black tee-shirt and work boots. With his wavy dark hair, rugged jaw and ironic smile, he'd struck her as a portrait waiting to be painted. She'd painted several portraits during the years he'd studied with Karl, but Rob was more than a willing model and a capable student. He'd become part of the family.

"You had your hood pulled up," she explained, "and I couldn't make out your face. And that SUV you were driving— I'm used to your truck."

"It's in the shop. The SUV's a loaner."

"Do you have any idea how scary you looked?"

He shrugged his shoulders. "Pretty scary, judging from the way things went down."

"I was sure you were the guy who broke in on Sunday."

"Hardly. When I saw the kitchen torn apart, I figured something awful happened, so I looked in the other windows and realized the whole house was a mess. I was about to call the cops, but before I knew it, your car was racing down the driveway, the cops were racing in my direction and knocking me to the ground. In no time at all they had me in cuffs and were stuffing me into their vehicle."

He looked over at her and grinned. "Kind of funny when you think about it." He shifted in his seat and his smile faded. "I wasn't just returning the axe," he said, his tone more serious than it had been. "I actually came here to apologize."

"For what?"

"For not showing up at the retrospective on Sunday." He looked down at the puddles dripping on the tiles from his muddy clothes. "The thought of seeing Karl's paintings—so many of them in one place. Somehow I couldn't face it."

Brooke felt a pang of sympathy for the sad-eyed person in front of her. "You don't have to explain. This past Sunday was one of the hardest days of my life. And when I got home…"

She swept her hand to indicate the cans and silverware and dishes strewn around the kitchen. "I had to face all this."

"That totally sucks. You okay?"

She took her time answering. "I'm a mess," she admitted. "I'm skittish and nervous, and when I'm here alone, I can't shake the feeling that somebody's watching me."

"That's completely understandable."

"Maybe. But I can't live this way. It was bad enough thinking of Karl all the time. But now…"

"Listen," he said, his voice tender. "If there's anything I can do, like replacing the basement window for instance, just let me know."

Brooke thought about his offer. There was so much to take care of, she hardly knew where to begin.

"Replacing the window? Sure. I could use some help with that."

Rob got his phone out of his jeans. "I've got some time tomorrow," he said as he scrolled through his calendar. "If it works for you, I'll breeze over here, pick up the window frame, and have it back in place early next week."

"That should work. The people installing the home security system will be here in the afternoon, but I doubt you'll be in their way."

They finished their coffee and put the mugs in the dishwasher. When they went outside, Rob looked up at the studio above the barn.

"I left a bunch of artwork up there. I should pick it up sometime." He glanced at his muddy clothes. "But not today."

"No hurry. It's not like your stuff's in the way. I haven't been up there since Karl died."

"I get it. You don't need to explain."

She watched Rob get in the SUV and head down the drive.

"*Rob's my best student,*" Karl used to remark. "*The best I ever had. He's got that je ne sais quoi that separates true talent from mere technical skill.*"

It was true. Rob was talented, but to Karl, he'd been more than a promising student. He was everything his own son wasn't.

Can you think of anyone who wishes you harm? Detective Radley had asked.

Certainly not Rob. Few people were as trustworthy or reliable.

Seven

Business was slow—dead, if the truth be known, but Madeleine didn't care. She'd started a new suspense novel and had just reached the part where a priceless Caravaggio had mysteriously vanished from the Vatican. The cardinals were in a dither, the pope was outraged, and then the buzzer sounded at the front of the store.

She tossed the book aside. This was no time for customers to show up.

She watched on the monitor as a slender woman with shoulder-length black hair entered the gallery. She wore a simple outfit of navy capris and a flowing white top, but even at this distance, Madeleine could tell the clothes were well-made and expensive.

She popped a breath mint in her mouth and watched the woman pause to look at one painting and then another. After five years of running a gallery, Madeleine had developed a formula for dealing with those who stopped by: give the customer time to form a connection with the artwork. Introductions and offers of assistance could wait.

Once the breath mint had dissolved into nothing, Madeleine touched up her lipstick and sallied forth to greet her customer.

"Welcome to The Hewitt Fine Arts Gallery," she began.

The woman turned and smiled, her perfect teeth gleaming in a bow-shaped mouth. Her lips were tinted in coral with subtle undertones of burnt sienna. Her silver necklace, earrings and bracelet revealed the touch of a New York designer whose pieces Madeleine coveted but couldn't afford. And the woman's fragrance? Hard to tell, but there were hints of lavender as well as something exotic that Madeleine couldn't quite place.

"I missed the retrospective on Sunday," the woman began. "I was out of town, but I promised myself I'd stop by the moment I got back."

"We had quite a crowd," Madeleine responded. "Karl Erikson was a beloved fixture in the regional arts community. Even so, the response far surpassed my expectations."

"Then it's just as well I wasn't here," the woman said, her eyes darting from canvas to canvas. "One needs space to fully appreciate the subtleties of an artist's work. That's not possible in a crowded gallery."

"Well, there's plenty of space at the moment. So, please— make yourself at home. And let me know if I can help."

"Perhaps you can." The woman reached into her bag, pulled out a card and handed it to Madeleine "Could you add my name to the mailing list?"

Madeleine glanced at the card: *Elena Voss, Writer/Producer. The Unveiling, A Production of ALN: the Art of Living Network.*

Well, wasn't this interesting? Elena Voss was exactly the sort of client a gallery owner longs for. In Elena's case the connections would include producers, celebrities, film makers and writers. The sort of sophisticated, well-heeled individuals Madeleine hoped to attract in the future when she opened a gallery in Manhattan. Assuming that ever happened.

"It's a thrill to meet you," Madeleine gushed. "My husband and I are big fans of the series. We watch it every chance we get."

That was a bit of an exaggeration. She and Sid had watched only a few episodes. The show was a lightweight bit of historical fluff that managed to imbue obscure topics with an aura of mysticism. It specialized in vanished treasures. Lost manuscripts that when unearthed had the potential to rewrite history. Enlightened beings who guarded ancient secrets. All quite interesting, and while factually suspect, each episode provided an hour of entertaining food for thought.

Elena crossed the room and stopped in front of a large canvas depicting boats docked at a marina. She stood a while, studying it in silence. "Charming," she finally said. "You can almost feel the boats bobbing up and down in the water."

"I'm fond of it," Madeleine said. She walked closer and pointed to one of eight boats tied up at the dock. "*The Lady Madeleine* was named for yours truly."

Elena looked back at her, puzzled. "How can you bear to part with the painting? It must mean a lot to you"

"Yes, but Sid and I get to keep the memories. Plus hundreds of pictures taken over the years. No, it's time to let it go. We've had lots of compliments on the piece, and I suspect it won't last long."

They walked together into the next room, and Elena's mouth dropped at the sight of Erikson's painting of Brooke, the same painting that had mesmerized David Price the day before.

"Brooke is the late artist's wife," Madeleine explained. "She's an accomplished painter herself. In fact, I have her booked for a show in February, but sadly, she hasn't painted a thing since Karl died. And then on Sunday her home was broken into and ransacked while she was here at the retrospective. The poor thing can't seem to catch a break."

"I'm sorry to hear that. My heart goes out to her. I hope things will soon be looking up." She left it at that and drifted over to a massive floral still life, examining it closely as though inspecting the brushwork. After that she retreated a few steps and walked back and forth, studying it from a variety of angles.

"I love this piece, but I'm not sure about the color palette. It's a bit bold, don't you think?"

"That's the idea. The colors exude optimism and vitality."

Elena turned to Madeleine, a wistful expression on her face. "I have a big favor to ask. I can't make up my mind which I like better—the marina or the floral still life. Could you possibly bring them to my home sometime and help me decide which one looks best in my office."

Madeleine smiled at the lovely creature. "My gallery specializes in the personal touch. Home consultation is one of the many services we offer."

"So you'd do that—really?"

"Of course. It would be my pleasure."

"We'll have lunch," Elena said enthusiastically."Nothing fancy. I'll have my chef throw something together."

"That's not necessary."

"No, I insist." She fell silent, her brow furrowed. "Perhaps you could ask the artist's widow to join us. I'd love to show her a nice time after all she's been through."

"That's very thoughtful of you, but I'm afraid Brooke's been a bit antisocial of late."

"Nonsense. We'll make an occasion of it. We'll have lunch and afterward the two of you can help me make up my mind. Give her a call, won't you, and see what you can set up? For this Friday if possible."

Madeleine felt doubtful. "Two days from now? That's rather short notice. And besides, I can't get Brooke to return my calls, even though I've left countless messages."

Elena seemed unfazed by Madeleine's arguments. "If you can't get through to her, we'll pick another date. But make it soon—before I have a chance to change my mind."

Madeleine watched Elena exit the gallery. How very thoughtful of this busy, successful woman to open her heart and her home in such a loving manner.

Alone again, Madeleine gazed at the painting of the marina and then at the floral still life. Unless Brooke was willing to step up to the plate, the sale would fall through and these large and very pricy canvases would still be hanging when the show closed.

She sighed at the thought. Given that the sale hinged on Brooke's willingness to cooperate, the deal was as good as dead.

▾ ▾ ▾

Brett was having trouble staying focused. Treasurer's report. Minutes from last month's meeting. Voting on new members. Announcements about the elections in November—important midterms given that lodge brothers were campaigning in certain key races.

Then there was the ceremonial stuff. Lots of guys got off on the mumbo-jumbo, but there were plenty like himself who just wanted to advance their careers while at the same time benefiting humanity. Not that Brett cared all that much for humanity. At least not the examples he encountered on a daily basis. Like the detectives who showed up while he was guarding the house the night before.

They'd elbowed their way inside and forced him to regurgitate the stuff he'd already told them. Instead of respecting a son's grief, they'd twisted his words like they were trying to trap him into saying he'd left the retrospective early on Sunday so he could search the house for whatever was supposedly hidden there. And then they'd hinted that the only reason he'd offered to watch the house in the first place was so he could pick up where he'd left off after ransacking it on Sunday.

Okay, so maybe he'd taken advantage of a chance to snoop around, a fact the cops didn't need to know. But overall, his motives had been above reproach. He was one-third owner of the place and had a duty to protect his property.

After that, they'd started prying into his relationship with his mom and his stepdad.

Brett wasn't exactly a fan of Greg Greenwood. Never had been. He couldn't stand the guy's slick style or the touchy-feely,

New Age garbage he dispensed in bucketsful. Energetic heal-ing? Chakra balancing? Aura readings? All a joke. But the past life regressions were the biggest con job of all as Brett had cleverly confirmed a year or so ago.

On a whim, he'd approached Greg for a hypnotic regres-sion. What Greg didn't know was that Bret had cooked up a story beforehand, a fabricated tale about a past life as a hooker named Jezebel who'd worked the streets of Victorian London. On a cold, dark night, according to Brett's supposed past-life memory, Jezebel had met up with Jack the Ripper and ended up in an alley with her throat slashed from ear to ear.

Throughout the session, Brett had piled on the gory de-tails, occasionally grabbing his neck and gagging to make the whole thing seem more believable. Afterward, he'd listened at-tentively to Greg's so-called 'professional analysis' of the ex-perience. Basically, Greg told Brett that his lousy personality was rooted in unresolved past-life, post-traumatic stress disorder stemming from the feelings of helplessness he'd experienced as a whore being murdered by Jack the Ripper. Greg added that until Brett made peace with his ordeal, he could expect to have painful sore throats and a fear of tight collars. Brett still laughed when he thought about it. But one thing was true. He didn't like tight collars.

But the detectives hadn't been particularly interested in Greg's life as a metaphysical con artist. They'd wanted to hear about his life as a possible thief and ransacker of homes. Sadly, Brett knew nothing about Greg's whereabouts on Sunday after-noon, and he honestly didn't care. And yeah, Greg liked to dig out the binoculars and have a look at birds now and then, but what of it? Everybody needs a hobby.

As far as Brett's mom was concerned, if she said she went to Philadelphia on Sunday, she went to Philadelphia. She had a thing for truth, like it was a religion or something.

An announcement pulled him out of his thoughts, and he returned his attention to the meeting. He wondered about the guy—whoever it was—who'd made up all this lodge stuff in the ancient misty past. Secret handshakes. Mystical symbols. Goofy rituals. It was nuts, but somehow it had managed to filter down through the ages. He looked at the men in their outfits. Mayors. Police chiefs. Bank presidents. CEOs. Each guy sopping it up like gravy.

He chuckled to himself. There's a sucker born every minute.

Eight

Brooke watched the pastor's face. The picture on her cell was one she loved. Karl's blue eyes exuded kindness. His smile hinted at his keen sense of humor. The firm line of his jaw suggested the determination and grit that had made him a man of integrity.

But none of that mattered, because Pastor Doug Ingram didn't recognize him. He passed the phone back and told her that a detective named James Burleigh had stopped by the day before asking similar questions with the same results.

The pastor went on to explain that his church had grown considerably in the last few years with new faces coming and going. There were times when he preferred the way things used to be when his congregation was a dozen or so gathered in his living room on Sunday mornings and again on Wednesday evenings for Bible study and prayer. Twenty years later he led three packed services and oversaw a staff of ten. The personal touch seemed a thing of the past.

"I wish I could be of assistance," he added sadly.

"Perhaps you still can." Brooke removed Karl's Bible from her bag and placed it on the desk. "My husband highlighted passages that seem to have a common theme. I'm trying to understand why they were important to him."

Pastor Ingram flipped through the pages and stopped at

several sticky notes to peruse the highlighted texts. He told Brooke the verses were familiar, and yes, she'd correctly identified a common theme. Ephesians 6 spoke of spiritual warfare. Deuteronomy 18 warned against sorcery, witchcraft and necromancy. Second Corinthians 11 alerted the reader to be on guard against deception. Ironically, these troubling words, as dark as they were, provided a glimmer of hope. He might be able to help her after all.

"We recently offered a series of lectures about occultism and paranormal activity," he said. "Given the flavor of these verses, I suspect that your late husband might have attended one or more of those sessions."

He picked up his phone, scrolled through his contact list, and jotted a name and number on a slip of paper. "I'm sure the leader of the workshops will be happy to speak to you. Give him a call and tell him I referred you."

Brooke shook the pastor's hand in parting.

"If you ever need to talk," he said, "the door's always open."

She thanked him and hurried out to her car.

▾ ▾ ▾

Ted Roslyn pulled the covers over his head and tried to ignore the phone squealing on the night stand. It had been a crazy month with back-to-back seminars up and down the West Coast and not much in the way of sleep. He'd taken a red-eye home, and now, all he wanted was to be in a coma for the next 48 hours.

But something—a still, small voice?—told him to answer. Sighing, he boosted himself on one elbow and mumbled a greeting. A woman identified herself as someone—in his present stupor the name slipped by.

"I just met with Pastor Ingram of Birch Hill Fellowship," she said. "He told me you taught a class my late husband might have attended."

"Yeah—I did a lecture series there a couple of months ago."

"Wonderful. Maybe you can help me figure out what my husband was thinking in the days and weeks before he died."

Ted fell silent. Was he a mind reader? How was he supposed to help her with that?

"Karl was an atheist most of his life," she continued. "But sometime in the spring he became obsessed with religion. He marked certain passages in his Bible and then..."

Her voice cracked like she was about to cry. He flopped back against the pillow and stared at the ceiling. He shouldn't have answered the phone. He wasn't in the mood for this. Not after three weeks of non-stop madness made worse by sleep deprivation.

"I know this must sound ridiculous," she continued between sniffles, "but I need to talk to you—as soon as possible. There's something terrible going on and I need to know what it is."

He noticed a crack in the ceiling. How long had it been there? He'd have to tell the property manager about it. Not that it would do much good. The landlord wouldn't lift a finger until the ceiling collapsed and killed him. He imagined the headlines: *Allentown Man Crushed to Death While Sleeping. Landlord Denies Responsibility.*

"Are you still there?" the woman asked. "I really need to talk to you."

He wanted to tell her he had more important things to do, like sinking into oblivion for the next two days. But the same still small voice that had prompted him to answer seemed to be urging him forward.

He let out a sigh. "I guess we can meet somewhere. Where are you?"

"In the parking lot outside Birch Hill Fellowship."

He gave her the name of a coffee shop in a local strip mall.

"I can be there in half an hour. How will I know it's you?" He paused to listen. "You'll be carrying a black leather Bible? Fine. I'll see you then."

Half an hour later he stared through weary eyes at a massive chalkboard. The choices were complex and a bit much to wade through given his present state of mind. There was Iced Vanilla Mist. Mocha Madness. Dark Chocolate Café Melange. And for fall, the inevitable seasonal blends like Pumpkin Streusel Latte and Praline Pumpkin Kiss. He ordered a Mocha Caramel Sea Salt Latte, and glanced around at the coffee shop patrons. There were exactly zero black leather Bibles to be seen, and having missed the caller's name, a black leather Bible was all he had to go on. Other than that, he was searching for an unhappy somebody with no name. A sad-eyed woman of mystery.

Latte in hand, he selected a table near the door, sat down, and took a sip and then another. He closed his eyes in anticipation of a caffeine rush, but nothing happened. Not even a vague flutter in his prefrontal cortex. No surprise. Given his recent sleep deprivation, it would take at least five gallons of the stuff to launch even a minor buzz.

He turned his sleepy gaze to the parking lot and watched the cars passing on the street. He sat up a bit straighter each time one pulled into the lot and slumped down again when someone other than a woman with a Bible emerged. After about ten minutes, a woman carrying a bulky, black book got out of a KIA Sportage. She wasn't bad looking and all in all was a pleasant surprise, given his expectations. As she came through the door, he noticed that her eyes were puffy, like she'd been crying. But if this sad-eyed woman of mystery wasn't on top of her game, neither was he, as she was soon to find out.

Nonetheless, he arose from his seat like the gentleman he was and walked over to the door. "Ted Roslyn," he said. "And you must be…"

"Brooke. Brooke Roberts."

Brooke. That was a nice name, like a happy little stream in summer. But he preferred Sad-Eyed Woman of Mystery. Hopefully he wouldn't slip and refer to her that way.

"Coffee?" he asked.

"I'll get it myself."

He knew better than to insist. Women were touchy these days and inclined to read twisted meanings into a guy's friendly overtures. He watched as she went to the counter and placed her order. Sad Eyes looked to be about his age or a bit younger—somewhere in her mid-thirties, he supposed. She was slender in a pair of black capris and a white tunic sort of top and totally young to be a widow. Not that husbands couldn't pop off at any moment, but to Ted the word *widow* suggested a feeble old thing watering African violets and looking sadly at photos of people who'd died a hundred years ago. This woman looked healthy enough to win the Boston Marathon.

After a few minutes, the sad-eyed woman of mystery slid into the empty seat across from him.

"Sounds like you've hit a rough patch of road," he said, in way of an opener.

"You might say that."

"Tell me about it."

He listened to a litany of troubles. Her marriage strained by her husband's religious conversion. His accidental death that was now considered suspicious. Her house broken into and ransacked. And then she'd come across his Bible.

She passed it across the table. "My husband's name is—was—Karl Erikson. He highlighted several passages, and the subject matter caused Pastor Ingram to think he might have attended your lectures. I'm trying to understand exactly what he was thinking before he died."

She looked at him, her blue-green eyes all watery and threatening to overflow. Thankfully she didn't cry—Ted was no good once the tears started flowing. Instead she turned her gaze out the window and sat there like the saddest person in the world.

He felt something tug at his heart. Something that awakened his inner knight in shining armor.

He took the Bible and flipped through the highlighted passages. Saul and the Witch of Endor. The prohibitions against sorcery in Deuteronomy. Spiritual warfare in Ephesians 6.

"Yeah," he said. "I would have referred to these passages."

"Was my husband in the audience? Did you meet him?"

He shrugged. "The name Karl Erikson doesn't ring a bell. But I didn't take attendance or pass around a sign-up sheet. People just showed up. Lots of them. Some I knew. Some I didn't. And unless someone stayed afterward to talk, I wouldn't remember them."

She handed him her phone. "Maybe this will help."

Ted studied the face on the screen. A warm smile. Sparkling eyes. Smart looking. And way too old for the hot tamale seated across from him. But that was none of his business—to each his own as the saying goes.

In spite of Ted's late-stage sleep deprivation, something shifted in his brain and he seemed to recognize the guy. He combed through his mental files, trying to recall where and when they'd met. A light flashed on. The end of a lecture. People filing out of the room. A man with graying hair and a closely trimmed beard.

"I remember now," he said. "It was a Sunday in mid-July. Your husband stayed after to ask questions."

"A Sunday in mid-July? That was the day..."

She didn't need to finish because her face said it all. They were talking about the day her husband died. After a bombshell like that, Ted felt pretty tongue-tied, so he waited for her to continue.

"What questions did he ask?"

Again Ted had to scan his mental hard drive, but eventually he recalled what the man had asked him. "He asked about occult ritual objects."

Sad Eyes seemed confused by the news. "Occult ritual objects? As in magic? As in pulling rabbits out of a hat—that kind of thing?"

"No. Definitely not rabbits. He told me he picked up a medallion at a Salvation Army thrift shop. Metal—possibly gold—with runic markings on one side. He thought it might have been used in occult rituals."

"Why would he think that?"

"He had somebody look at it. An appraiser, I suppose. The person—whoever it was—said that if the thing was genuine, it would be valuable."

She turned and looked out the window, and when he followed her gaze he realized there was nothing out there of interest. She was just trying to piece things together in her head. He took a sip of his Double Caramel Sea Salt Latte and waited for her to speak which she eventually did.

"What else did Karl talk to you about?"

He took a moment to frame his answer. Sad Eyes was upset, and his words weren't going to make her feel much better.

"Your husband wanted to know if occult ritual objects possess powers of their own or if their alleged powers are derived from the imagination of the user."

"And you told him the latter was true—right?"

"Yes and no. I explained that in many cases a practitioner expects a ritual object to deliver a certain outcome, so he or she inadvertently skews the results to match those expectations. We call that 'confirmation bias.'"

Brooke nodded. "Karl would have agreed with that. And so would I."

"But there's more to it, and that's what your husband was most interested in."

She waited for him to continue.

"Imagine, if you will, that reality exists in more dimensions than the human mind can perceive. And imagine that at least one of those unperceived dimensions is populated by unseen beings."

"Angels and demons?"

"Bingo." He watched the expression on her face. Skepticism on steroids. The skepticism would only deepen before he was through.

"Practitioners use occult ritual objects to access these unseen realms," Ted continued. "The problem is that these practices—even those that appear benign—are governed by dark entities—demons—who wish us harm. They promise a favorable outcome, but over time they deliver just the opposite.

"And that brings us back to your husband's question about the source of power behind an occult ritual object. Demonic entities often attach themselves to specific objects and use them as tools to manipulate and deceive the person handling them."

He watched her face. She was analyzing. Processing. And definitely not buying any of it. He waited for her to speak, and she did so almost immediately.

"This is the twenty-first century," Brooke announced, as though he was unaware of the fact. "Belief in demons died out with the Dark Ages. Nowadays, only religious fanatics and crazy people buy into this nonsense." She glared at him like he'd committed a crime. "I was hoping for concrete information I could share with the police. Instead you're telling me nonsense."

"Really? You'd be surprised at the occult activity cops have encountered over the years. Some of it pretty creepy."

"Like what? Chicken bones and pentagrams and black candles? That's nothing but kids fooling around and trying to scare each other."

She picked up the Bible and flashed him the defiant sort of look a woman gives a guy when she's about to hit him between the eyes with a verbal two-by-four. "I appreciate your taking the time to meet with me," she said, her voice snotty like she could care less that he'd dragged himself out of bed to answer her questions. "Now, if you'll excuse me…"

She got out of her seat and marched toward the door, but instead of storming into the parking lot, she stopped in her tracks, frozen, like an ice sculpture. It took her a moment to thaw out, and when she did, she returned to the table and sank down in the seat she'd just vacated.

"One last question. Was someone with Karl when he spoke to you? A woman, perhaps?"

Ted hadn't seen that coming. All the above and now adultery? The plot had thickened fast, like quick-drying cement.

He thought back to the moment in question. "The room was crowded. If someone was with your husband, I didn't notice."

Brooke sat silently, and he couldn't tell if she was relieved or upset by the lack of information.

"So where do I go from here?" she asked.

He reached into his pocket, got out a business card and handed it to her. "Check out my website and YouTube channel. If you'd like to talk further, feel free to give me a call."

Nine

Detective Burleigh was surprised to find Brooke's place humming with activity. Vans sporting *Stay Safe Security Systems* logos crowded the driveway while workers in *Stay Safe* tee-shirts roamed the property, stringing wires and mounting electronic gizmos to the house and surrounding trees. The detective was familiar with *Stay Safe*'s products. They cost a pretty penny but were well worth it. Brooke would indeed be safe once the system was up and running.

He got out of the car and when he approached the house, he found Rob Tate kneeling on the porch helping a red-headed guy connect some wires. He looked up, and if Burleigh was reading him correctly, Tate wasn't overjoyed to see him again. Who could blame him after the rough treatment he'd received the day before?

Rob's expression softened and his face broke into a grin. "You decided to arrest me after all?"

Burleigh pretended to be stern. "So far you're in the clear. Make sure it stays that way."

He left it at that. No point in mentioning that as one of Erikson's students, Rob was on the list of people yet to be interviewed.

The detective navigated his way through the clutter of tools and wires on the porch. A quick knock brought Brooke to the door, and he noticed that her eyes were puffy like she'd been crying or not sleeping. Or, as was more likely, both.

She pushed a strand of hair behind one ear and stepped aside for him to enter the house. And then she hesitated as though noticing Rob Tate for the first time.

"Why are you still here?" she asked. "Is there a problem with the window?"

"Nope. It's in my truck. I'll have it fixed and back in place in no time."

The red-headed guy spoke up. "Your friend here's a quick study. I show him something, and he's got it in two seconds. I might have to offer him a job before the day's over."

Burleigh followed Brooke into the living room. The furniture had been righted and some of the clutter picked up. "I see you've been busy," he commented.

"Karl's son has been staying here and keeping an eye on things while I'm at my uncle's. Last night he actually straightened up a bit, and I've been slowly putting things away." She looked around and sighed. "There's still a lot to do."

She gestured toward the sofa and the detective took a seat. The cushions—or what was left of them—sank beneath his weight. Brooke sat down in the chair across from the sofa and began with an apology for the previous day's false alarm. He assured her that she'd done the right thing and then he waited for her to proceed. He was there at her invitation, after all.

"I learned something new this morning," she finally said. "But it's pretty crazy."

"I hear lots of crazy stuff."

She shifted her gaze toward a closed door on the other side of the room. "There's something I need to show you. I'll just be a minute." She got out of her seat and returned with a book that she handed to him.

"Karl's Bible," she explained. "He marked some pages with sticky notes and highlighted several verses. See if you can detect a theme."

"Not my specialty," Burleigh remarked as he took the leather-bound book from her hand. "I was basically a Sunday school dropout."

His comment elicited a smile. "Me too. Still, I think you should take a look."

He flipped to the pages indicated. She was right. While the texts were unfamiliar, the theme was crystal clear. Powers of darkness. Forces of evil. Demons. He turned to a passage in Deuteronomy and mentally ticked off a list that included divination, sorcery, and witchcraft.

He looked up at her. "Was your husband interested in these topics?"

She shook her head and said that discovering these texts had come as a surprise. She went on to explain that she'd spoken to Pastor Ingram at Birch Hill Fellowship, and he'd referred her to a guy named Ted Roslyn who led seminars on these kinds of topics. They'd met at a coffee shop, and when she showed him a photo of her late husband, he remembered speaking to him about an occult ritual object Karl had purchased at a thrift shop.

Burleigh felt the hairs bristling at the back of his neck. He hadn't anticipated the investigation taking this turn. Some of the darkest cases he'd handled in his thirty-five-year career had their roots in occult practices. He recalled crimes so brutal, so inhuman, and so terrifying that they defied description.

"Did Roslyn say which thrift shop?"

"Salvation Army. I'd imagine there are only a few in the area."

He made a mental note to visit every Salvation Army thrift shop within a thirty-mile radius.

"And there's something else," she said. "The day Karl spoke to Ted was the same day he died."

The detective struggled to maintain his trademark poker face. Brooke's words had just opened up a sea of possibilities, including ones that implicated Ted Roslyn in Erikson's death.

"I'll need Roslyn's contact information," he said.

She went into an adjacent room and returned with a business card. He jotted down the information, returned the card and extricated himself from the slashed sofa cushions, feeling old and clumsy as he struggled to his feet.

He thanked Brooke for the information and excused himself. Outside the work crew seemed to be wrapping things up. Rob Tate was still there and was still lending a hand to the Stay-Safe team. Burleigh studied him from a distance. Had Karl Erikson shown Rob this occult ritual object? Was it something he coveted, and if so, did that explain his fascination with the home security system? Was he hoping to enter the house without triggering the alarms so he could search for it?

Burleigh decided to pay a visit to Rob Tate. Sooner rather than later. And that went for Ted Roslyn as well.

▾ ▾ ▾

Brooke watched from the kitchen window as Burleigh's car disappeared down the drive. She'd expected him to scoff at the notion of demons and dismiss the matter as superstitious nonsense. Instead, he'd taken it seriously.

She'd have preferred scoffing. His somber reaction had only added to her uneasiness.

There was a knock at the door. "Everything's hooked up," the red-headed installer announced. "Time now for the grand tour and a tutorial on how this stuff works."

She followed him outside to a small rectangular sign next to the driveway: *This Home is Protected by Stay-Safe Security Systems.*

"Our first line of defense is low-tech but highly effective," he began. "When an intruder sees our sign, he typically backs off. If he doesn't, he'll be sorry."

He pointed out signs placed here and there around the property. After that, he directed Brooke's attention to video cameras and motion detectors tucked among the branches of evergreens and near the roofline of the house and barn. From there, they moved inside where he showed her how to access the display monitor next to the front door as well as similar monitors in her home office and master bedroom. Finally he demonstrated the settings on the alarms near the doors and gave directions for setting them each time she went out and came back in.

"Think you'll sleep better tonight?" he asked, once the tour was complete.

"That's the plan," she responded, although she had her doubts.

He told her a user's manual was available on the company's website and said she should call the 800 number if she had any questions.

They left and Rob followed a few minutes later. Brooke felt a deep loneliness as his truck disappeared down the drive. If Karl were still alive, Rob would have stayed for dinner. They'd have lit candles and then the discussions would have begun. Politics, history, art. Their conversation would have lingered well into the night.

She went back inside and touched a video monitor, watching as the scene shifted from the porch to the barn to the woods at the rear of the house to the trees on the south side of the property to the length of the driveway.

All was well, and she was safe inside a high-tech fortress.

And yet she still felt vulnerable.

The object might still be in the house and until she knew for certain, she'd have no peace.

Her phone squealed in her pocket. She glanced at the screen and saw Madeleine Hewitt's number. Normally she would have let it go to voicemail, but in her present distress, she welcomed the sound of a human voice.

The conversation was brief. A potential client had expressed interest in two large canvasses. She'd invited Madeleine and Brooke to her home on Friday to offer their opinions. Madeleine knew Brooke was unlikely to accept, but she was extending the invitation anyway.

"I'll go," Brooke said abruptly. "I need to get out of the house."

For a moment there was silence. "Well, that's a surprise. I'd prepared a dozen arguments to persuade you, and now I won't need any of them. I'm sure Elena will be pleased. She's asked us to have lunch after which we'll help her make her decision. I'll pick you up at 11:30."

As they hung up, Brooke heard a faint noise through the open window. She reacted accordingly. Sweaty palms. Racing heartbeat. Shortness of breath. She dashed to the monitor and saw a trio of deer grazing near the barn. No demons. Just Bambi and friends.

She chided herself for her fears and set about getting the bedroom ready for the night. She threw the bedding in the washing machine, picked up the clothes from the floor and tossed the jewelry in a drawer without sorting through the various pieces. Hours later she lay beneath freshly laundered sheets, listening to the chirping of crickets outside the open window.

Brooke missed the warmth of Karl next to her, and she missed his strength and his quiet self-assurance that let her know that all was well. She'd never considered needing a man to keep her safe. There'd been no need to think that way because the world she and Karl had shared had been a safe place, a place filled with art and music and the laughter of friends. Danger existed somewhere out there in worlds that had no bearing on their own. But she was alone now, and the safe world she remembered was a thing of the past.

It took a while but she eventually fell asleep. And then she was suddenly awake, every nerve on edge and every sense attuned to her surroundings. She glanced at the clock. Two-thirty.

She threw off the covers and crossed the room to the monitor. The first screen showed the barn and the surrounding trees. No one was there, not even a deer or a rabbit or a raccoon. The same was true at the side of the house and in the back.

She brought up a view of the driveway, rewound the video and watched, her heart racing as a man dressed in black walked toward the house. A hooded jacket shaded his face, but she could see his closely trimmed dark beard and mustache. He stopped at the first *Stay Safe* sign and after staring at it, he reached into a pocket for his phone. He kept his gaze fixed on the house, and when the call ended, he headed back down the driveway toward the road. The sound of his steps on the gravel was what had awakened her.

She touched the screen to trigger an alarm. In minutes a policewoman and a male officer were at the door. They watched the video, searched the property, and came up empty-handed. The policewoman praised the home security system for providing protection, and she told Brooke to put the incident out of her mind and get some sleep.

Easy for the cops to say.

Instead of going back to bed, she made a cup of mint tea and took it into the living room.

Can you think of anyone who wishes you harm?

Yes, she could. Not a demon, but a flesh and blood man who'd approached the house and vanished in the night.

Ten

B it by bit reality filtered back. Flecks of light through stained glass. A blue jay's raucous chatter from a nearby tree. Fragrances wafting up from the kitchen.

Elena Voss opened her eyes and gazed at the lacquered box open before her. Inside were the rarest pieces in her collection. A jeweled falcon from Egypt's Nubian Dynasty. A Thai Buddha in gold and jade. An ancient Canaanite idol. A small, first century carving of Artemis from the temple in Ephesus. And many more.

Some she'd acquired in crowded marketplaces teaming with merchants and thieves. Others had found their way to her from vendors known only to those who could meet their price. Others had filtered through a network of shady characters who trafficked in stolen artifacts. But each of these pieces, however noteworthy, was nothing compared to the one that had slipped through her fingers.

The medallion and eleven others like it had changed hands many times over the centuries. One day each would find its way to one of twelve individuals deemed worthy. She intended to be one of the twelve.

She rose from her prayer rug and gazed at a stained glass window that depicted angels descending from heaven. The window was only one of the many details she loved about the charming Lehigh Valley Victorian she'd purchased a year ago, but mostly she loved the house's provenance. Its previous owner had been a personal friend and confidant of renowned Theosophist Alice Bailey. Elena had heard stories about the rituals and secret ceremonies conducted within these walls, and having heard the stories, she understood why the place had immediately felt like home.

She smoothed her gray slacks and inspected her image in a full-length mirror. Her flowing white top was cut shorter in the front than in the back, creating an air of graceful fluidity when she walked. Moonstone earrings set in silver glistened against the background of her lustrous black hair and matching pieces graced her neck and wrists. Her appearance, like the meal her chef was preparing, was striking yet understated, chosen to impress but not intimidate.

Her plans had come together quickly, and she wondered if she may have omitted a detail or overlooked something of importance. To add to her uncertainty, her spirit guide had been late in arriving and minutes had ticked by as she'd sought its presence. When he finally arrived, his message had been brief but clear: *Build bridges, not walls.*

The housekeeper's voice over the intercom announced her guests.

She glanced again at her image in the mirror. She was nervous, and she wasn't accustomed to being nervous. But with so much riding on this occasion, it was all she could do to settle the butterflies fluttering wildly in her belly.

She hastened down the stairs and found Madeleine and Brooke in the sitting room off the foyer. She greeted Madeleine with a quick hug, but her approach to Brooke was more measured. She didn't want to frighten this wounded bird—not if she hoped to lure her into a gilded cage and lock the door behind her.

So how should she proceed? Normally she'd have begun by praising Karl Erikson's artwork. That, of course, was the reason for the luncheon. But the gallery owner had made it clear that Brooke's grief was still raw, and Elena feared that reminding Brooke of her husband's passing would cast a dark spell over the conversation. She decided on small talk and aimless chatter to lighten the mood. After that, her guide would help her build bridges, not walls.

She began with casual remarks about the weather. So unpredictable this year. Dreary days punctuated by occasional crisp mornings and bright, warm afternoons. Planning what to wear under such changeable conditions was a nightmare.

She continued the pleasant banter as she escorted her guests to the dining room. Once seated, she endured Madeleine's effusive compliments: *So elegant—so French—so straight out of Versailles. And the china—Limoges? Family pieces? You must tell me where you shop for antiques. And the glasses? Irish crystal or Venetian?*

And so on.

Eventually Madeleine ran out of praise for Elena's dining room and its accoutrements and moved on to other topics. "I want to hear all about that exciting cable series you're working on. I don't know which season I liked better. *The Unveiling of the Pyramids* or the series about the secrets of the Himalayas. And I'm so looking forward to the coming season: *The Unveiling of the English Renaissance*. How exciting."

Elena took a taste of lobster bisque and watched Brooke's face. There seemed to be a shift in her demeanor. A slight brightening of her expression at the mention of the English Renaissance. Had the subject aroused her interest? Elena would have to explore further.

"I've bitten off a lot with this next season," she remarked. "In spite of the volumes of material about Elizabeth I, she was a highly secretive woman who left behind countless unanswered questions. For starters, was she really a virgin? Some would say a definite 'yes' while others claim she bore a child in her early teens to a rogue named Thomas Seymour. Some claim the child grew up to be Edward de Vere, who, incidentally is believed by many to be the true author of Shakespeare's plays."

Again she watched Brooke's face. There was no misreading her expression. She was definitely interested in the topic.

Elena continued in that vein. "We can't forget Elizabeth's scandalous flirtations with Robert Dudley and the question of whether or not she conspired with him to murder his wife. And there are some—if you can believe it—who actually suggest that Elizabeth was a man."

"Nonsense," Madeleine scoffed. "That would have been impossible."

"I've heard that theory," Brooke spoke up. "It was popularized by Bram Stoker, the author of *Dracula*."

There was no doubt about it. The ice princess was warming up. The more her reserve melted, the easier it would be for Elena to draw her in and bend her to her will.

She smiled at the unsuspecting creature. "You're absolutely right. Based on his research, Bram Stoker felt confident in claiming that Elizabeth died in childhood of a plague. Her caretakers, fearful of being accused of negligence and beheaded by an irate Henry VIII, substituted a young boy with similar features, but needless to say, the subterfuge became difficult to hide as the boy became a man. The queen's closest advisors and her personal physician were the only ones entrusted with the secret."

"That's absurd," Madeleine said, clearly not persuaded by what she'd heard.

"Of course it is," Elena agreed, "but it's one of many lingering mysteries about her life. And the secrecy didn't stop with the queen. Her entire court was a hornet's nest of intrigue. Her astrologer claimed direct communication with angels. Her spymaster created a network of spies stationed all over England and the continent. And as I already mentioned, there's the enduring question as to who really wrote the plays attributed to William Shakespeare."

"My uncle considers himself an expert on the authorship question," Brooke commented as the housekeeper removed the soup bowls.

Elena felt a tingle of excitement. Was this the bridge she was meant to build? Shakespeare via Brooke's uncle?

"Your uncle must be an intelligent man," Elena remarked.

Brooke rose to the bait, her reserve melting as she spoke of the man who clearly meant everything to her. She described Dr. Nelson Roberts as a retired professor of mechanical engineering with interests that encompassed a variety of subjects ranging from Shakespeare to Bach to early twentieth-century art. She spoke of him as a stabilizing force in her life, and a support when her father vanished years ago and again when her mother died. More recently he'd been an anchor following her husband's death and the upheaval of Sunday's break-in.

And with that, she fell silent as though she'd revealed too much and was regretting the fact.

Elena refrained from probing. She wanted Brooke to be comfortable and at ease when she made her move. If that required steering the conversation out of murky waters and into a brighter estuary, that's exactly what she'd do. Soon her guests were laughing at Elena's stories about her co-workers in New York and smiling at her description of an outlandish new boutique and promising to visit a perfumery on Fifth Avenue that created made-to-order fragrances.

She maintained a light touch as they worked their way through grilled salmon with asparagus followed by chocolate crepes topped with strawberries and whipped cream. After coffee, they adjourned to Elena's second floor office and discovered that the canvases had already been delivered by the chef who'd grumbled about being asked to transport them from the back of Madeleine's van.

The gallery owner eyed the paintings that leaned side by side along one wall. "I prefer the marina," she announced. "The mottled blue of the water, the variegated colors of the boats, the hints of pink and pale orange in the sails work together to provide a sense of serenity." She smiled at her hostess. "Just the thing for jangled nerves facing deadline pressures."

Elena narrowed her gaze and studied the paintings. "Serenity isn't quite what I was going for. When I'm under deadline pressure—which is basically every day of my life—I need to feel energized."

She turned to the floral still life. "I like the vitality of this piece. It's bright and cheerful, like a splash of sunlight on a winter's day."

She glanced at Brooke. "I'm torn. Tranquility or energy. Which do you prefer?"

She watched Brooke glance around the room with its prayer rug, home altar, crystals, statuettes of ancient goddesses, and the stained glass angels descending from the heavens. Brooke's gaze came to rest on an image of John Dee, alchemist and court astrologer to Queen Elizabeth I.

"To tell you the truth," she said slowly. "I don't think either canvas is right for this room."

Madeleine's hand flew to her heart. "You can't be serious! They're both stunning. The colors! The lighting! They're perfect. Either would be charming."

Elena watched Madeleine's reaction with amusement. She was clearly mortified that Brooke was threatening an important sale.

"The room has an ethereal feeling," Brooke explained. "Neither painting supports that sensibility."

She was right but it hardly mattered because Elena had little interest in either canvas—at least for their usual purpose as decorative items. They were merely a means to an end that she would soon explore.

She smiled at Brooke. "I appreciate your honesty."

Brooke returned the smile. There it was. A connection. A bridge. Things were proceeding according to plan.

"She's right," Elena told Madeleine." We'll take a quick

tour of the house, and if we find suitable locations, I might decide to buy not one, but both."

The news seemed to revive Madeleine's spirits. The women returned to the first floor and once the tour was complete, they agreed that the library was the ideal spot for the painting of the marina while the floral still life was best suited for the sitting room looking out over the rose garden.

After that they said their goodbyes and Elena escorted them to the van in the driveway.

"I'm thrilled with my purchases," she said to Madeleine. "Just like that, we've transformed two rooms—as if by magic!"

Madeleine nodded toward Brooke who'd lagged behind to admire the roses. "That's not the only magic that happened here today. Other than the retrospective, this is the first time Brooke's socialized since Karl's death—and the first time I've seen her smile. It's wonderful what you were able to accomplish."

Elena followed Madeleine's gaze. Brooke seemed much more relaxed than when she'd first arrived and perfectly at peace among the roses.

"She's a talented painter," Madeleine remarked. "And an accomplished editor as well. Hopefully she'll find her footing and get back to both."

Elena felt a prickling sensation at the back of her neck, a sure sign that her spirit guide was calling her to attention. "If you'll excuse me," she murmured, "I'd like to tell Brooke how glad I am she joined us today."

She approached Brooke and thanked her again for being honest, even though it meant risking a sale. After that, she invited her to come back to see the paintings once they were hung.

Brooke made no response. Not an acceptance. Not a refusal. Nothing.

Elena felt a momentary panic. The woman was about to slip away, and if she hoped to solidify their relationship, she needed to do it now.

She touched Brooke's arm in an intimate gesture like those shared by friends. "Madeleine mentioned that you're an editor. A good one. I could use some help sifting through the volumes of information our researchers have compiled for the upcoming season. You have a background in Renaissance history, and you've proven you can render an honest opinion. I'd be grateful if you'd agree to help out."

She watched Brooke's face but saw no response. "Of course, if you're not interested..."

Brooke shook her head. "I'm sorry, but since Karl's death, I've neglected my own clients. I appreciate your offer, but now isn't the time."

Elena reached into her pocket and withdrew her business card. "You don't have to decide right away. Give me a call when you're ready. We'll get together and talk."

She watched as her guests got into the van and departed. The afternoon had been a success. She'd melted Brooke's icy reserve, and as a bonus, she had two paintings done by Karl Erikson. She didn't care about the subject matter; she only cared that the canvases were vessels for his energy. Before long, her spirit guide would put that energy to good use.

▾ ▾ ▾

Ezra Simmons gazed out the display window of Mordecai's Antiques and Oddities. The guy with the reflecting sunglasses was back again. He'd noticed him staring at the store and walking up and down the block with his phone pressed to his ear. At one point Ezra had stood close to the window to get a better view, and to his surprise, the guy had smirked and nodded a greeting. Since then, Ezra remained at a distance from the window.

Once the man was gone, Ezra went to the office at the rear of the store to look in on his dad. Satisfied that the old man had enough tasks to keep him occupied, he returned to the front room to shelve some items he'd acquired at an on-line auction.

He was setting up a Halloween display when the door opened and the man with the reflecting sunglasses walked in. His hair was dark, his features hard and angular, his narrow, unsmiling mouth surrounded by a dark, neatly trimmed beard and mustache. He wore black jeans, a black tee-shirt and a black jacket. A tough guy outfit. An outfit that said, *don't mess with me.*

The man paused to look at some vintage Barbie dolls dressed like nuns. He picked one up and scowled at it, like it brought back unpleasant memories. After that, he moved on to a set of gargoyle bookends and then to a crystal ball that had once belonged to a carnival fortune teller. Finally he crossed the room and stopped in front of a 1920's beaded peacock lamp.

"Can I help you?" Ezra asked.

"Maybe. I'm looking for Ezra Simmons."

"That would be me."

The man gave him the once over, or at least it seemed that way. All Ezra could see was his own image reflected in the man's sunglasses. Make that two images. One in each lens.

"Interesting place you've got here," the man said. "Quirky, if you know what I mean."

"That's how we like it."

"I understand it's been in the family a long while."

"I'm the third generation."

"It'd be a shame if you were the last."

A chill snaked up Ezra's spine. "Are you looking for something specific?"

"Yeah. A place where we can talk. In private."

Another chill. "You're the only customer in the store. We can talk right here."

The man poked the finger at the lamp, watching as the beads swayed back and forth. "I understand this store's got a reputation for playing fair with buyers and sellers," he remarked. "Confidentiality. Discretion. That sort of thing."

"I like to think so."

"I'm here for a client of mine," he said without taking his eyes off the lamp. "She spoke to you a while back about a medallion."

Ezra drew in his breath. This guy worked for Elena Voss. Ezra had always dealt directly with Elena and the fact that she'd dispatched a lackey didn't bode well. He decided to bluff and pretend he had no clue what the guy was talking about.

"I speak to lots of people about lots of objects," he said casually, like none of this mattered. "That includes medallions. Could you be more specific?"

"Sure, I can be more specific," the man said as he watched the beads sway back and forth. "The object in question belonged to an artist who brought it here for a quick appraisal. He had no intention of selling the thing and no intention of releasing his contact information to a potential buyer. Even so, you gave the guy's information to my client in exchange for a handsome fee and an understanding that this was an exclusive arrangement and she would do her own negotiations. Imagine her surprise when she found out somebody was in line ahead of her."

Ezra felt tiny beads of sweat break out on his upper lip. "There was no one else," he stammered. "Your client is the only one I dealt with. When I say an arrangement is exclusive, that's exactly what I mean." There, he'd told the truth but how could he convince this man to believe him?

The guy appeared to lose interest in the lamp and its beaded fringe. He took a few steps closer to Ezra, and as he did, Ezra could see his own reflection—his graying hair, thick brows, worried expression—growing larger and larger in the man's sunglasses.

"Say what you like," the guy said with a smirk, "but we both know you played dirty with my client and she's not one bit happy about it. But since she's a nice lady, she's willing to make you a deal. Get your hands on the medallion and deliver it within a week and nobody gets hurt. Understand?"

Ezra's knees turned to jelly. "I've got no control over the matter. The individual who owned the item is dead, and I heard that his house was robbed. I don't know where the thing is, so how am I supposed to get my hands on it?"

"A challenging problem, indeed. I hope you come up with an answer."

"I'm telling you, I gave the contact information to only one person."

"My client thinks otherwise. Find the medallion and we'll drop the whole thing."

The man was about to leave, but he stopped at the door and took his phone out of his pocket. He came back to show Ezra a photo of a thirty-something woman with blue-green eyes and chin-length chestnut hair.

"The artist's widow," the man told him. "If she walks through your door, let us know right away and we just might go easy on you."

Eleven

adeleine raised a glass of white wine in a toast to herself. Two large canvases sold in the blink of an eye. It was time to celebrate.

She took a sip, swallowed, and stared at the empty seat across from her. Sid should be here to share the moment. Honestly, how long could a trip to the men's room take?

She leaned out of the booth to get a better look at the bar in the next room. There he was; a glass in his hand and a grin plastered across his face as he laughed it up with the bartender. Madeleine knew her husband's methods. He'd figured he could enjoy at least one drink she wouldn't be able to count.

She thought about calling him to task for his sly tomfoolery, but decided against it. She wanted him in a good mood tonight, especially if and when the topic of money came up. And if that meant tolerating his being pie-eyed by the time they left Antoine's, so be it.

She watched as he expanded his audience to include his fellow drinkers. She had to smile in spite of herself. Wherever her husband went, a party followed. At sixty-five he was still an attractive man with a welcoming smile and lustrous hair that had only recently began to turn silver at the temples. And he was still fit and trim while most men who drank as much as he did had bloated bellies to attest to their bad habits.

She watched him drain his glass, place it on the bar and exchange a conspiratorial wink with the bartender. Madeleine turned away to avoid being seen, and when he joined her she pretended to be looking at her phone.

"Did you order the filet?" he asked as he slid into the booth across from her.

"Of course. Medium rare, the way you like it." She nodded toward the bar. "Did you order me a drink?"

He looked at her sheepishly. "You saw me over there?"

"You weren't exactly hiding in a corner."

"Okay then. Guilty as charged." He held out both hands. "Slap on the cuffs."

"No cuffs tonight. We're here to celebrate."

"I'll drink to that. But what, pray tell, are we celebrating?"

She smiled at the charmingly goofy guy seated across from her. It was hard to believe he was a history professor and a respected one at that, who also taught archaeology and had conducted fieldtrips to digs around the world. There was nothing stuffy or pedantic about him. Sid was a professor who made his lectures entertaining as well as informative.

"Tonight we're celebrating a fabulous sale," she announced. "Two large canvases on the walls of a brand new client. One with money, prestige and power."

"Money, prestige, and power? I like the sound of that. Who are we talking about?"

"TV producer, Elena Voss. You've heard of *The Unveiling* series?"

Sid chuckled. "You mean that wacky show where they twist the facts until they scream for mercy?"

She frowned at the remark. "The series is very successful. People love that kind of stuff."

"That's because they know absolutely nothing about history. But that's a rant for another time. Go on with your story. Exactly which paintings are we talking about?"

"The large floral still life and the one of the marina."

Sid sank back in the booth, his expression stuck some-where between a smile and a frown. Bittersweet might describe it. *"The Marina in Summer,"* he mused, a faraway look in his eyes. "I always loved the way Karl caught the feeling of that place. All those boats bobbing up and down and the sunlight sparkling in the water." He smiled at his wife, his expression tender. "I named our boat for you—*Lady Madeleine*."

She smiled at the memory. "We had wonderful times out on the lake when the kids were small."

He laughed to himself. "I still remember the time Karl fell overboard. Boy was he mad. He came up sputtering and swear-ing, and he got even madder when I made like I was going to sail off and leave him to swim back to shore." He shook his head. "Hard to believe the good times are gone forever."

Madeleine hastened to change the subject. Once Sid started mixing alcohol with memories of Karl, the evening was done for.

She proposed a toast to her successful day, and her hus-band, who would never refuse a drink, beckoned for the server who soon appeared with a scotch and soda.

He clinked his glass against Madeleine's. "To you, my charming lady."

"To us," she clarified. "And to Elena Voss's ongoing rela-tionship with Hewitt Fine Arts Gallery."

The toast concluded, she set her glass on the table and got down to business. "Today marks a milestone in our history. Think about it. A client like Elena Voss opens the door to a whole new class of patrons: high-powered media types with more money than they know how to spend."

Sid looked skeptical. "Because this woman bought a couple of paintings, these high-powered media types are about to knock down our doors?"

Madeleine heard the cynicism in her husband's voice and rose to her own defense. "All I'm saying is that Elena's patron-age will give us a bump in prestige."

Sid swished his drink around in the glass and watched it catch the light from the candle. "Forgive me my dear, but I think I'll restrain my enthusiasm until the aforementioned media types show up with their checkbooks wide open."

She didn't like the direction this was headed. She'd hoped Sid would share her vision and agree that it was time to expand the gallery. With a bit more space they'd have room to bring in edgier artists—like Karl's protégé, that handsome, young Rob Tate. His recent paintings, though a bit dark, were brilliant. Artists like Rob would attract a trendier clientele and there'd still be space in the gallery for the more conventional artists her established patrons preferred. If the expansion went well, she'd be ready for the next step—a gallery in New York.

She cast a glance in Sid's direction. No, he hadn't caught her enthusiasm. Perhaps a different approach was in order. Something softer with a touch of sadness thrown in.

She emitted a sigh. "Ever since we started the gallery, I've dreamed of taking it to the next level. I thought that with Elena Voss as a customer…" She let her voice trail off. "I guess I'm chasing fantasies. Wishful thinking and all that."

She glanced at her husband's face. Yes, he'd picked up on the shift in mood. She said nothing. Instead, she gazed at her glass and tried to look wistful and dejected.

It must have worked because Sid reached for her hand across the table. He sat in silence, stroking her fingers and toying with the marcasite ring that had once belonged to his mother. This was more like it. Her bold enthusiasm had intimidated him, but the damsel in distress routine was producing the desired effect.

"Of course we'll consider expansion," he conceded. "When the time's right. What's that saying? *There's a tide in the affairs of men that leads on to fortune but when omitted all the something of life is bound up in something else.* What I'm trying to say is that timing is everything.

She smiled at his words. He was so handsome, this man

she'd married. And so adorable for trying to soothe her with a quote from Shakespeare, even though he'd bungled it beyond recognition.

"Whatever you suggest will be just right," she said softly. "You always were the brains of the operation."

He grinned and raised his glass. "A toast to the powerful Elena Voss, producer of utter and complete nonsense, and to her friends with money to burn."

▾ ▾ ▾

Ted stared at his computer screen. He needed to write the script for his next online video, but he was having trouble getting started. And no wonder. A pair of detectives had shown up an hour ago to question him about his conversation with Brooke. He hadn't been surprised; he'd been expecting them. It was only natural that they'd want to follow up on the things he and Brooke had discussed.

Once he'd run through the details about their meeting at the coffee shop, the discussion had shifted to the brief encounter between Ted and Karl Erikson. From there the questions headed in a direction Ted hadn't anticipated.

Had he been curious about the occult ritual object Erikson described? Did he have a sense of its value? Was it something he might have desired?

Ted told them he didn't collect occult ritual objects and wasn't about to start.

After that they focused on his activities for the rest of that Sunday afternoon in mid-July. Where did he go after Erikson left the church? Could anyone vouch for his whereabouts?

He told them he'd gone to a diner like he did every Sunday, but he doubted anyone could verify the fact because he'd been alone and two months had passed since that day. After that he went home and since he lived alone and wasn't particularly chummy with the neighbors, there was nobody who could vouch for him in that department either. He referred the cops to his pastor and a few people at church who could attest to the fact that he was basically a decent guy who, to the best of their knowledge, wouldn't steal an occult ritual object and push its owner to his death down a steep embankment. And no, he knew nothing about the place where Erikson's body had been found.

Eventually the cops ran out of questions and left.

Since then he'd been trying to put together a video script. His subscriber list was growing, and his audience expected new output every few days. At the moment he was working on a presentation about Theosophist Alice Bailey, Lucis Trust and the UN. He had hours of research ahead of him but he couldn't stay focused. Not that the topic wasn't important. Unbeknown to most, Alice Bailey had been an extremely influential figure of the 20th century.

But it wasn't just the weird conversation with the cops that kept bugging him. The sad-eyed woman of mystery was taking up space in his head and try as he might, he couldn't chase her away. At first he'd figured it was the story she'd told him—it wasn't every day a guy got drawn into a tale about murder, theft, adultery and magic, and anyone would be intrigued. But there was more to it than just that. He'd been touched by her situation. She was lonely and afraid, and she needed a friend.

He played around with that concept for a while, picturing himself as the hero who'd offered assistance and would continue to offer assistance should she request it.

Eventually he faced the facts. He was attracted to her. Big time.

He recalled the way she'd looked at him from across the table in the coffee shop with her eyes a curious mixture of green and blue with tiny hints of golden brown around the pupils. Those eyes reminded him of turquoise or a kaleidoscope with colors shifting in the changing light.

And then there was her smile. Not that she'd smiled often

that morning, but a smile had slipped through on occasion. Not a happy smile, but an odd, sad little smile. A Mona Lisa smile that spoke of pain and heartache while at the same time hinting at other things. Intelligence. Curiosity. And under better circumstances, humor.

He thought of her hair—waves of chestnut tinged with gold. Ted's ex-wife used to pay beaucoup de bucks to make her hair look like that, and he had to laugh at the memory. "A woman's hair is her glory," Becca used to say to justify the expense. He suspected that was the only Bible verse she knew.

Finally he thought of the occult ritual object that seemed to be at the heart of this mess. If it could speak, what stories would it tell? Provenance meant a lot with these occult trinkets, and if this medallion possessed a notable history, it would be highly desired by those with the power and influence to obtain it. Objects possessed by famous occultists typically brought massive prices at auction—if they ever made it to auction. More often deals were conducted in private and there was usually a devil's bargain to be made in the process.

All this added up to a narrative that just might be bigger than anyone—the cops included—could possibly dream. But more to the point, if that medallion was still in Brooke's house, she might be in serious danger, but he suspected that she'd already figured that out.

▼ ▼ ▼

Madeleine excused herself and went to bed early with a novel she'd been reading. There was nothing interesting on TV, so Sid decided to take a walk.

Twenty minutes later he unlocked the door to the gallery and stepped inside. He liked being there when no one else was around. Solitude provided an opportunity to relate to the paintings in a more personal way. To study them from afar and from a variety of angles and to move in close to examine the nuances of each brush stroke. And solitude gave him a chance to have a heart-to-heart discussion with the deceased artist who'd been his lifelong friend.

He pulled a flask from his pocket, "I'm here to share a drink," he said as though Karl were right there in the room with him and not moldering away in the cemetery.

"We sure had some fine times back in the day, didn't we?" He held the flask high and took a sip like this was a toast and Karl was next to him at their favorite bar.

"Earlier tonight I thought about the Irish pub we went to on St. Patty's Day—jeez, how many years ago was it? The kids weren't born yet, so it's been a long time. I can still taste the meat and potato pie and smell the corned beef and cabbage boiling on the stove in the kitchen." He smiled at the thought, and for a moment he could almost hear a Celtic fiddle playing off in the distance. "Remember how the guys in the band coaxed me out of my seat? There I was, demonstrating the finer points of Irish dancing with people cheering me on and tossing coins at my feet. After that, it's all a blur."

He paused, recalling those devil-may-care days before time and trouble came knocking.

"Yes indeed, those were mighty fine times, and it's hard to believe you and I will never raise a glass together, my friend. Not on this side of the grave." He took another swig to drive home the point and then he crossed the gallery to the space where the painting of the marina had hung.

"I can't believe Madeleine let some prima donna come waltzing in here and buy my favorite painting right out from under me. Just a glance could take me back to summer days out there on the lake with the sun sparkling and the sails catching the wind and sending us racing through the water. It was all laughs except for the day when the wind died down and we sat there with the lake all glassy and still like the whole world was holding its breath. That's when I told you about the dig in Bangkok and Cindy, that cute little grad student who'd caught my eye."

The thought filled him with a soul-crushing remorse. It had been fifteen years ago, but the repercussions of it were with him to this day.

"You were the only one who knew about the hush money I paid to keep Madeleine from learning about that situation. And the child support? Try keeping something like that off the books! I didn't tell Madeleine about any of it, and then a year went by and then another and by then it had become like a game, trying to keep it from her. You stood by me through all of that, and you backed me in every lie I was forced to tell."

A moan escaped from some wounded, desperate place inside of him. "Madeleine wants to expand the gallery and bring in new artists and she's hoping to open a second gallery in New York. She thinks it's just a matter of waltzing into a bank and signing up for a loan and then I'll make all her dreams come true."

He took a swig from his flask and wiped his mouth on his sleeve.

"You should have seen how upset she was when she told me she'd misplaced her mother's emerald brooch. I scolded her for losing track of where she put her things. 'You shouldn't be so careless,' I said."

He let out a cynical laugh. "Little does she know I've been selling her jewelry and getting rid of treasures my dad and my grandfather collected over the decades. If I sell anymore, it'll be obvious things are missing, but I'm staring at three more years of child support, and after that, Cindy's lawyers will be after me to help with college tuition."

He turned from the empty space and walked across the gallery to gaze at Karl's photo and the bio posted in a frame that hung near the door. True to form, the sight of his buddy's face choked him up like it always did.

"Remember when I approached you early last summer?" he demanded of the silent photo. "I asked you to spot me some change until I got my head above water. You could have helped me out. You could have sold a painting or some of that pottery you collect or even that trinket you bragged about picking up at a thrift shop. Would it have hurt you to sell a stupid trinket to help a pal out of a tight spot?

"But what did you do? You sprang religion on me. And then you told me to go to AA and get sober, like that was something I'd never tried before.

"You blind-sided me that day," he shouted. "I thought you were too smart for that tent-meeting revival stuff, but you came on to me like a crazed holy roller. Repent! Get right with God! Tell Madeleine what you've been up to and set things straight.

"I couldn't sleep from then on thinking that you might work yourself into a frenzy and tell Madeleine the whole story. I never thought I'd have to worry about a thing like that. You and I were lifelong friends—womb to tomb we used to say. I knew your secrets—every last one of them. I pledged to carry them to the grave and I had a right to expect the same from you! But instead…"

He ripped Karl's photo from the wall and hurled it to the floor, sending shards of glass flying in all directions. He kicked the frame across the room and then he stomped over to it and ground his heel into his old friend's face, ripping the paper and tearing it to shreds as he shouted curses and disavowed the friendship that had carried him through the years.

Once his anger dissipated, he sank to his knees, his head in his hands as a towering wall of remorse crashed down over him. Madeleine waited for him at home. Madeleine—his wife and his soul mate. The woman who loved him and trusted him and still believed in his power to make her dreams come true.

He didn't know how long he sat like that, but eventually he struggled to his feet and went to the supply closet for a broom and a dustpan to clean up the mess. His secrets were buried with Karl in the grave, but the weight of them lay squarely on Sid's shoulders and it would be a long, lonely journey until he finally put them to rest.

Twelve

The house was quiet except for the sound of rain against the windows. Elena slipped into a long, white dress, a flowing, diaphanous creation she wore on nights when she hoped to make contact. She brushed her hair aside and secured a necklace at her throat—lapis lazuli mounted in silver and handcrafted long ago by Spanish gypsies in caves near the Palace of the Alhambra. She added matching earrings and arranged a series of bracelets on her wrist: ceremonial ornaments reserved for special occasions.

The buzzer sounded from the first floor. She blew out the candles and went into the upstairs hallway. The housekeeper looked up at her from the foyer.

"I've lit a fire in the library like you requested. If it's all right, I'll be on my way."

"Of course. I'll see you in the morning."

The woman hesitated. "You're sure you won't need me?"

Elena shook her head. "I'll be fine. Really. I have to handle this alone."

The older woman raised her umbrella and with a nod of her head, disappeared into the rain.

Elena went down the stairs and slipped into the library. A fire danced in the grate, its flames creating a cheerful glow. She stopped to gaze at a photo of her parents on their wedding day.

Her father, a blue-eyed, blond-haired German, the quintessential Saxon, her mother, a dark-haired beauty of gypsy extraction. Elena had inherited her mother's dark hair, olive skin and deep, brooding eyes. But more importantly, she'd inherited another attribute: the ability to see things others couldn't.

But so far, her second sight had not yielded the answers she sought. On rainy nights like this one with visions to cast and realms to explore, her thoughts returned to Jeremy. To this day she couldn't accept that he was dead. He'd been a powerful figure—a poet, a wizard, a madman, and a tech genius. Without him the world seemed a sad and desolate place.

For years she'd clung to rumors that he was still alive. That, like the phoenix of old, he'd risen from the ashes of the California wildfires and taken flight to parts unknown. She'd pursued him in trances and meditations, clutching to her heart the ring he'd given her—a fire-red ruby encircled by a jade dragon. But in all those hours of searching, she'd seen only vast acres of woodland. Hills teeming with trees. Forests stretching endlessly across a broad horizon. Images, she presumed, of the land through which those wildfires had raged and the soil on which his ashes had fallen, tossed and driven by fiery winds.

She let out a sigh, her longings awakened by the mere thought of him. She recalled his voice whispering in her ear and his touch against her cheek and his strength and his power and the intoxicating madness of his love for her. But it was an illusion. If it were otherwise, she would have made contact by now.

She drove the thoughts away as she'd done countess times in the last three years There was no point in thinking of him. Not when urgent business required her attention.

Over the decades, Elena's remote viewing skills had enabled her to penetrate the throbbing heart of vast cities, peer into isolated villages and scale mountains to explore distant and hidden sanctuaries. Success depended upon possessing an item energetically related to the subject of the quest. The more significant the object, the greater her ability to home in on the subject. Karl Erikson's paintings possessed multiple layers of energy: the energy of the artist who'd created them, the energy of his wife who'd watched them take shape, and the energy of their lost passion, shattered by his death.

She crossed the room to the fireplace and stood gazing at the painting of the marina that hung above it. She had no interest in the subject matter or the manner in which it was painted; what mattered was the energy with which the painting was infused. She touched the canvas, and with her eyes closed, began the slow, measured breathing that would launch her journey. A minute turned into two and then three before she felt a presence. "Are you there?" she asked her guide.

A sound emanated from the flames. Embers crackling and sputtering as they swirled upward from the burning logs. And then, a tingling in her spine.

"I've built bridges, not walls," she whispered into the flames. "Lead me, I pray, to the object of my desire."

For a while she saw nothing, but gradually an image took shape. And then other images and then others until a scene lay before her. Trees on either side of a rutted lane. On her left, a timber-frame house. To her right, a barn.

The artist's property, of course. She'd been there before, in visions as well as physically—on nights when she'd stood among the trees, watching, listening, sensing.

Something prompted her toward the barn. In an instant she was inside, brushing back cobwebs as she adjusted to the murky darkness. A tremor of excitement took hold of her. She'd never gotten this far before. The energy contained within Erikson's painting was indeed making a difference.

She proceeded across a rough, earthen floor and came to a stop before a flight of stairs.

"Ascend," her guide instructed, and so she did, one foot following the other until she came to a landing and a closed door. She drifted through it and into a cavernous space. A circle of easels dominated the center of the room while on the perimeter, counters overflowed with brushes, sketch pads, paints, and various art supplies. And then the vision began to wobble. She strained to hold onto it, but it grew faint and indistinct like a scene viewed through a rain-drenched window.

Pins and needles prickled at her fingertips. Icy chills raced down her spine. A cold wind wafted against her neck.

And then she was back in present reality—alone in the library with embers crackling and the smell of burning logs tickling at her nose.

What had gone wrong? Had she somehow blocked the flow of energy and shut down the vision? That wasn't possible. There had to be another explanation.

She breathed in deeply and tried to clear her thoughts. One minute dragged into two. And then three, and she was back in the studio, fighting to regain focus.

"Reveal what's hidden," she whispered to her guide.

All at once she understood. Nothing was hidden there. She'd been misdirected by the energy of the painting to the studio where it had originated.

Again she sought her guides, her arms outstretched like a child reaching for its mother. Her yearning was soon satisfied.

"Descend the stairs and exit the barn," a voice instructed.

The dusty stairs seemed to sway beneath her feet as she made her way downward. And then she was out of the barn and standing in front of the house. With a few deep breaths, the scene shifted and she was on the porch, gazing at the door.

At her bidding, the door swung open, and she smiled with amusement at the surveillance equipment mounted along one wall. Foolish little people to think their toys could block the entry of that which was unseen.

She glided through the foyer and into a space she assumed was the living room. A touch on her shoulder directed her to a closed door. She approached it with bated breath.

And then she knew. The item she sought was beyond that door.

She willed it to open, and when it didn't, she pictured herself floating through it. When that failed to produce results, she visualized herself reaching for the doorknob, extending her hand, grasping with her fingers, her skin touching metal. And then…

A searing pain radiated up her arm and down her spine and she heard her voice somewhere off in the distance, crying in anguish. Suddenly weak, she sank into a chair, her body wracked with spasms and every nerve on fire.

She reached for a bottle of brandy on the table next to her, poured a glass and drank. The liquid caught in her throat, burning and blistering, and the ensuing coughing fit tore at her lungs.

The fire in the grate flared up suddenly, the flames raging like the conflagration that had taken Jeremy's life. Dazed, Elena sank deeper into the chair and remained that way for an hour, maybe two. When she finally arose, the fire had been reduced to ashes and the room around her was as dark as midnight. She struggled out of the chair, and unable to climb the stairs, she sank down on the sofa, listening to the wind and the rain as it beat against the house.

Thirteen

Brooke watched the steam rise, ghostlike, from her coffee mug. She sat on a porch rocker, staring blankly at the surrounding trees. A chilly Saturday morning like this one was a reminder that September was marching toward October, and there'd soon be nothing but dreary vistas and the bitter cold of winter to remind her of what her life had become.

She pulled up the hood of her sweatshirt and stifled a yawn. She'd lain awake last night thinking of Elena Voss's offer and wondering what to do about it. Under normal circumstances she would have jumped at an opportunity to be part of the editorial team of a successful cable documentary series. She was comfortable with the subject matter, and if push came to shove, she could always rely on Uncle Nelson's vast store of knowledge as a backup. But while the offer had been tempting, her emotional state was too fragile for such a weighty undertaking. Months of grieving lay ahead of her. Months of winter sunsets and cold lonely nights before spring would dawn again.

And yet, a change of focus might be therapeutic. Something new to brighten her days.

No. Grief and loneliness defined her every waking moment and there was no escaping from its clutches. And yet she couldn't help but wonder what Karl would have told her to do. The answer was easy. He'd have told her to seize the moment and run with it. That offers like this were rare and she'd be a fool to walk away.

But the timing was bad, and she couldn't take on obligations she'd be unable to fulfill.

On the other hand, she was a woman alone in the world with her whole life ahead of her. She had enough money to get by for a few years, but eventually those resources would be drained away keeping up with day-to-day expenses. Was that wise? At some point she'd need to think of her future.

Maybe she should call Elena to discuss the matter. Elena had been more than generous in welcoming Brooke to her home and showing her kindness. More than that, she'd bought not one, but two of Karl's paintings. The least Brooke could do was express an interest in her offer.

She reached for her phone and within minutes it was arranged. Elena would email some files for Brooke to peruse. If she found the assignment interesting, they'd proceed from there. If not, Brooke could refuse and Elena would understand. For the moment, there was only one principle to guide her as she looked over the material: when forced to choose between dull facts and exciting uncertainties, Elena advised her staff to err on the side of exciting uncertainties. This was television, after all.

Brooke was soon wading through piles of information submitted by five different scholars. The first file dealt with the life and death of 16th century playwright and poet, Christopher Marlowe. Her task, assuming she accepted the assignment, would be to weave the research into a cohesive narrative focused on the odd set of circumstances surrounding Marlowe's death. The official story was that he'd died in a tavern brawl. A more interesting possibility was that he'd faked his own death and had been smuggled out of England to avoid execution for heresy.

There was a term for this phenomenon: *the philosopher's death*. A heretic faking his or her death and escaping into self-imposed exile.

She moved on to a folder about occultist John Dee. In addition to being an expert on mathematics, navigation and astrology, Dee was reputed to have been one of Elizabeth's cleverest spies. He'd devised a cipher to identify himself to the queen using the image of a mask mounted on an inverted L-shaped rod, like the masks people hid behind at costume balls. The two eye holes appeared as o's and the rod reaching across and supporting the mask appeared as a seven, with the horizontal stroke of the seven extending across the o's and the vertical stroke continuing below them, hence, 007. According to legend, John Dee had been the inspiration for Ian Fleming's famous secret agent.

Hours later Brooke rose from her desk and stretched her cramped limbs. Where had the time gone? While she'd been working, the clouds had broken up, the sun had reappeared, and she'd waded through volumes of material, some of it ponderous and academic, some of it fresh and stimulating. For the first time since Karl's death, she felt connected to something other than grief.

A wave of guilt swept over as she reflected on what she'd just experienced. An entire afternoon had passed and in all that time she hadn't thought of Karl. Was his memory already fading? Was she letting go of him so easily?

She looked out the window toward the barn and the wide, empty windows of the studio. Everything that had been her life and Karl's was up there, and she'd avoided the painful recollections that would rise up to greet her in that space. But now, with Karl slipping from her thoughts, maybe it was time to go up there, if for no other reason than to keep his memory alive.

She got up from her computer, went out to the barn and unlocked the door. The fragrance of cool, dank earth came rushing to meet her, bringing back memories—not only of Karl, but of his students—Rob—Jessie—Angela—Chris—and others through the years. It was like they were there with her, their chatter lingering in the air as they made their way up the steps.

She continued to the staircase. One step, two, and then the rest. She arrived on the landing, and a strange sensation swept over her. She almost believed that when she opened the door, she'd see Karl, a brush in his hand, his denim shirt streaked with paint and his gray hair disheveled as he smiled at her.

She threw open the door and the illusion vanished.

The vast open space lay bathed in the shadows of late afternoon while here and there, a ray of sunlight cast its glow on tiny dust particles hanging in the air. A dozen easels stood at attention in the center of the room, gathered in a silent circle around an empty platform where models once posed. Normally each easel held a canvas or a drawing board, but by now all the students except Rob had claimed their work.

She crossed the room to her own easel and the canvas that sat, unfinished, on the tray. She remembered Karl lugging his French easel and a picnic basket to the grassy dunes that rose and fell along the sea. While he painted, she'd gone exploring, making quick sketches of sandpipers and gulls and shooting reference photos like the one that inspired the painting of Karl that stood unfinished in front of her.

A sudden wellspring of tears turned the studio into a sea of wobbling shadows. She wiped her eyes and looked toward the wall where his most recent works hung, finished except for his final, masterful touch. She shifted her gaze to his easel and the painting he'd started just before he died. It was a landscape on an eleven-by-fourteen canvas, roughed out in sepia and tinted with a first thin layer of paint. While the location looked vaguely familiar, she couldn't quite place it.

And then she recognized it. The trees. The embankment. The stream. It was the spot where he and Sid Hewitt used to play as kids. The place where Karl and his ex-wife used to hang out and smoke pot with friends during high school. The place where, as an adult, he'd retreated to think and dream and imagine the future. And more recently? It was the place where he'd died.

Why had he been painting that spot just a day or so before his death? Did he have a premonition of things to come? A sense of destiny that drew him to that location? He'd painted the scene before, plenty of times, like Cezanne who'd filled multiple canvases with images of Mount Sainte-Victoire. But Cezanne hadn't been found dead at the foot of Mount Sainte-Victoire, and that's what made Karl's final work-in-progress so disturbing.

Should she mention it to Detective Burleigh? He'd urged her to report anything that seemed suspicious, and while this might not qualify as suspicious, it was an odd coincidence and possibly significant. So it wouldn't hurt to call. The detective could decide if a visit was in order.

Their conversation was brief. Burleigh thanked her for the information and offered to stop by and take a look.

That done, Brooke glanced at a solitary easel near a rear window. In the last year Rob had withdrawn from the circle of students, claiming he needed privacy while he painted. The enormous canvas on his easel was turned away from the rest of the studio, making it necessary to cross the room to see what he'd been working on.

For the last two years, Rob's paintings had been characterized by vivid use of color, bold brushstrokes and a geometric treatment of ordinary subject matter. But the images Brooke saw in front of her were nothing like his earlier work. What she saw was a composite of images drawn from world mythology and portrayed with raw, brutality. She recognized Medusa, her hair a tangle of snakes. Pandora unleashing evil upon the world. Moloch, the Canaanite deity surrounded by sacrificial fire. A horned deity, part man, part wolf, part goat. Phaeton, his chariot crashing in flames. Questzalcoatl, the feathered serpent. In the center of it all, an enormous phoenix ascended from the hellish landscape as flames licked at its heels.

Rob's sketchbook lay on the floor next to the easel. When Brooke opened it, a host of ghoulish entities leaped from its pages. Chimeras. Ancient gods and goddesses. Wraiths. Satyrs. Winged creatures and giants. Demonic beings from somewhere inside a nightmare.

My name is Legion, the drawings seemed to shout, *for we are many.*

▼ ▼ ▼

Burleigh sat in his car outside the barn. It was getting dark, and he could see lights on in the studio, but before he went up there, he needed to wrap things up with Jason Radley. The younger detective had interviewed Rob Tate earlier in the day and some interesting details had emerged.

Rob hadn't attended Erikson's retrospective on Sunday, in part because of a family obligation, but mostly because he claimed to be distressed about Erikson's passing. He'd left the family gathering around noon that day to go back to his loft apartment and paint, but there were no witnesses to verify that claim.

When asked, he'd sworn up and down that he knew nothing about occult ritual objects or about anything occult-related, but Detective Radley had spotted a book among his art supplies, and when he casually checked, it turned out to be something called a *grimoire*—a collection of spells and incantations. So Rob had lied about his lack of knowledge of hocus-pocus stuff, and that meant he could have lied about the break-in as well.

Radley described the paintings in Tate's studio as huge spooky things that incorporated occult symbols with figures drawn from folklore and mythology.

"So anyway, Boss," Radley concluded, "I think we should take a serious look at Rob Tate. He's just the kind of guy who'd be interested in this medallion thing."

Burleigh agreed with his sidekick. They hung up and the detective sat for a moment thinking about the other day when Rob showed up with an axe. Who's to say that he hadn't come back to finish the job as Brooke had originally feared before she'd recognized him and assumed his innocence? The matter certainly merited further study.

That decided, Burleigh got out of his car and walked across the drive to the barn. The door was locked, so he rattled the handle a few times and called out. A moment later Brooke let him in, and he followed her across a dirt floor to a set of stairs leading to a large room filled with easels and art supplies. When she pointed out her husband's easel, he went over to take a look at the canvas. There was only the bare outline of trees and an embankment above a stream, but he recognized the streambed as the place where Karl Erikson's body had been found.

"When did your husband start this painting?" he asked Brooke.

"He must have roughed it out the Friday before he died. That Saturday he went with me to an art festival, and I went back by myself on Sunday while he went to church."

Burleigh wondered if Erikson's students had watched him rough out the painting. Perhaps they'd asked him about the location, and perhaps he'd mentioned that he'd be going there the following Sunday afternoon. Could one of his students have met him there with disastrous results?

"Since you and I spoke," Brooke said, "I discovered something else you should see."

He followed her across the room to a solitary easel. He recognized the subject matter from Radley's description of Rob Tate's work.

"Rob never used to paint like this," Brooke said. "He did mostly landscapes and figure studies, but this stuff..." She seemed to shudder as she gazed at the huge canvas. "Rob was like a son to Karl, and I keep wondering if the subject matter of Rob's paintings had something to do with Karl's religious conversion."

"It's hard to say," Burleigh responded, but he made a mental note to discuss the subject with Rob.

He slipped behind the easel and stood where Rob might have stood while painting. There was a clear line of sight from his easel to Erikson's. Had Erikson mentioned that he'd be going to that spot on Sunday afternoon, and had Rob just happened to be waiting for him when he arrived? Had there been an angry discussion that ended in a fall—possibly an accident—that Rob had been too guilt stricken to acknowledge?

"Your husband's painting," Burleigh said nodding toward the easel. "Mind if I borrow it for a few days?"

"Not if you think it will help."

"It might. But then again, it might not." He went back to his car for an evidence bag. Back upstairs, he wrapped up the canvas and followed Brooke down the stairs, waiting while she locked the doors behind them.

"I hope I didn't drag you out on another false alarm," she said.

"Not at all. Like I told you before, if anything strikes you as significant, I need to be the first to know about it."

He placed the painting next to him in the car. As he drove away, he saw Brooke in the rearview mirror. She stood on the front porch with the trees towering overhead and the night wrapping itself all around her. She looked small and vulnerable, and his heart went out to the poor thing. It was hard enough to deal with the fading ghosts of lost loved ones, but demons were another matter all together.

Fourteen

A final chord echoed from an acoustic guitar. That quick, Ted was out of his seat and headed for the door. It wasn't that he wasn't sociable. He was—to a point. And it wasn't that he faulted the single women at Birch Hill Community Fellowship for the fevered quest that at times made him a target. Creating a home and a family was a worthy goal, but he'd been down that road before—not the family part; just the marriage and home part—and it hadn't turned out well. So if he'd taken to being a tad selective in the company he kept, that was his business, and he was sorry if anyone was offended.

Twenty minutes later he slid into his favorite booth at his favorite diner. He ordered the meat-lovers omelet with home fries and rye toast, and as he waited for his order, he surveyed the people seated around him. He couldn't help but feel a pang of loneliness as he saw couples—some with kids, some without—chatting and laughing in the surrounding booths.

When he'd met Becca ten years earlier, he'd been a full-time writer for a regional newspaper. In his spare time, he and a buddy had shared a joint venture producing podcasts and YouTube videos that debunked paranormal phenomena. Becca, a computer programmer, had shared his skepticism about such things, and they'd hit it off right from the start. But after their marriage, things began to change. Once Ted became a Christian and left journalism for his lecture and video gig, his income took a nosedive, and it wasn't long before Becca started dropping hints about his less than lucrative career.

His mother-in-law hadn't helped matters.

Your husband's a fanatic, she'd been fond of telling her daughter. He'll never make enough money to support a family.

Ted chased a mouthful of home fries with a swig of coffee and thought about his present circumstances—meaning Brooke. If he hadn't answered the phone the other morning, he wouldn't be wasting time thinking of her when he knew there was no future in it. She didn't share his beliefs—far from it—and that meant a relationship—at least one that worked—wasn't even a possibility. Somehow it figured that the first woman he'd been attracted to since his divorce was one he couldn't have.

He was still brooding when he paid the tab and went out to his Jeep. He headed for home—nowhere else to go—but the thought of spending the afternoon in a melancholy funk wasn't exactly tempting.

He decided to take a detour and twenty minutes later he left his Jeep in the municipal parking garage in downtown Bethlehem and made his way to Hewitt Fine Arts Gallery. Not that he cared all that much about art. He was just curious about the paintings done by Brooke's late husband.

The space he entered was comprised of three well-lit rooms, and there was a classy feel about the gallery that made Ted feel uncomfortable. He'd stayed up late working on his video and had barely taken time to wash his face and throw a blazer over his tee-shirt and jeans before running off to church. His hair was an unruly mess and his face was covered in overnight stubble. There was no way to deny it: he looked like a slob.

He glanced around at the collection. He didn't know a lot about art other than what he'd picked up in college humanities courses, but he knew enough to realize that while not exactly realistic, these paintings weren't completely abstract either. And therein lay their charm.

He stopped in front of an image of cows grazing in a meadow. He liked the way Karl Erikson had exaggerated the purples and blues of the shadows, making them richer and fuller than they might actually have been. Next to it was a painting of a waterfall surrounded by fall foliage. The rocks in the foreground were dotted with pinks, corals and shades of turquoise—not like real rocks at all but somehow more so.

He entered the second room and found himself in front of a canvas depicting a tent at dusk. Embers glowed in a fire pit and smoke rose into the surrounding trees. It brought back memories of camping trips and wild drunken nights with his buddies—back in the day when he used to have wild drunken nights and when he used to have that particular set of buddies. Strange how art could awaken thoughts long forgotten.

He turned to his right and came to a huge canvas of Brooke sitting in a canoe, her hand dangling in the water. The light surrounded her like a halo, bringing out golden highlights in her hair. Her white dress was shadowed in lilac, teal and rose, colors that seemed to capture everything enchanting about a summer afternoon. Her expression was hard to read. Thoughtful. Ironic. Haunting. Even on canvas she was a woman of mystery.

A buzzer from the front of the gallery announced another visitor. The sound brought an older woman—the owner?—scurrying from a room at the back. She hastened in the direction of the front door, and he could hear her greeting the newcomers. Must be people with money because she sure hadn't come running when Ted walked through the door. Pathetic that his strained circumstances were so easy to read.

He turned his attention back to the portrait, his eyes probing the subtle interplay of light and shadow in the blue-green eyes that had been haunting him for the last few days. Okay, so if he couldn't gaze into those eyes for real, then he'd have to be content to stare at the portrait.

A poem came back to him right then and there with words he'd probably picked up in some long-forgotten English class:

Shall I compare thee to a summer's day? The answer was yes. A summer's day was a perfect comparison.

▾ ▾ ▾

Uncle Nelson paused in front of a painting. "Another one marked sold," he said to Madeleine Hewitt.

"The retrospective was a huge success," she responded. "And you can see why. The show is breathtaking."

Brooke tried to ignore their chatter. This was Karl's life's work on these walls. The paintings would hang for a few weeks, and then those marked *sold* would be claimed by those who'd bought them. Soon they'd disappear into private collections and she'd never see them again.

But even more overwhelming was the memory of that day seven years earlier when she'd attended an opening at the Hewitt Gallery. She hadn't recognized the name of the artist, but she'd been an emerging artist herself, and she liked to see what others were doing.

She'd been studying the details of an autumn landscape when an older man asked her opinion of the work. She told him she liked the energy of the composition but she'd have enjoyed seeing the colors deepened a bit, especially the alizarin crimson and the yellow ochre. He'd gazed at the painting as though contemplating her remarks and then he said he wondered what the artist would make of her critique. She'd told him she had no intention of telling the artist, whoever he was, and he'd assured her that her remarks were safe with him. As she'd been preparing to leave, she was approached by gallery owner Madeleine Hewitt who said the artist asked to be introduced to her. She was surprised and somewhat flattered by the request and then mortified when she realized the artist was the man to whom she'd been speaking.

Karl had laughed with obvious pleasure at her embarrassment and assured her that he intended to take her comments to heart. The next day he called and asked her to have coffee so they could continue their discussion. That was the first of countless cups of coffee and she'd been counting on many more cups of coffee as the years unfolded.

Brooke suppressed a sigh at the thought of that moment, and then she wished with all her heart that she were anywhere but the gallery. She shouldn't have let her uncle talk her into coming here today. He hadn't attended the retrospective and he'd suggested stopping by on their way to an afternoon concert. She'd agreed because he'd been kind and generous, but it had been a huge mistake, and she couldn't wait for the ordeal to be over.

She paid little attention to the conversation as she and her uncle followed Madeleine from canvas to canvas. Madeleine was in a chatty mood as was Uncle Nelson, and the two wouldn't quit. Why were they going on like this? Couldn't they see it was upsetting her?

In the second room she noticed a solitary, scruffy-haired individual with his back to them. He was staring at the large portrait Karl had done of her, and at the sound of voices, he turned around. His eyes met hers and his mouth fell open.

It was the religious fanatic, Ted Roslyn. What was he doing here and why was he studying her portrait when there were so many other paintings to see?

His face reddened. "I was curious about your late husband's work," he stammered. "I thought I'd stop by to take a look. The paintings are interesting. I mean good. Very good. Not that I know much about art. But this one…" He nodded toward the portrait. "Looks just like you."

She was at a loss for words. She hadn't told her uncle about meeting Ted at the coffee shop, and she certainly hadn't told him about the occult ritual object allegedly hidden in her house. It would have upset him and so she'd kept quiet, and now she was worried that Ted would blurt out the details of their conversation—especially the part about demons. Her uncle would be alarmed by such thoughts, and there would be questions to follow. Questions that Brooke didn't want to answer.

Thankfully, Ted didn't broach the subject. Instead, he told Uncle Nelson and Madeleine that he was a friend of Brooke's, and after some brief remarks, he said goodbye and beat a hasty exit.

Brooke was glad when he was gone. There was something voyeuristic about the way he'd been ogling her portrait. What had been going through his mind as he'd studied her face and her eyes and her wistful expression from a lovely day that now seemed to have been in another lifetime?

Eventually Madeleine and Uncle Nelson wrapped up their conversation. Brooke and her uncle said their goodbyes and headed off to a concert of works by Bach and Vivaldi. They joined others chatting in the lobby prior to the concert, and Uncle Nelson stopped now and then to introduce his niece to a friend or a former colleague.

A familiar face emerged from the crowd. Director of the Tri-County Historical Conservancy David Price. He stopped to chat and Uncle Nelson took a moment to introduce them.

"I've already had the pleasure," David responded. "Once at an arts festival. Again at the retrospective where I managed to make an ass of myself. And later when your niece graciously accepted my apology."

Uncle Nelson glanced curiously at Brooke. "There's a story there. I'll look forward to hearing it."

"Did you contact the antiques appraiser I recommended?" David asked Brooke.

"I did. She's coming to the house tomorrow afternoon."

"Wonderful. I'm sure you'll be pleased with her work. Julie's a real pro."

Brooke glanced at her watch. "The concert's about to begin," she said. "Perhaps we should find our seats."

David Price excused himself, but before he could make his departure, he turned back to speak to Uncle Nelson. "I just had an idea. Why don't you and Brooke make a trip to our offices sometime soon?" He turned to Brooke. "If you've never visited, I'm sure you'd enjoy a tour."

She made no response. She had no desire to be in this man's company, or any man's company, other than Karl's and that was impossible. But the eager look on her uncle's face was impossible to ignore. He'd been kind in so many ways, and so she reluctantly accepted the invitation.

"I promise you won't be disappointed." He got his phone from his pocket and searched briefly. "I've got an hour at ten tomorrow morning. Is that too soon?"

Uncle Nelson glanced at Brooke. "I've got nothing planned."

She shrugged. "My schedule's open as well."

"That settles it," David said. "I'll see you tomorrow at ten."

▼ ▼ ▼

Rob paged through the grimoire that lay open on the coffee table. He'd picked it up at Mordecai's Antiques and Oddities, a place where his late mentor, Karl Erikson, had worked back in his student days. One step through the door and Rob had felt right at home in the place. It was packed to the rafters with weird stuff scrounged up from carnivals, churches, Masonic temples and who knows where else. It was just the kind of junk Rob found fascinating, and he'd decided on the spot to start a collection. He'd begun by purchasing this grimoire. A second visit had netted another grimoire, this one based on the teachings of Elizabethan mathematician, alchemist and conjurer, John Dee. Dee and his sidekick claimed to have conjured angels—spirit beings—who'd taught them a secret language.

This language, when correctly uttered, was alleged to open portals to other realms.

Sadly, John Dee's secret language was nearly impossible to master, especially when a person had little time to devote to the task. But Rob was giving it his best shot, and while no spirits had visibly manifested—at least not yet—there were times when he could sense a presence in the room, as though something was next to him, watching and directing his steps. In recent weeks he'd begun experiencing keener than usual insight into the minds of those around him. So keen that at times he felt like he'd crawled right inside a person's head and was reading their thoughts and guessing what they'd do or say next.

He'd tried to tell Karl about his experiences. About the ascended masters and unseen guides who spoke to him. His mentor's reaction was not what Rob had expected.

He'd been prepared for cynicism and mockery. Instead, Karl had set off on a quest of his own. A quest that led—against all odds—to Jesus. Not the cosmic Jesus waiting to take his place among the ascended masters, but the regular Jesus Rob had no interest in.

"I found this church," Karl said one day after the other students had gone. "The pastor's a smart guy who's been around the block a few times. They're offering a series of lectures that address some of the things you're into. Why don't you visit with me some Sunday? It never hurts to get a fresh perspective."

But Rob didn't want a fresh perspective. Not if it involved church.

From there the preaching had begun. Repentance. Forgiveness. Grace: the unmerited favor of the Lord.

He heard the rumbling of the elevator in the hall outside his door. No one ever came up to the loft except a model on the rare occasions when Rob had extra money to spend. Other than that, the only visitor was the landlord stopping by to collect overdue rent. This month he'd paid on time and he wasn't expecting a model, so there was only one explanation. The cop was back.

He heard a knock at the door and rose to answer it.

It was the older guy this time. In his hands was a canvas wrapped in plastic.

When Rob let him in, Detective Burleigh pointed to the grimoire that lay open on the coffee table. "I came here today to discuss art, demons and God," he announced. "Not necessarily in that order."

Fifteen

It was after six and dusk had already settled in when Brooke got home from the concert. She rewound the video footage, set it to play at triple speed and watched birds streak like missiles through the sky, deer gallop through the underbrush and squirrels erupt from the leaves and vanish into the treetops.

And then a surprising sight appeared. A red SUV tearing down the drive and grinding to a halt in front of the house. A tall man emerged and careened toward the door. Madeleine's husband, Sid. What was he doing here?

She slowed the video to normal speed and watched Sid knock on the door. He waited a bit, knocked again, and instead of returning to his vehicle, he crossed the driveway and looked up at the studio. He tried the door to the barn and when he found it locked, he headed toward the rear of the house and out of sight. Brooke adjusted the monitor to access the video for the back of the property, and there he was—circling the house, his eyes raking over walls and windows. He trudged up on the rear deck, looked inside and then he turned and headed into the woods.

Another camera picked up his image as he made his way through the undergrowth and came to a stop beneath a large oak. He knelt down, brushed away some leaves and stared at the spot he'd just cleared.

Brooke wondered if the medallion was out there, not hidden in the house as she'd assumed, but buried in the woods beneath the oak tree. Had Karl revealed its hiding place to his closest friend? She expected Sid to start digging, but instead, he knelt and made the sign of the cross, an unexpected gesture from someone who claimed to be an atheist with no love lost between himself and a God in whom he didn't believe. He stayed like that for a few moments with his eyes closed and then, instead of unearthing this alleged occult ritual object, he trudged back to his car and drove off.

Twenty minutes later Detective James Burleigh and his sidekick stood next to Brooke, watching the video footage.

"We'll need a shovel and a flashlight," the senior detective announced with a glance out the window at the gathering dusk. "And a garden trowel if you've got one handy."

Brooke found a flashlight in the kitchen and showed the men where the gardening tools were kept on the first floor of the barn. Burleigh selected a shovel and handed it to Radley. "You're young and strong. I'll let you do the honors."

A thick blanket of humidity had settled over the landscape and distant flashes of lightning warned of an impending storm. Burleigh led the way, the flashlight blazing a trail. Finally the beam came to rest on a patch of dark earth where the leaves had been brushed away.

"This is the spot," he told his partner. "Start digging."

Radley rolled up his sleeves and got down to business One hole. Two. He scooped up another shovelful and paused to wipe the sweat from his brow and brush away the gnats. "There's nothing here but dirt and bugs," he announced. "What do you say we pack it in?"

"Keep digging."

Another ten minutes and the flashlight revealed a change in the color of the soil—flecks of lighter brown were mingled with the rich, dark earth. Radley picked up a handful of what appeared to be wood chips and Brooke watched as they crumbled at his touch. He made a few remarks about finding the remains of a treasure chest and resumed digging.

A few more shovelfuls and he brought up a bone. "Okay, not a treasure chest," he said, a trace of disappointment in his voice. "Would you believe a coffin?"

Brooke hoped he was joking.

He dug some more and reached down and held up a skull. Not human but canine.

He looked over at Brooke. "Did you and your husband lose a dog?"

"Yes, a year ago but we had her cremated."

"Somebody's pet departed this earth," he said, "and the owner made sure it had a proper burial."

Burleigh turned to Brooke. "I guess that's it for tonight. We'll have a word with Sid Hewitt to see what he knows about all this. I'll get back to you once we've got some answers. In the meantime, leave things as they are in case we need to take another look."

She watched as they departed. She'd been certain they'd find this occult ritual object out there beneath the tree, but it remained hidden. She went back in the house and listened to the stillness. The object was somewhere inside, she knew it. She locked the door and double checked the alarms to make sure they were set. If anyone tried to get in, the police would be instantly alerted. So why was she so afraid to be alone?

▼ ▼ ▼

The Hewitt residence had once belonged to Sid's father and his father before him. The study where Sid presently sat was a masculine room with masculine appointments. Chairs upholstered in dark leather. Walls paneled in walnut. A rug purchased nearly a century earlier from a merchant in Istanbul. It was a place for sipping cognac and smoking an occasional cigar.

For studying ancient maps, perusing forgotten texts, and pondering secrets buried in the sands of time.

The most prominent feature was the floor-to-ceiling cabinet that showcased artifacts the Hewitt men had collected over the decades. Tiny Egyptian burial figures. Ancient Hittite deities. Phoenician amulets. Babylonian cylinder seals. A fragment of a Scythian spear and a host of other small treasures. Some Sid had inherited from his father and grandfather. Some he'd purchased in the antiquities markets. And there were a few he'd smuggled out of sites when no one was looking. Unethical, to be sure, but more significantly, illegal, with penalties varying from country to country.

He couldn't sell the stolen items, at least not through legal channels, so he'd been forced to unload treasures his father and grandfather had acquired long ago. Both men must be rolling over in their graves at the thought of how readily Sid had dispensed with the items they'd prized. It had pained him each time he'd sent a piece to auction. But there'd been no choice. Not with a clandestine child support check to be handed over each month.

The only blessing was that Madeleine had never taken inventory of the pieces in the collection. If she had, he'd have been hard pressed to explain their disappearance.

He thought of the piece Karl had told him about. A phoenix surrounded by red stones—possibly rubies—and on the other side, strange runic carvings. Its provenance was unknown, and Karl had died before Sid had a chance to take a look and render an opinion. But the description had awakened his curiosity. How old was this thing? Where had it been made? Who created it and under what circumstances and for what purpose? An occult ritual object, Karl had told him. And what was its value. That was the question Sid had been most anxious to answer. If only he could find it—but how?

Across from him on the desk was a photo of himself and Madeleine taken on the first dig they'd gone on together.

They'd been a good-looking couple back in the day. Thirty-eight years later Madeleine was graceful and elegant, but at age twenty-five, she'd been a knockout. Blonde hair, blue eyes and a classic profile that hinted at aristocratic bloodlines. A head-turner, he'd always said.

And Sid? The picture portrayed a lean and lanky individual in well-worn khakis and an over-sized fedora to keep the sun from his eyes. Handsome with more than a touch of bravado. And now? Did people still see him as dynamic and dashing? Probably not. While the younger version of himself might live on in his mind, a much older and sadder version had moved into his body and taken up ownership.

He turned his gaze to the portrait above the fireplace. Max, the Bernese mountain dog who'd departed this world 20 years ago today. Karl had painted it two-and-a-half decades earlier, and after all these years, the sight of it could still get Sid all choked up.

He thought back to that September afternoon. The sun had lain low on the horizon and the evening had been humid, much like tonight. He and Karl had eased poor, old Max into a wheelbarrow, and Sid pushed it into the woods with Karl trailing behind with a shotgun, prepared to do what Sid couldn't even contemplate.

For a moment he'd almost turned back. He could have taken Max to the vet's. The process would have been clean. A falling asleep. A silent passing.

But Max was born and bred for the outdoors. He'd scrambled up rocky hillsides and followed winding paths on countless treks through state parks and national forests, He'd been a friend to the last, every pitiful, wheezing, agonized breath testifying to his fighting spirit. No, Max didn't deserve to spend his last moments surrounded by steel and chrome in a cold, sterile clinic. He deserved to die in the vast outdoors with all of nature witnessing his passing.

But at the last minute it was all too much.

"*I can't go through with it,*" Sid had said, a sob clutching at his throat.

Wait near the house, Karl told him. *It'll be over in a minute.*

A single shot exploded out of the woods.

As the last echoes faded, Sid staggered into the forest and found Karl, shotgun at his side, gazing at a mound of fur. Sid hadn't realized there'd be so much blood nor had he pictured the matted fur, the gaping wound, and those warm, gentle eyes now glassy and vacant.

Somehow he'd managed to help Karl lift the bulky form into the pine box they'd nailed together that morning. After a final goodbye, they closed the lid, nailed it shut, and lowered it into the hole. Karl handed Sid a shovel and waited while he heaped mounds of earth onto the coffin.

Later, Madeleine and Janine had joined them. They'd lit candles and shared a moment of silence as the late September twilight wrapped its arms around them. Afterward, they made their way back to the house, a fairy procession of flickering light against the vast and boundless darkness. Inside they poured drinks, toasted their departed friend, and swapped stories of his life.

And that was why he'd had to go to the property today. A twentieth anniversary pilgrimage. A journey he had to make.

He glanced at the mantle clock.

By now the police would have reviewed the digital images on Brooke's security system. It was only a matter of time before they appeared at his door.

Sixteen

Storms had swept through the night before, driving away the humidity and leaving behind a bright, clear morning. Detective Burleigh had called late the prior evening to tell Brooke not to worry—the dog buried in the woods had once belonged to Sid Hewitt. The detective promised to have someone stop by to fill in the holes, and so the matter was settled.

Brooke walked down the porch steps and into the woods. The mounds of earth surrounding the freshly dug holes had turned to mud in last night's rain. Other than that, everything was as it had been except for the sunlight filtering through the trees.

She was about to walk away when something shiny caught her eye. Her pulse quickened. Had the medallion been buried out here all along and they'd somehow missed it last night?

She scrambled into the hole and fished it out of the mud. And then her heart sank. It was just a piece of painted tin, an anti-war button to be precise, the sort of thing someone might pin to their jacket to make a statement. This one depicted a raised fist superimposed over an armored tank. Scratches on the surface revealed metal beneath the paint, suggesting it had been buried awhile. It must have belonged to Karl—a relic of his rebellious youth. Or maybe it hadn't been Karl's at all. Maybe it had belonged to a friend or to some random person passing through the woods.

She carried it back to the house and left it on her desk. A busy day lay ahead of her. There was the visit to David Price's office at ten followed at one-thirty by the antique appraisal. She hurried to shower and change out of her muddy clothes and then she left to pick up her uncle.

He was waiting for her outside his apartment building. She followed his directions, and half an hour later they came to a long driveway guarded by a pair of enormous concrete lions. Ahead of them lay a Tudor-style mansion with mullioned windows, massive chimneys, and ivy-covered, half-timbered walls.

"This is lovely," she murmured. "I feel like I stepped into a time machine and stepped out in the English Renaissance."

Her uncle smiled at the remark "I thought you'd like it."

She parked the car and they followed a brick sidewalk to a massive oak door that creaked as they entered. The director was waiting for them and after a few pleasantries, David Price began the tour by directing their attention to a portrait of the original owner, a man named Alden Marshall whose wealth had come from ventures in shipping and munitions. He'd built the mansion in the early 1900's and his heirs had lived there until it was sold in the mid 1970's. After that a series of owners gradually let the house and grounds fall into disrepair

"The house has a rather sad history," their host explained. "The last of the Marshalls to live here had a 16-year-old daughter who sneaked out of the house one night to meet a boyfriend in the garden shed. Somehow the shed caught fire, and both of them perished in the blaze. The evidence hinted at arson—the family had enemies—but the point couldn't be definitively proved. The grieving parents were desperate to escape the memories, so they sold the property for much less than its appraised value. A succession of future owners lacked the means to keep it up, but I think you'll agree that the Conservancy has captured its original grandeur."

He led them into a spacious living room featuring high

ceilings with exposed beams, an immense fireplace and assorted pieces of period décor. The most prominent feature was a huge stained glass window depicting St. George, patron saint of England, slaying a dragon. The rest of the first floor, with the exception of a contemporary kitchen, was much the same. Expansive spaces with furnishings that could be easily re-arranged and stored to accommodate weddings and conferences scheduled at this popular venue.

The tour of the downstairs complete, David led them up the broad staircase and down the second-floor hall to his office. Like the rest of the building, the room exemplified the Tudor era. There was a suit of armor in one corner, tapestries on the walls, a portrait of Henry VIII and one of Elizabeth I above a marble fireplace.

"Don't tell the other board members," David said to Uncle Nelson, "but this room was what convinced me to take the job."

The elderly gentleman didn't seem surprised. "There aren't many corporate heads with offices as grand as this," he commented. "You should consider yourself lucky."

David served coffee and proved to be a genial host as he chatted about the Conservancy's on-going projects. "There's an idea I've been turning over in my head," he remarked as the conversation drew to a close. "We're embarking on a study of eighteenth century structures in the Lehigh Valley. I've got three researchers on the project—one full timer and two interns. Once their work's completed, I'll need an editor to tie the pieces together." He directed his attention to Brooke. "Madeleine Hewitt tells me you're an editor. Perhaps we could convince you to lend a hand."

Brooke glanced at her uncle. The keen expression on his face suggested that he hoped she'd say yes.

"There's a lot on my plate at the moment," she said, as much for her uncle's benefit as David's. "I've just taken on a challenging assignment and I can't imagine committing to anything else."

"There's no pressure," their host assured her. "We've barely begun the research phase, and once that's complete, the contributors will need time to write up their findings. Any actual editing wouldn't begin until well into the new year."

"By then your current project will be wrapped up," Brooke's uncle said, gazing in her direction. "The arrangement sounds perfect."

"Give it some thought." David left it at that and rose to his feet. "We'll conclude with a tour of the grounds. There aren't many days left before the frost sets in, so we should enjoy the gardens while we can."

The tour began in a topiary garden at the rear of the house. From there they followed a path to an Elizabethan knot garden, so-called because the bushes, flowers and herbs were arranged in manicured knots around a central fountain.

"Best seen from the air," Price informed them.

They continued into a rose garden and after admiring the heirloom varieties, they ventured into a formal garden with a chapel at one end. Their final destination was a raised mound that provided a broad view of what David laughingly referred to as a deer park—acres of woodland named for the hunting grounds of Tudor kings and queens.

Afterward he escorted them to the car, and as they drove away, Brooke glanced in the rearview mirror and saw him watching their departure.

"He likes you," her uncle said.

She frowned at those words. She'd seen this coming, and she'd even wondered if her uncle had arranged beforehand for David Price to bump into them at the concert and set up today's visit.

"Don't do this to me," she said. "It's too soon after Karl's death to start playing matchmaker."

"Of course. But at some point life will go on, my dear."

"Will it?" She felt tears well up in her eyes. "I'd prefer not to discuss this again."

"As you wish."

The remaining miles passed in silence.

▾ ▾ ▾

Janine placed her hands a few inches above the lumbar region of the woman stretched out, belly-down, on the Reiki table. Sandra was a first-time client who'd come to the Center for the Mystic Healing Arts seeking relief from lower back pain. Janine was anxious to ease her suffering, and in the process she hoped to establish her as a steady client who'd return for regular treatments.

She felt her fingers tingle as her hands move back and forth across the lower vertebrae. "The energy's beginning to shift," she said. "Can you feel the warmth?"

"Of course I feel the warmth," Sandra snapped back. "Room temperature is 70 degrees. Body temperature is 98.6. Your hands are only a few inches above my back, so I'm experiencing a completely predictable increase in temperature. It has nothing to do with magical energy and everything to do with the transfer of physical, measurable heat."

Janine stifled a sigh. Someone had given Sandra a gift certificate for a Reiki session, otherwise, she wouldn't be there. In all likelihood, Sandra had come to the session determined to prove that Reiki was a joke, and unless Janine could override her skepticism, Sandra wouldn't be back for further treatment.

"If I feel better at all," the woman continued, her tone a bit less caustic, "it's not because you're chasing some non-existent energy around my body, but because the music, the candlelight and the incense are incredibly soothing."

Janine grabbed onto those words. "You've identified an important starting point. Every one of us needs to learn methods of quieting ourselves in these troubled times. What begins as relaxation can lead to deeper healing if you allow it to."

Sandra let out a laugh. "If I allow it to? You mean if I allow you to brainwash me, I might get fooled into thinking there's something to this nonsense?"

Nonsense? How dare this woman spout such negativity? Didn't she know that a positive attitude was essential if healing was to take place?

For a fleeting moment Janine was tempted to tell her to get out of there and take her nasty attitude and her bad manners with her. She was angry, really angry and it took a number of deep breaths before the anger gave way, not to tranquility, but to worry and self doubt.

Why was she feeling this way? There'd been too much of this sort of thing of late.

She forced her thoughts back to her original intentions for the Reiki session, the intentions she'd established before Sharon had shown up and poisoned the atmosphere. She'd wanted Sandra to experience deep and satisfying relief. She wanted her to know wellness and joy. She wanted her to radiate abundant health and prosperity.

But if Sandra's intention was to cling to her pain and use it as a tool to manipulate others, then the two of them were working at cross purposes and all of Janine's good intentions wouldn't matter in the least. She had no power over the intentions of others. What mattered was that her own intentions were noble and true. Popular wisdom stated that the road to hell was paved with good intentions, but Janine believed the opposite. Good intentions were everything and those with good intentions couldn't be blamed for the freakish moments when fate intervened and skewed the outcome in an undesirable direction.

The session wound up, and Sandra struggled off the table. "The pain hasn't abated," she announced, "but I feel much more relaxed."

"That's a good starting point. I hope I see you again."

"Don't hold your breath."

Janine stood at the window and watched Sandra's car pull out of the parking lot. She felt a charitable sadness at having failed in her attempt to ease the woman's suffering, but Sandra's toxic energy had proven to be an insurmountable obstacle.

It was so frustrating. Janine's kids were the same way. Stuck in their energetic ruts and their father had been much the same way. Was it genetic? Could children inherit their parents' negativity? Was it hard-wired and thus impossible to overcome?

Both Stephi and Brett needed something to dispel the gloom and bring a bright new vitality to their lives. A vacation might help. No, that wasn't it. Vacations inevitably ended and life resumed its same dull routines. What the kids needed was something adventurous to jolt them out of their lethargy and give meaning to their lives.

She closed her eyes and pictured them being excited about something that had yet to materialize. She imagined Stephanie's face aglow with an inner fire, and saw Brett energized by pursuits that shook him out of his self-centered arrogance.

And then she let it go. She'd set her intentions. It was up to the kids to set theirs.

▼ ▼ ▼

Brooke made a sandwich and set it aside after a single bite. She had no appetite and was in a miserable funk after so many nights of fitful sleep. She resented her uncle's not-so-subtle attempts at matchmaking, and at the moment she was in no mood for an appraiser to barge into the house and paw through Karl's family heirlooms, shaking loose ghosts as she made her way from room to room.

Tires crunched on the gravel drive and she glanced at her watch. One-thirty. Julie Franklin was right on time.

The appraiser was young—in her late twenties perhaps. She wore a gray sweatshirt trimmed in lace with calf-length skinny jeans and a pair of high-topped red sneakers that matched the red tote bag over her shoulder. Her long blond hair was swept back in a loose ponytail that bounced against her neck as she made her way from her van to the house.

After some words of introduction, she followed Brooke into the living room and eyed her surroundings. I like the timber lodge feel of the place," she remarked. "It's rustic without relying on mountain house clichés like moose lampshades and tables made out of fake antlers. It's got an authentic feel."

"My husband's doing," Brooke acknowledged without elaborating. She explained that she was interested in learning the value of Karl's family pieces—the things that belonged to his kids that would soon be sent to auction.

Julie reached into her bag, brought out a tablet and explained that she'd be providing two estimates for each item. Retail: what a piece might fetch in an antique shop and hence its replacement value for insurance purposes. The lower price would be the auction estimate based on prices realized in the last year.

An hour later they'd catalogued most of Karl's family heirlooms and the last stop was his study. Brooke had straightened up, but while the room appeared orderly, the books and the art pottery were no longer arranged with the meticulous care Karl had insisted upon.

As Brooke might have expected, Julie was immediately drawn to the pottery collection. She selected a vase in variegated shades of blue and green and took it to the window to examine in the light. She did the same with each piece and made notes in her tablet as she went.

"Ceramics have lost considerable value in the last few years," she remarked as she worked, "but the better items still bring healthy sums at auction. I've counted three pieces of Newcomb College, two Van Briggles, three Wellers, and a Teco. Together they're probably worth…" She took a moment to do to the math. "Approximately twelve thousand dollars for insurance purposes. Eight thousand at auction. The remaining odds and ends should bring an additional two thousand as well. I'll need to confirm that with records, of course."

Brooke found the news interesting, but troubling. The pieces were worth more than she'd expected, and yet the intruder had left them behind. More proof that money wasn't the object of the break-in.

Julie put the ceramic pieces back in the cabinet and turned her attention to an old, slant top desk that seemed to disappear into a dark corner.

"That couldn't be worth much," Brooke commented. "Karl only kept it around because it's a family piece."

The appraiser ran her fingers over the wood. "Don't be so sure about that. It's mahogany and the hardware appears to be original." She pulled back the slant top and examined the small interior drawers and cubby holes. After that she slid the desk away from the wall so she could study the back and then she removed each of the four main drawers and examined the details. "The dovetails are irregular, which means they're handcrafted. The nail heads are square instead of round and that means they're handmade as well."

She put the drawers back where they belonged and stood gazing at the piece. "It's unsigned, so I'll need a second opinion, but if it's what I think it is, it was made in New England by an important furniture maker working in the late eighteenth century. If that's the case, it should bring a hefty sum at a major auction house like Christie's or Sotheby's."

Brooke was surprised. "I had no idea. Karl's kids will be pleased."

"Back in the eighteenth and early nineteenth centuries," Julie continued, "desks like this one were sometimes made with secret compartments where wealthy folks stashed their valuables. Mind if I do some snooping?"

Goose bumps prickled up Brooke's arms. Could Karl have hidden this mysterious occult ritual object somewhere inside the desk?

She gave Julie the go-ahead and watched her expert fingers explore the intricacies of the cubbyholes and tiny drawers beneath the slant top. Before long two cubbies popped loose revealing an opening. Julie measured the interior space and did the same with the exterior of the desk.

"A false back," she announced. The desk is deeper on the outside than the inside."

She returned to the front of the desk, pulled out the small drawers beneath the cubby holes and probed the openings. After a minute or two, she was rewarded with a faint clicking sound, and within seconds, a panel slid to one side. She reached inside and when she turned to face Brooke, she held a small wooden box out in front of her.

"Go ahead. Open it."

Brooke's fingers trembled and it took several tries before the lid slid open. And then her heart sank. The box was empty.

She held it out for Julie to see.

"No diamonds or rubies? Too bad, but don't be discouraged. Where there's one hidden compartment, there's bound to be others. That's how they made these things back in the day."

Julie returned to the desk and resumed her search. This time she closed her eyes as though relying on her sense of touch to provide the clues. A minute later she opened her eyes and smiled at Brooke.

"There's a tiny crack splitting the space in two, and that indicates there's not one, but two hidden enclosures. All I have to do is find the spring that releases them."

She repeated her earlier actions and when nothing happened, she stood back and stared at the desk as though pleading with it to give up its secrets. Finally she pulled out the first of the four large drawers and felt inside. She did the same with the second drawer and then the third.

"There it is," she said. "A raised bump. If I could just get it to..."

She fell silent and then *Click!* A second later she reached into the space where the small drawers had once been and withdrew a tiny wooden box.

Brooke felt breathless as she stared at the object in Julie's hand. Was she about to find something Karl had hidden? Or was this just another wild goose chase like the previous night's adventure among the trees?

She took the box and slid back the lid. It was empty.

This time Julie seemed disappointed, but she quickly rallied. "There's another box. so we've got one last chance at buried treasure."

For the third time Brooke took a small wooden object from Julie's outstretched hand. She attempted to slide back the lid, and when it refused to budge, she handed it back.

"You do it. If I force it, it might break."

Julie fiddled with the lid for a few seconds with similar results. "The person who made this desk was way too clever," she said with a frown. Even so, she persisted and soon her frown gave way to a smile as the lid to the box slid open. "There's something inside," she announced. "Take a look."

Seventeen

The wooden box sat in Julie's hand, waiting for Brooke to possess it and whatever it contained But she was frozen. Immobilized. All she could do was stare.

"Take it already," Julie said. "The suspense is killing me."

Brooke reached out her hand, her heart pounding. She felt her fingers close around the box. Felt the smooth worn surfaces of the wood. Felt time grind to a halt as she held it in her hand. Dare she look inside?

A sense of dread washed over her. A sense that life would never be the same once the object was revealed. But there was no turning back and no pretending it didn't exist.

She looked inside and saw a crumpled mound of tissue paper. She fished it out and felt the heaviness of something wrapped up and protected in the paper's feathery lightness, like a snowball wrapped around a rock.

"The tissue hasn't yellowed," Julie remarked. "It hasn't been there long."

Brooke unfolded the paper—one fold. Two. And then another.

There it was: a golden phoenix encircled by red jewels.

"Yo, Brooke," Rob Tate's voice shouted from the foyer.

As he appeared in the open doorway. Brooke thrust the medallion behind her back. Had he seen it? The ominous silence suggested that he had.

His eyes swept the room and came to rest on the desk pulled from the wall. "Sorry to interrupt, but I wanted to let you know that I'll be in the basement replacing the window."

Brooke clutched the medallion behind her back. "Go right ahead. We were just finishing in here."

The appraiser approached Rob, a smile on her face, her hand outstretched. "I'm Julie. And you are…?" He completed the introduction. After a few pleasantries, he disappeared to take care of business.

Julie crossed to the window and watched him get his tools from his truck. "He's not hard to look at," she remarked. "Maybe I'll break something at my place so he can come over and fix it. What do you think?"

Brooke nodded but paid little attention. All she could think of was the phoenix in the center of Rob's canvas. Had Karl shown him the medallion, and had it been the inspiration for the painting?

She was about to hand Julie the wooden box when she noticed something else inside. A duplicate of the anti-war button she'd found earlier in the day.

"Funny the stuff people hang on to," Julie remarked. She quickly moved on to the medallion. "Mind if I take a look?"

"Of course not."

She took the object over to the window and studied it awhile in the light. "The bird's a phoenix, and if you're lucky, the metal is gold and the jewels are rubies. The carvings on the back are Greek to me, and I don't see anything to identify the maker." She handed it back. "I don't specialize in antique jewelry, but I'd be happy to set you up with someone who does."

"That won't be necessary. And please, don't mention this to anybody. Including Karl's kids. I'll tell them myself."

Julie appeared offended at the request. "Discretion is part of my job." She turned her attention to putting the desk back together and then she and Brooke returned to the living room.

Julie promised to get back to her in a day or so with estimates and said she'd arrange a second appraisal on the desk.

Their business concluded, Brooke escorted her to the door and watched the van drive away. A sound from the basement reminded her that she was alone with Rob.

Her fingers stole to the medallion in her pocket. Rob had seen it—she had no doubt of that. The timing of his approach. The look on his face. The silence that had spoken volumes.

Just a few days earlier she'd attested to his character, but that was before she'd watched him ponder the intricacies of her home security system and before she'd seen his painting and his drawings.

She glanced toward the door leading to the basement. Soon Rob would join her and it would be just the two of them. What would she say to him? Would he mention the medallion? Would he ask to see it? Would she need to defend herself, or was she panicking over nothing?

She forced herself to get a grip. She wouldn't mention the medallion unless he did and she'd cut their conversation short by explaining that the last few days had worn her out, and she needed to rest and collect her thoughts.

She heard his steps on the basement stairs. And then he was with her in the living room. His handsome face. His kind smile. His strong hands that gripped axes and made paintings of demons.

To her surprise, the conversation went smoothly. She thanked him for replacing the window, they exchanged a few words and he excused himself.

She locked the door behind him and leaned against it. How much had Rob learned about the security system? Enough to disable it? Enough to hide his tracks? Enough to silence the alarms and erase the video footage so no one would know he'd broken in?

She took the medallion from her pocket and studied it in the lingering light. Should she call the police and tell them of the discovery?

Yes, of course.

But what would she learn? Detective Burleigh wouldn't be able to explain the medallion or its meaning. At best, he'd put it in an evidence bag, take it to the station and return it once the case was solved. *If* the case was solved.

She forced herself to think clearly. What did she want, or better yet what did she need?

Safety to be sure, but she needed something else as well.

She gazed at the runic markings on the back of the medallion. The characters were indecipherable, but surely they had a meaning, and she wanted to know what it was. She got her phone out of her pocket and put it back. Not once, but twice.

Should she call him or would she be inviting trouble if she did?

▼ ▼ ▼

Twilight settled across the lawn beneath Elena's window, blanketing the roses in shadow. All was quiet except for the breeze rustling through the treetops. So why was she so unsettled?

The answer came in the form of a vague prickling at the back of her neck.

Something was wrong. Terribly wrong. But what?

The luncheon had been a huge success. She'd disarmed Brooke's icy reserve and lured her into her web. Brooke had taken on the editing assignment, and it was only a matter of time before the unsuspecting creature would welcome Elena into her heart and her home. Elena should be celebrating, but instead she was pacing back and forth with her thoughts spinning wildly through her head.

She knelt on her prayer rug and tried to quiet herself. She breathed in slowly, held the breath and released it. It took longer than usual, but bit-by-bit the world receded and a dark mist arose in her mind, swirling and eddying around her.

"Where are you?" she called out to her guide. "I can't see you in the darkness."

She listened for the inner voice that directed her steps, but was greeted with silence. Even so, she groped through the mist alone, without a light to guide her.

And then she knew.

The medallion had been found. It was in Brooke's possession and there was no telling what the stupid woman would do with it.

Wild with rage, Elena shook off the trance, grabbed her phone, and waited impatiently until her contact answered. "Move fast," she ordered. "And be sure to cover your tracks."

▼ ▼ ▼

Ted was feeling irritable and for good reason. His thoughts kept returning to Brooke and that miserable, awkward encounter in the Hewitt Gallery. His inane remarks had shown how little he knew about art, and he could only imagine what she thought of him now.

Get over it, he told himself, but the thoughts continued to assail him.

He stared at the computer monitor. His script was nearly complete. Just a few more hours of research and he'd be able to tie the pieces into an airtight presentation. He scrolled through a few more sources and was finally getting into it when the phone rang. Should he let it go to voicemail? No. He was short on cash these days, and if this was someone calling to book a lecture, he needed to answer before they disconnected and changed their minds.

"Dispelling the Darkness Ministries," he said. "Ted Roslyn speaking."

"I hate to bother you," a woman's voice began, "but something's come up and I didn't know who else to call."

"I'm sorry. I didn't catch your name. Who's calling please?"

"This is Brooke."

Brooke? The Sad-Eyed Woman of Mystery? Was it possible? He didn't know any other Brookes, so it must be the same one.

"It's no bother at all," he stammered. "I'm glad you thought of me. What's up?"

She explained that an antiques appraiser had come across a medallion in an old desk. She thought it might be the occult ritual object her late husband had described and she wanted Ted to take a look at it.

He glanced at his watch. It was 9:00 and he'd already put on sweats and a tee-shirt before hunkering down for the night. But none of that mattered. He could get changed and be on his way in minutes. "I'm not doing much right now," he said even thought he actually was. "I could stop by tonight or whenever it's convenient."

"Tonight would be wonderful. I'd like to get this figured out as soon as possible. If it's no bother, I mean."

"It's no bother at all. Just give me your address and I'll be there."

Half an hour later, he got out of his Jeep in front of a rustic timber frame house. It was pretty creepy out there in the woods with the trees towering overhead and no one around for miles. No wonder Sad Eyes was freaked out.

He walked up on the porch and when he knocked, there she was. Her blue-green eyes. Her half-hearted smile. Her chestnut hair. Granted, she seemed a bit worn around the edges. Hassled and frazzled and in need of sleep, but charming nonetheless.

She stepped aside to allow him to enter. "Thanks for running over here so late."

"Glad to be of service."

He followed her into a living room with a vaulted ceiling. The décor was rustic like you'd expect in a timber frame structure. For a moment he felt like he'd just come home after a long hike in the woods. No more than that. He felt ready to split logs, bring down an eight pointer with a bow and arrow and pull trout from a raging stream.

But not right now.

Right now he was here to listen.

Brooke didn't bother with small talk. Instead, she reached into her pocket and held out an item for him to inspect.

And there it was, in the flesh, so to speak. A phoenix on one side. A bunch of strange carvings on the other.

He ran his fingers over the edge of the piece and inspected it beneath a light. It was worn down, the details diminished with time, but there was no mistaking the creature slithering around the perimeter.

He invited Brooke to take a closer look. When she did, she glanced back at him in surprise.

"A snake. I can't believe I didn't notice it before."

"It's an occult symbol known as the Ouroboros," Ted explained. "A snake—sometimes a dragon—swallowing its tail. It appears over and over in ancient cultures. Hindu texts describe it as the power of Kundalini. Norse cultures saw it as the world serpent. The Aztecs viewed it as the feathered serpent god, Quetzalcoatl. To Renaissance alchemists it signified the merging of opposite forces. Light and dark. Wisdom and folly. Good and evil. Male and female."

She turned the object over. "At first I thought the carvings on the back were Hebrew or Greek, but I looked up both alphabets online and neither was a match."

"I imagine it's a cipher of some kind," he said. "Back in the day sorcerers could literally lose their heads for practicing magic arts, so they developed secret alphabets to transmit their messages. Nowadays, only a handful of serious scholars and practitioners know how to interpret their codes. I'm not one of them, but I've got a friend who might be able to shed some light on the subject. If you're interested, I'll get in touch with him."

"Of course I'm interested. And the sooner the better. I'll eventually need to show this thing to the police, but I'd like to know more about it first."

"That settles it. I'll send my buddy a text and see what he thinks. It might expedite things if I included some pictures."

She agreed to the plan and so Ted took a couple of shots of each side of the piece. The more he looked at the carvings, the more familiar they seemed. Not that he could interpret the symbols, but rather that something about them rang a bell.

He dispatched the pictures with a brief message. As he was finishing up, he heard a vehicle rumbling up the drive. When he looked at Brooke, her eyes were wide with fear.

"It's Rob!" She pointed at the medallion. "Put it in your pocket. If he asks about it, pretend you don't know what he's talking about."

"Slow down," Ted said. "Who or what is this about?"

"Rob Tate," she said impatiently, like he was supposed to know who the guy was. "He was here today putting in a window. He walked into the study just as the appraiser found the medallion. He saw it—I know he did, and I keep wondering if Karl showed it to him and if he's wanted to get his hands on it ever since. I think he figured how to work the security and I'm afraid he'll break in to steal it."

"It's okay," Ted said, although he had no way of knowing it that was true because Brooke's story wasn't entirely clear. "Look at it this way. I'm here so you won't have to face this guy alone."

His statement was punctuated by a thump, thump, thump on the door. Brooke grabbed onto his arm like it was a life preserver, and it took a few seconds for her to calm down and let go.

"Wait here," she said. "If I need help, I'll let you know."

Eighteen

Brett knocked again, more forcefully this time. He'd risked his life camping out at this place and had even straightened up a bit to show Brooke he could be a nice guy when he chose to be. He'd waited all afternoon to hear what the appraiser had to say, and when he got sick of waiting, he'd called Brooke for the details. Not once, but five times. The least she could have done was call back, but did she? No.

He was just about to shout her name when the door flew open and she stood there staring at him. She seemed flustered, like he'd barged into the middle of something and taken her off guard. Or like she was expecting someone else.

"I assume the appraiser was here today?" he began.

"Of course. I forgot to call you."

"Is that an apology?"

"Not exactly. But for the record, I'm sorry. It slipped my mind."

"So, for the record, are you going to invite me in, or am I supposed to stand on the porch all night?"

She seemed confused by the question. "It's late. I'll give you a call in the morning and go over the details."

"It's not late. It's not even ten. And it's not like you have to get up and go to work like normal people. Just tell me about the appraisal and I'll be on my way."

He made an attempt to enter, but she refused to step aside.

"The appraisal was interesting," she said. "I learned a lot."

"Bravo. So you're smarter than you were before. Now, cut to the chase. How much money are we talking about?"

"Julie will get back to me in a day or so with the estimates. The only thing she said for sure is that the art pottery's worth around eight thousand at auction."

Brett gave a whistle. "Not bad for a bunch of ugly vases. Not bad at all. Anything else?"

"She's getting a second opinion on the slant top desk in your dad's study, but she expects it to bring a decent price at Sotheby's or Christie's."

Brett brightened at the thought. "That piece of junk? I can't picture it."

"Me either. But she seemed pretty convinced."

He chuckled to himself. The other night he'd pulled the drawers out of that clunky old thing, hoping to find somebody's will stuck between the drawers or stock certificates wedged inside the cubby holes. He hadn't found a thing and it had never occurred to him that the desk itself might be worth a bundle.

"Let me take a look at it," he said, curious as to what the appraiser had seen that he'd missed.

"Some other time."

"What do you mean, some other time? The desk belonged to my dad's family and now it belongs to Stephi and me. I have a right to check it out."

"I said, not now."

He could tell she was ticked because her lips were drawn in a straight line—the classic Brooke's-in-a-snit look he and Stephi always made fun of.

He took a step forward and was surprised when she raised an arm to block him. Enough of this, he decided. If she wanted to get physical, he'd give her physical.

He shoved her aside and strode through the foyer and into the living room.

And then he stopped in his tracks. So this was why Brooke had tried to keep him out on the porch.

A scruffy-haired guy stood in front of him. "I'm Ted Roslyn," he said. "A friend of Brooke's."

Before Brett could say a word, Brooke completed the introductions, all nice and proper like this was a tea party and they'd been waiting for him to arrive.

The guy extended his hand, but Brett was having none of it. Instead he glared at Brooke. "What's going on here?"

"Ted stopped by to help me with something."

"Yeah, I'll bet he did."

"It's not what you think."

"Really? That's interesting, because I think it looks bad. Really bad. No wonder you didn't want me in the house. You didn't want me to learn your dirty little secret."

"There's no dirty little secret."

"Oh, really?"

"She's telling the truth," the shaggy-haired creep insisted. "I'm just a friend."

"Yeah, and I'm the president of the United States."

He noticed Brooke exchange a glance with the creep— just a brief moment of eye contact, but it's meaning was clear: *Keep your mouth shut and with any luck, he'll soon be gone.*

"Ted stopped by to help me with a problem," she informed him.

"Oh yeah? What kind of problem? The problem of being alone and scared in the deep, dark woods. The problem of sleeping all by yourself in my dad's king-size bed?"

"That's not fair and you know it."

"Oh, no? Well, let me tell you what's not fair. It's not fair that you've spent the last two months soaking up everyone's pity when all the while you've been…"

He couldn't bring himself to continue. Not when he wanted to punch the scruffy-haired guy in the face. Brett's dad didn't deserve this. He deserved to be remembered. To be mourned and honored and missed and loved.

"My dad was too good for you," he shouted at Brooke. "You weaseled your way into his life and took control of everything he and my mom built together. And now that he's gone, this is the way you show your thanks."

Seized with the same grief that had assailed him at the retrospective, he turned and headed out the door, and he made sure that it slammed behind him.

▾ ▾ ▾

Ted was the first to break the silence. "I seem to have caused a problem."

"It's not your fault. If I'd called Brett earlier like I was supposed to, this wouldn't have happened. He'll forget about it in a few days."

Her words weren't convincing.

"He's not like his father," Brooke added. "Karl was thoughtful and kind. Brett's belligerent and arrogant and…"

"And grieving."

The word seemed to catch her by surprise. "Grieving. Of course."

And not much younger than you, Ted observed. It must be weird having an attractive stepmom so close to your own age. A real challenge when it came to family dynamics.

He took the medallion out of his pocket and handed it back to her. "Like I was saying before we were interrupted, I'll get back to you as soon as I hear from my friend."

The remark was followed by silence. Where to go from here? He glanced toward the foyer. "I guess I'll be on my way. I hope I haven't caused too much trouble."

She hesitated before answering, and he could sense her thoughts careening back and forth in her head as she tried to figure out what to do.

"Could you stay a while longer?" she asked. "The other

night I woke up and there was a strange man in the driveway. He left when he saw the signs for the security system and when the police checked the property, he was gone. They said I was safe, but I can't get him out of my head. And I keep picturing Rob showing up and disabling the security system while I'm asleep."

Her blue-green eyes were begging him to stay, so how could he say no? He couldn't. But that didn't make things exactly comfortable. He sat down on one end of the sofa and she sat on the other, and all he could think about was Brett's crack about the king-sized bed, and he wondered if Brooke was thinking the same thing.

"How does someone become a born-again ghost-buster?" she asked out of the blue.

"A born-again ghost-buster? That's not how I think of myself."

"Okay. So, how do you think of yourself?"

"I'm a Christian apologist."

"Apologist? As in saying you're sorry?"

"As in defending the faith. The word *apologetics* comes from the Greek word, *apologia*, which means a defense or an answer. My area of expertise is occult phenomena which includes the New Age movement, alternative spirituality, UFOs, paranormal experiences—that kind of stuff."

"Crazy stuff."

He nodded. "Indeed. But this crazy stuff, as you call it, represents a significant trend in modern thought."

"So how did you get started doing this? It's kind of a specialized area, isn't it?"

He listened to the inflection in her voice. It was hard to tell if she was serious or if she was mocking him. But it hardly mattered. It was something to talk about. At least until she felt less fearful and asked him to leave.

He explained that he used to write for a regional newspaper, and over time he'd noticed a bias: some stories got lots of coverage while others were mentioned briefly before vanishing. He started looking into the stories that vanished, and in several instances he'd stumbled on stuff the public needed to know. He'd approached the editors about doing some investigative pieces—that's the reason he'd wanted to be a journalist in the first place—but they wouldn't bite. Even worse, they loaded him down with garbage assignments and took him off the better ones.

He recalled his editor's angry face. *Conspiracy theorist,* he'd *called him. Don't bother me again until you get your facts straight.*

But Ted's facts had been straight. The things he'd discovered could have unseated powerful local politicians, but the paper wanted none of it.

"Anyway," he continued, "in my spare time I hooked up with a guy who hosted a YouTube channel that debunked hoaxes, urban legends, UFO sightings—crazy stuff as you call it. Eventually I left the paper and went with him full time. Soon I was running into cases I couldn't explain."

"Like what?"

"Like a popular medium I was determined to expose as a fraud. We selected the individual the medium would meet with and made sure the controls were in place so she couldn't cheat. To my amazement, the stuff she spewed out was spot on. She knew what kind of dog the subject had when he was a kid. The color of his first bike. His favorite teacher in elementary school. His first girlfriend. After that she described a crime the guy had seen in the woods when he was six-years-old. He'd repressed the memory and as she talked about it, he started sobbing and we had to end the session. I followed up by taking the story to the police, and to my complete surprise, the information helped solve a case that had gone cold forty years earlier.

"I had no explanation for what I'd witnessed. Either the woman possessed unusual powers, or unusual powers possessed her.

"As time went by I encountered other stories I couldn't explain. Not many, but enough to make me skeptical of my own skepticism—if you follow what I mean. And then I had an experience that's difficult to describe."

He watched her face cloud over. "I'll spare you the details because you're spooked enough already. It was pretty horrific, and afterward I started having nightmares and feeling like someone or something was watching me. I thought I was going crazy, and then I started running into people who—out of the blue—began telling me about Jesus. Being a debunker, I was determined to find the flaws in their arguments, but the day came when I bent the knee, and my life hasn't been the same since."

Again he watched Brooke's face. She wasn't buying it.

They moved on to other topics, and bit by bit she seemed to relax. Or maybe she was just exhausted. When she stifled a yawn, he glanced at his watch. It was nearly three in the morning.

"I probably should be going."

She had to be pretty tired, because the idea seemed to suit her. "I'm glad you stopped by. You've been a huge help."

"Glad to hear it. I'll be in touch as soon as I hear back from my friend." At the door he gazed one last time into her blue green eyes. "If you need anything," he said. "I'm just a phone call away."

▾ ▾ ▾

Brett tried to shake the cramp out of his leg, but ended up banging his knee against the steering wheel. He let out a frustrated yelp. He's about had it with playing sentry, but after all this time, he hated to give up on his mission.

Instead of going home, he'd parked his Lexus behind a bunch of trees just across the road from Brooke's driveway. From this vantage point he had a view of the house and the cars parked in front of it. He'd been passing his time on his phone reading up on antique desks and checking out auction websites. In the process he'd learned a few things like the names of important furniture makers from long ago and their price ranges at auction. But by now he was bored to death, and the shaggy-haired creep still hadn't emerged from the house.

He noticed a black SUV cruising by for the fifth or sixth time. Like before, it slowed down as it passed the driveway. He considered following it—it might be the person who'd ransacked the house, but at the moment, he had other matters on his mind. Even so, he took a few photos of the car to show to the cops, but he doubted they'd turn out. It was too dark out here in the middle of nowhere and using a flash would have been a dead give-away.

A few minutes more and he decided it to throw in the towel and go home, There was no point in waiting for the creep to exit. Not if he and Brooke were snuggled down for the night.

The thought made his stomach turn. How long had this been going on? Did it start before his dad died? He could imagine his old man's reaction if he'd found out Brooke was messing around. Fire and fury at first. Hopeless despair later on. Was that why he'd gotten so weirdly religious there at the end? Had he turned to God because his marriage was falling apart?

Brett pounded his fist against the steering wheel at the thought of it. Too bad it wasn't Ted Roslyn's face.

A thought occurred to him. He'd never paid much attention to the old junk his dad had accumulated over the years. What if Brooke had already cashed in on valuable goodies belonging to him and Stephi? He chided himself for not being more diligent. He should have kept an eye on things while Brooke was playing the grief-stricken widow.

He'd talk to Stephi about this first thing tomorrow. No. Second thing. First he'd call the appraiser to verify the things Brooke had told him. Once he had those details sorted out, he'd phone his baby sister and together they'd come up with a plan.

He was surprised when headlights beamed from the end of

the driveway. Looks like Romeo was on the move. He watched through the trees as the vehicle approached. A Jeep Renegade turned out of the drive, and Brett gave it a head start before easing his Lexus out of the hiding place with the headlights off. When Roslyn's taillights disappeared around a bend, Brett turned on his low beams and picked up speed until the Renegade came back in view. He followed it all the way to Allentown and watched as the beat-up piece of junk came to rest in front of a squalid looking row house. From all appearances the neighborhood was a dump and probably home to drug-dealers, hookers and assorted low-life scum.

He watched Roslyn exit the Jeep and disappear inside a corner property.

So this is what Brooke had wrecked her marriage for. A creep, who judging from his address, had barely a nickel to his name.

Nineteen

Ted called Brooke around nine Tuesday morning. His friend had found the photos interesting, but he wanted to see the medallion in person before passing judgment. He was a busy guy, but he was willing to work them in the following day around noon. Since he lived three hours away in Pennsylvania's Endless Mountains, they'd need to be on the road no later than nine the following morning. Brooke agreed to meet Ted at the same coffee shop where they'd met a week earlier, and when they finalized their plans, she said goodbye and hung up.

Afterward, she turned her attention to Christopher Marlowe and the question of his death, but as intriguing as the topic had seemed a few days ago, all she could think of at the moment was the medallion and the people—whoever they were—who wanted it.

She checked the video monitor for the second time that morning just to make sure she hadn't missed anything. There was no sign of Rob or anyone else, but security system or no security system, she wouldn't feel safe as long as the medallion remained in her possession.

So what should she do? The more she thought about it, the more she wanted to get away from the house and spend the day where no one would think to look for her. But where would that be? Her uncle's apartment was out of the question—she didn't want anyone following her there and she didn't want to put him at risk.

So what were her options?

She fretted about it for a while and then an idea struck her. She'd take the train to the city and visit Mordecai's Antiques and Oddities, the store where Karl had worked as an undergrad. He'd told her about the owner's fascination with the mysterious and the arcane, and she wondered now if someone at the store might be able to tell her something that would supplement what she'd learn on tomorrow's trek to the Endless Mountains.

She looked up the train schedule on her phone. After that, she placed the medallion in her pocket and grabbed her bag from the floor. If someone chose to break in while she was away, they'd be at the mercy of the security system and the alarms. And if someone managed to get past the security system and the alarms, Brooke would assume it was Rob Tate, and she was certain Detective Burleigh would agree with her.

Forty-five minutes later she boarded a SEPTA train and in another fifty minutes she got off at Jefferson Station. She took the escalator up to the ground floor and joined the pedestrians on Market Street. Here in the city she was anonymous, and for the first time since the break-in, she knew she was safe.

▼ ▼ ▼

Brett held the phone to his ear and leaned back with his feet on the desk. He liked sitting like this. It made him feel important, like he was VP in charge of marketing instead of a lowly peasant chained to a cubicle.

"This is Brett Erikson," he said when a woman's voice answered. "I'm calling about the appraisal you did yesterday at my dad's house."

Julie Franklin's response was dodgy. She confirmed that

she did an appraisal yesterday, but since she didn't know the person to whom she was speaking (him) she wasn't willing to discuss the details.

"Take my word for it," he said in a no-nonsense voice. "Karl Erikson was my dad. Brooke Roberts is my stepmother. There's a bunch of old junk in the house. Blanket chests and bureaus and statues and lamps and a bunch of pottery and so forth. I need a ballpark estimate of their value."

Julie's response was basically a rehash of what Brooke had already told him. She was working up the numbers and would get back to Brooke in a few days.

"There's a beat-up desk in the study," Brett continued. "I understand it might be worth something."

Again Julie's comments matched what Brooke had said last night. And then she said something that was news to him, and that quick his feet dropped to the floor and he rocketed out of his chair, stunned by what he'd just heard.

"Brooke never mentioned a secret compartment in the desk."

There was silence on the other end. When Julie finally spoke, he could sense that she was trying to wriggle out of a corner she'd just painted herself into.

"I don't care that you promised not to discuss it with anyone," he informed her. "The desk is a family heirloom—not Brooke's family, but mine and my sister's. If there was something hidden in it, Stephi and I have a right to know."

Julie hemmed and hawed until Brett said the magic word.

Not *abracadabra*, as one might expect, but *lawyer.* The most magical word in the English language, bar none. After that Little Miss Antiques Appraiser was a whole lot more cooperative.

"So," he said once she'd filled in the details. "You found a medallion—possibly gold—with a phoenix surrounded by a bunch of red stones—possibly rubies. What's it worth?"

Her response floored him. "What do you mean you don't

know? You're an appraiser. It's your job to know what stuff is worth."

She explained that jewelry wasn't her specialty and that she'd offered to give Brooke the name of an expert, but Brooke wasn't interested in learning its value. Oh, really? Did that mean Brooke already knew how much this thing was worth? He'd have to find out.

"Thanks, Julie," he said. "You've been a huge help."

He terminated the call and sat down to think things through. He understood now why Brooke had been so cagey last night. She'd found a valuable trinket that she and lover boy intended to keep for themselves. How long had she known about this thing? And who else knew about it and who had broken into the house to find it?

He picked up the phone and made another call.

"Hey Steph. How about we meet for lunch at noon? My treat."

▾ ▾ ▾

Brooke walked up six steps to a green door. In front of her was a brass knocker featuring a monkey's face that grinned broadly, as though daring her to enter. She took the dare and when she went inside Mordecai's Antiques and Oddities, she found a dark and dusty room decorated for Halloween. Directly in front of her was a taxidermied black cat with its back arched and its teeth bared. Surrounding it were vintage devil masks; papier-mâché jack-o'lanterns; cardboard cutouts of witches, demons and owls; and a smattering of Ouija boards. A table to her left displayed Civil War medical equipment including a saw used for amputation. She wondered how many limbs it had severed.

A middle-aged man with salt and pepper hair looked up from his Sudoku puzzle. "Can I help you?" he asked, his eyes studying her intently, or so it seemed.

"I'm looking for Mordecai Simmons."

"That's my dad. He's theoretically retired, but he can't seem to keep his hands out of the business. He's working in the office today. Whom shall I say is calling?"

"My name's Brooke Roberts. My late husband worked here a long time ago. Karl Erikson. Maybe you knew him."

The man looked at her strangely. She couldn't explain it, but something in his lingering gaze made her feel ill-at-ease, more evidence, she supposed, of her distressed state of mind.

He emerged from behind the check-out counter. "This way."

She followed him through a tangle of rooms, past festival masks, magic lanterns, carnival memorabilia, religious statuary and occult paraphernalia—a jumbled assortment of the bizarre, the sacred, and the profane. A door at the rear of the shop stood open. He ushered her through it and into a tiny office where an old man sat hunched over a desk.

"You've got a visitor, Dad. Brooke Roberts. Karl Erikson's widow."

Mordecai Simmons' mouth dropped open, and he stared, somewhat rudely. He quickly collected himself and pointed with his cane toward a chair piled with folders. "Move that stuff," he instructed his son. "Mind your manners and offer the lady a seat."

Mordecai's son did as instructed and then excused himself and went into the adjacent room. Brooke glanced out the door and saw that instead of returning to his Sudoku puzzle at the front of the store, he lingered within earshot of the office.

She began to explain the reason for her visit, but the old man cut her off. His eyes darted toward the door, and when he pointed with his cane, his hands shook so badly it was a wonder it didn't fly from his grasp. "Close the door and lock it," he ordered, his voice a hushed whisper.

She eyed him curiously. She'd expected Mordecai Simmons to offer a few words of introduction followed by some fond remembrances or her late husband from years gone by. This was not the reception she'd anticipated.

She did as he'd commanded and returned to her seat. "I took the train to town today," she stammered, "because of ..."

"Because of the phoenix medallion. I already know."

She looked at him, perplexed. How did he know that?

"I'm not psychic, if that's what you're thinking. Your late husband paid me a visit not long before he died. He said he'd bought a medallion at a thrift shop and he asked me to eval-uate it."

She fished the object from her pocket and held it out for him to see. "Is this what he showed you?"

The old man recoiled at the sight. "That's not a trinket to toss in your pocket and drag all over town. It belongs in a vault under lock and key."

He placed a quivering hand on his chest and closed his eyes. For a moment, Brooke thought he might be ill, and she was just about to open the door to ask his son for help when the man resumed speaking.

"When your late husband first showed me the medallion, I believed it to be a reproduction. Since learning of his death, I've come to wonder if it might actually be authentic."

"And if it is?"

"If it is, it's worth a king's ransom, and there are plenty of individuals who would kill to possess the medallion and its power."

Brooke stared at the object in her hand. She should have taken it directly to the police, but then she'd never be able to learn its meaning. That, after all, is why she'd made this trip to the city and why she'd be headed in the opposite direction the following day.

"Can you explain the carvings on the back?"

"I can't translate them, if that's what you mean. The words are written in a language Renaissance occultist John Dee be-lieved to have been given to him by angels. Few have mastered this tongue and many have gone mad trying. The object is believed to have been created by Dee himself, from alchemical gold. The former assertion is entirely possible. The latter is entirely absurd, but it lends to the lore associated with the piece."

The object sparkled in the glow of the single light on Mordecai's desk. Alchemical gold? The language of angels. She'd never have imagined such things—not in a million years.

"An expert is looking at it tomorrow," she said, her gaze fixed on the carvings. "Perhaps he'll be able to add to the things you've just told me."

"An expert?" the old man looked doubtful. "And who exactly would that be?"

"I'm not sure. A friend arranged the meeting."

Mordecai's smile was condescending. "I wouldn't count on much from this alleged expert of yours. The individual with the greatest knowledge of the phoenix medallion was turned into ashes in a California wildfire three years ago. It was, however, a less torturous death than the one certain people had marked out for him."

"Less torturous?" Brooke pictured innocent women burned as witches. Martyrs dying for their faith. The *auto-da-fe* of the Spanish Inquisition. "What could be more torturous than being burned alive?"

"Jeremy Stokes had broken faith with the esoteric societies to which he'd pledged allegiance. There were rumors circulating that he intended to betray powerful individuals who preferred that their secrets remained secret. Believe me, death by fire would have been speedier than the prolonged agony that would have been inflicted by those intent on silencing him. Curiously, I've heard stories that he survived the inferno and is living elsewhere under an assumed name. I think, however, that he'd be a somewhat difficult person to keep hidden."

"Why's that?"

Mordecai offered a brief description to prove his point. Stokes was tall—six-foot-three or better. Broad shoulders. Imposing physique. Wild black hair and a beard to match. Dark eyes that breathed threats. A perpetual scowl. Eccentric with a passion for opera.

"If you'd met him, you wouldn't soon forget him."

He dismissed the ghost of Jeremy Stokes with a wave of his hand. "Enough of this chatter." He leaned across his desk, his eyes boring into Brooke's. "You are in danger, my dear. There are persons in this city and elsewhere who would gladly do you harm if it meant getting their hands on the object in your possession."

He held up his cane, his hands trembling as he pointed toward a door at the back of the office. "Leave by the rear exit. Get out of the city as quickly as possible. Don't return home— not until this so-called expert has an opportunity to inspect the medallion and help you decide how best to dispose of it. Watch your back at all times, and if you sense someone following you, find a way to elude them. Stick to the alleys as you flee, and may the God of Abraham, Isaac, and Jacob go with you."

Twenty

Stephi glanced over the menu. She'd arrived at the restaurant on time, but Brett was nowhere in sight. Figures he'd be late.

She pulled her phone from her bag. No message from Brett, but was she surprised? It would be just like him not to show, and meanwhile she'd already ordered white wine at eight dollars a glass, and now she'd be stuck paying for it.

To her surprise, Brett showed up seconds later. He sauntered through the door and stopped to kibitz with the hostess, a cute little thing in a short skirt and tight sweater. She led him to the booth where Stephi waited and gave him a flirtatious smile before making her exit.

"Hey there, little sis," Brett said as he slid into his seat. "You look terrific. Doing something different with your hair?"

Stephi glared at him. "I've worn it this way for the last three years."

"Really? Well, it looks even more terrific than usual."

She eyed him suspiciously. "Did I hear you correctly this morning? You said you were treating?"

"I invited you to lunch, didn't I? Of course, I'm treating."

Her suspicions deepened. Brett never treated. That must mean he was prepping her for a massive favor. Well, if that was the case, she'd order something really expensive. No way was she going to let her brother take advantage of her. Not this time and not like all those times before.

She eyed the menu. Lobster bisque would be a tasty starter, followed by crab cakes with steamed asparagus. She gave her order to the server and listened while Brett ordered a cheeseburger and diet Coke.

"So which would you like to hear about first?" he asked as the server departed for the kitchen. "Should I tell you about Dad's old slant-top desk that's worth a bundle and has a secret compartment where a valuable medallion just happened to be hidden that Brooke doesn't want us to know about? Or would you rather hear about Brooke shacking up with a shaggy-haired creep from Allentown?"

Both questions knocked Stephi for a loop. She gulped down a mouthful of pinot grigio and tried to process what she'd just heard. "Tell me those choices again."

Ten minutes later she stared at the lobster bisque congealing in the bowl in front of her. "You're telling me that the appraiser found a totally valuable medallion in a secret compartment in that dilapidated old desk?"

Brett nodded.

"And Brooke conveniently forgot to tell you about it even though it might be what the thief was looking for when he ransacked the house?"

"That's about the size of it," Brett said, matter-of-factly. "Brooke said the desk is worth a ton of money, but she never mentioned the secret compartment and the medallion. Apparently she coerced the appraiser into keeping it quiet, and I had to threaten Julie Franklin with a lawyer to get her to cough up the information."

Stephi's thoughts were reeling. "This guy you saw at the house with Brooke? You're saying they're an item?"

Brett nodded and laughed sardonically. "For two months Brooke's been crying boo-hoo and making everybody walk on eggshells because she's oh-so fragile and oh-so grieving and oh-so tragic and sad. Meanwhile she's shacking up with this creep and scheming to steal our inheritance out from under us."

Stephi set down her spoon and forced back the anger welling up inside her. "I knew the day I met her she was trouble. I never understood what Dad saw in her."

"Other than her incredible hotness?"

She felt her face flush. "Don't talk about Dad like that. I can't bear it."

"Well, learn to bear it, because it's reality. Brooke is way hot, and you're a fool if you think Dad wasn't aware of it."

Stephi shuddered and took a quick sip of wine to chase away the thought.

"And that brings us to the subject of this Roslyn idiot," her brother continued. "I don't know how long he was at the house before I showed up, but he sure stayed a long time after I left. They had plenty of time to—you know."

Stephi pounded her fist on the table. "It's wrong! All of it. And if you hadn't gone to the house last night, we still wouldn't know a thing."

She took a quick bite of bisque and swallowed hard. And then a thought hit her. Had Brooke been seeing this creep while their Dad was still alive? She asked Brett, and he said he couldn't be sure, but he'd wondered the same thing. After that she wondered aloud if their father might have known about Brooke messing with this guy, and then a third question occurred to her, one she could barely express but managed to choke out anyway.

"What if Ted Roslyn followed Dad into the woods that Sunday in July, and what if they got in an argument over Brooke, and what if the argument turned into a fight and then..." She left the thought dangling. The picture in her mind was too terrible to consider.

Brett gazed at his placemat that by now was dotted with ketchup that had dripped from his burger. "All I'm saying, little sis, is that the whole things smells fishy. I wanted to tell you about it so we can put our heads together and get to the bottom of it." He reached his hand across the table. "Are we a team?"

Stephi felt her resentment vanish. From now on, she and her brother were comrades facing a common foe. She took his hand in hers. "We're a team. And for Dad's sake, we're going to find out the truth."

▾ ▾ ▾

Brooke raced down the alley behind the store, and when she arrived at the intersection of Spruce Street, she drew back into the shadows to check out the activity on the block. She saw nothing alarming, and so she merged with the pedestrians, hoping to blend in with the crowd.

Just a short time ago she'd felt anonymous—one of many faceless individuals in a busy city. But the sense of anonymity had vanished, and now she felt exposed and vulnerable—like snipers lurked in every doorway, weapons raised and ready to fire when she walked by.

She made her way toward Tenth Street, her eyes scanning the people milling past. A street vendor held out a falafel and shouted the price. A woman hastened by lugging a brief case and a bulky portfolio. Bicycles wove in and out of traffic. A road crew filled a pothole. And thankfully, no one paid her any attention.

A block farther and she noticed a man on the other side of the street dressed in black with dark hair and a neatly trimmed beard. Something about him seemed familiar, but it was hard to tell because of his reflecting sunglasses. She studied him a moment and lowered her eyes. It was him—she was sure of it. The man she'd seen on the security footage a few nights earlier.

She hurried along the block. The man was talking on his phone and seemed oblivious to her presence, but that would change if he caught sight of her.

She darted down an alley to avoid detection. Ahead of her was an overflowing dumpster. Not the best place to hide, she realized as she swatted at yellow jackets, but there weren't many options. She crouched behind it, trying not to gag at the odor of rotting meat and sour milk. A minute ticked by and then another. Was it safe now?

She inched slowly forward and looked toward the street. And there he was with his back to the alley, watching people passing by, his cell phone pressed to his ear.

She drew back and bumped her cheek against something sharp and metallic. She touched her face and was relieved to discover that it wasn't bleeding. Even so, she'd have a bruise as a souvenir of the day's adventures.

But bruises were the least of her worries. At the moment she was terrified that the man who'd staked out her house knew she was in the city. Had he followed her from her house, or did he have contacts who'd notified him of her whereabouts? Had he seen her duck down the alley, and if so, was he on his cell summoning reinforcements to watch and wait for her to emerge from the other end?

She heard a noise. Footsteps. Left-right, left-right, left-right. Was she about to be detected? If so, she'd surrender the medallion and hopefully her pursuer would leave her alone. But she knew he wouldn't. Not when she'd seen his face and could ID him.

She held her breath and wished she could disappear, but the most she could do was wedge herself more tightly between the dumpster and the adjacent brick wall.

A peal of girlish laughter rang out and a teenager in jeans and a tank top walked by, chatting on her phone. She gave Brooke a curious look and continued on her way.

A sigh of relief escaped her lips. It wasn't the guy dressed in black—just a teenager talking to a friend. Brooke got her phone out of her pocket and checked the train schedule. She wouldn't make the next one and would have to wait around for the next. That meant hiding out in the women's restroom at Jefferson Station and when the time approached, making a mad dash down the escalator and onto the loading platform, hopefully with no one seeing her.

She did a quick inventory of her surroundings and eased out of her hiding place. She kept her face turned toward the sidewalk and as she neared Market Street, she paused to take shelter in a doorway that provided a clear view of the people entering and exiting the station. She noticed a brawny Black guy in dark jogging pants and a tight tee-shirt. He wore sunglasses, but even though she couldn't see his eyes, she could tell from the way he turned his head that he was watching the passers-by. Was he looking for her, or was he waiting to meet someone? She had no idea, but she realized it was ridiculous to think she could make it to the station without attracting attention.

Macy's was just a tad west of where she stood, so she doubled back around the block and headed in that direction. She entered the store through a side entrance and emerged fifteen minutes later in a different outfit that included a Phillies baseball cap and a pair of dark glasses. By now there was no time to hide out in the restroom at the train station. She'd be lucky to get to the boarding platform in time.

She paused at the traffic light and pretended to fiddle with her phone. In reality, she was shifting her gaze back and forth, trying to scan the faces outside the station. The brawny Black man was nowhere to be seen nor was the man she'd recognized earlier.

She merged into the crowd, her eyes straight ahead, her steps hurried. At the entrance to the station she hesitated and looked around. A bad move as she soon realized.

The dark-haired man stood in a doorway on the other side of the street, partially masked by shadows. His reflecting glasses shifted in her direction and in an instant, he bolted toward the street and into the path of traffic. Tires screeched, horns blared, curses rang out, and a police whistle shrieked into the chaos. A cop darted toward the guy and grabbed him by the collar while people gathered to watch.

Brooke took advantage of the confusion to race into the station in the direction of the escalator. She dodged shoppers lugging heavy bags and skirted people ambling along with phones pressed to their ear. She bumped into a woman with a couple of kids and after a quick apology she darted off, only to collide with a large man who'd bent over abruptly to tie his shoe. She finally made it to the escalator and endured the curses and angry stares of people she squeezed past as she descended the moving stairs.

The marquee announced that her train was due at any second. She glanced down the track and saw an approaching light. In an instant, the train whooshed into the station, the doors rattled open and a throng of passengers began the clumsy process of disembarking.

Bit by bit Brooke made her way forward, ignoring the stares and angry remarks of those she slithered past. Once inside the train, she claimed the nearest empty seat and hunkered down facing the wall next to her with her face well beneath the window. It seemed to take an eternity for people to board, but eventually the train lurched forward. As it gained speed, she raised herself up and looked back toward the platform.

And there they were, the tall Black guy leading the way while the other guy followed close behind. She watched them shove people as she'd done just a few minutes earlier, and when they got to the platform they waved their arms and shouted for the train to stop.

Too bad for them. The train kept going.

She let out a sigh and sank back in her seat, her eyes closed as she waited for her heart rate to return to normal.

"You all right?" asked a voice. Brooke turned to see a heavy-set Black woman seated next to her.

She said yes, but the woman didn't seem to buy it.

"Am I right in thinking a man had something to do with that bruise on your face?"

Brooke touched her cheek. She'd tried to hide the injury with makeup back in the Macy's fitting room. Obviously she'd failed.

"No need to answer," the woman said. "It's plain to see you're running from some no account and hiding the fact behind a pair of sunglasses and a brand new baseball cap."

Brooke looked at her, surprised. "How'd you know? About the hat, I mean."

The woman chuckled. "Easy. You forgot to take off the price tag, and I figured you must've bought it in a hurry. If you don't mind me saying so, you paid too much."

Brooke removed the cap. Sure enough. A tag revealed the price: $27.00. No point in mentioning the 30-percent discount.

"I know how these men are," the woman continued. "All lovey-dovey one day and crazy with their fists the next. Just ask my baby girl. It took a hospital bed and a bunch of machines going beep, beep, beep to get her to wise up to that no-good-for-nothin' she swore she loved. But, Hallelujah! Jesus stepped in and now my baby's about to be married to a decent, church-going man."

She gazed at Brooke. "Do you know the Lord?"

Brooke shook her head and instantly regretted it. She'd just given her neighbor *carte blanche* to start preaching.

The woman wasted no time getting down to business. "Now, listen to me and listen good. When you get home tonight, I want you to get down on your knees and ask Jesus to be your Lord and Savior, you hear? Confess your sins and invite the Holy Spirit into your heart. Once you've done all that, go out and find yourself a decent man. One who loves God and doesn't slam his fist in your face."

Brooke's eyes filled with tears. She'd had a decent man. A wonderful man. A man who loved God and didn't slam his fist in her face. But God took him away.

She fought back the urge to tell the woman what she could do with this God of hers, but before she could find the words, the woman placed her hand gently on Brooke's arm. The gesture was so tender that it took her off guard. Yes, that's what she'd been missing through these sad, lonely months. She'd needed to be mothered and comforted like the scared, lonely child she was. Instead, she'd put up walls and barricaded the doors to keep people out.

"I'll be praying for you, honey," the woman said. "And what's more, I'll get my prayer group praying for you as well. Tonight while you're going about your business, a hundred saints of God will be lifting you up to the Father, praying for your safety and asking Jesus to hold you in his tender, loving hands."

The conductor called out the first stop, and the woman gathered her bags and struggled to her feet.

"Now you do exactly as I told you. And you stay safe, you hear?"

"I'll try," Brooke said. "Thanks for caring."

▾ ▾ ▾

Stephi leaned against the steering wheel and closed her eyes. She couldn't go back to work. Not with three glasses of pinot grigio swooshing around in her belly and wreaking havoc with her brain. She'd have to call in sick. A white lie about a stomach virus or a food-borne illness that came on suddenly.

She made the call at the next traffic light and managed to get home without incurring a DUI. Inside the apartment, she leaned against the door and turned her eyes toward heaven. "I begged you not to marry her, Daddy, but you wouldn't listen! And now look what's happened."

When no response was forthcoming, she staggered over to the futon and sank into the cushion. She leaned forward, her face in her hands and before long, sobs erupted and set her whole body trembling. She missed her father so much. Missed his smile. Missed hearing him call her Sweetness and Light—not that he'd called her that very often in the last few years. Not since Brooke stole his heart away.

She needed to talk to someone—but who? It was terrible being a therapist and listening to kids spew out endless stories of angst and torment while she had no one who cared enough to listen to her problems. The only one who might be remotely interested was her mom—assuming she wasn't in the middle of one of her phony healing sessions.

When Janine answered, Stephi let it fly. Brooke's new boyfriend. The slant-top desk. The hidden medallion. Lies and murder and her inheritance being stolen away.

Afterward Janine was strangely silent.

"Mom," Stephi barked into the phone. "I'm crying my heart out and you're not even listening."

"Of course I'm listening. It's just, I don't know, I'm a bit shaken, that's all. Maybe I should have mentioned this earlier, but in the chaos of the police interviews last week…" She hesitated. "This has been a very trying time for me and Greg."

"Oh really? Well, I hate to tell you, but it's been a trying time for me too. And for Brett and for everybody involved. So, why don't you stop feeling sorry for yourself and think about me for a change?"

Her mother offered apologies mixed with the usual excuses about her intentions being something other than the way things actually turned out. And then she launched into a saga about her experiences on the Sunday of the retrospective. The trip to Philadelphia. Coffee at a diner. A visit to Mordecai's Antiques and Oddities.

"What I neglected to mention earlier," Janine continued, "is that Mordecai told me that your father stopped by the store shortly before he died to ask about a trinket of some sort. It was probably a reproduction, but had it been real, it would have been valuable. And possibly dangerous in some way that I didn't quite understand. Mordecai got pretty upset about it, but I at-tributed his reaction to old age and dementia."

Stephi couldn't believe her ears. "Are you telling me that all this time you knew there a was a trinket or a medallion or whatever hidden in the house and yet you never said a word about it to me or Brett?" Her mind reeled at the thought. "You told the police about it—right? Please tell me you told the police."

Again there was silence. "I didn't want to plant suggestions that might lead in the wrong direction. Greg convinced me that it probably wasn't important."

"Are you crazy? The thief was probably looking for this possibly valuable, possibly dangerous thing. And since you didn't bother to mention it to the police, I'll have to do it."

"But what about Greg?" her mother gasped. "It was his idea not to mention it and I promised to support his decision."

"Greg is always bossing you around and you put up with it without a word. Aren't you ever going to start thinking for your-self?"

She wrapped up the call and made another, this time to Detective Burleigh who promised to stop by within the hour. At least someone cared about the story she had to tell.

She wondered if the detective's sidekick would be with him. She'd sensed that Jason Radley had been flirting with her on their first visit. She recalled his kind expression, and the in-terest he'd shown as he wrote down her remarks. She wondered where this next visit might lead. Nice to think that something good might come out of this terrible mess.

▾ ▾ ▾

Brooke glanced out the window as the train pulled into the station. Cars idled in the parking lot, waiting to swallow up passengers returning from the city. Her eyes darted from windshield to windshield, trying to see if her pursuers were behind one of them. They didn't seem to be, but that didn't mean much. They could have dispatched someone else to watch out for her.

The thought made her feel exposed and vulnerable as she joined the others exiting the train. She kept her eyes to the ground and hastened to her car. Once inside she locked the door and clutched the steering wheel, uncertain as to her next move.

Mordecai Simmons had urged her not to return home. But where would she go? Uncle Nelson's apartment was out of the question—there was no way she'd risk putting him in danger. That left a hotel and that meant she'd have to pull the baseball cap low over her eyes and hope that no one was in the lobby watching as she checked in. After that, she'd have to lock herself in her room and barricade the door with chairs and whatever else she could pile in front of it. In the morning, she'd meet Ted Roslyn at the coffee shop as planned and they'd speed off to the Endless Mountains to see this person who might or might not be the person who might or might not have died in a California wildfire.

But perhaps she should call Ted first.

He picked up after the first ring and listened as she recounted the events of the day.

"Forget the hotel," he said, once she'd finished. "They could follow you there and make a mess of things."

"But that's the only option I can think of."

He was silent a moment and she wondered if he was praying. That would be just the way of a fanatic like him, wasting time when matters demanded quick, decisive action.

"Head directly to the coffee shop—the same one where we met before," he finally said. "Go inside, order something and take it to a table as far away from the windows as possible. Sit there until I call your cell."

Brooke recalled the woman who'd shown such kindness on the train. "I met a woman this afternoon who said a hundred saints of God would be praying for me tonight. For what that's worth."

"Don't knock it," Ted commented, "The way things are going, you need all the help you can get."

Twenty-one

Detective Burleigh could tell that Stephanie Erikson had been drinking—there was no mistaking the slur in her speech as she greeted him and Radley at the door. His suspicions were confirmed by the sight of a wine glass on a table next to the futon—the fresh red circle in the bottom was a dead giveaway. But as the saying goes: *in vino veritas—in wine there's truth*—and truth—or a semblance thereof—was gushing out of Ms. Erikson like water from a hydrant.

She began by claiming that it had come to her attention that Brooke Roberts and a man named Ted Roslyn were lovers. She was one-hundred percent sure of this because her brother had caught the couple together in the house the night before. Not in a compromising position, so to speak. Just that Brett had found them hanging out together in the living room. After that he'd parked his car nearby to keep an eye the house and it was way late—around two in the morning—maybe later—yes, probably later—when Roslyn finally left.

She went on to embellish the saga with layers of supposition and innuendo about Brooke and Roslyn having been a thing before her father died. Supposedly his death was the result of the two men having fought over Brooke.

He noticed Radley giving him a sideways glance as the narrative unfolded. Both men knew that Brooke had met Roslyn only a few days earlier in response to a referral given by the pastor of Birch Hill Community Fellowship. They'd checked out the story and it had held up under scrutiny. There'd been no longstanding relationship, and that meant that whatever might have developed between Brooke and this fellow was of extremely recent vintage.

Furthermore, they'd checked out Ted Roslyn's background starting with his website and ending with interviews with his pastor and several acquaintances from church, and he'd come up squeaky clean. He wasn't as kooky as one might have expected given the nature of his specialty. There'd been no exorcisms or weird religious practices that anyone could recall. Just thought-provoking videos, lectures and discussions. He was a man of strong convictions who enjoyed a good debate in a country where folks were entitled to their opinions and entitled to express them.

Burleigh was about to thank Ms. Erikson for the information she'd provided, flaky as it was, when she blurted out something about her mother's visit to Mordecai's Antiques and Oddities. Apparently the store owner had told Janine about an occult ritual object Karl Erikson had shown him months earlier. Greg Greenwood had advised his wife to keep the information quiet and she'd had fallen in line with the plan.

That was the first worthwhile information to come out of this cockamamie interview. Given the Greenwood's New Agey, hocus-pocus proclivities, an object like that would have made a nice addition to their collection of crystals and other weird junk. Funny that they'd never mentioned it, and in Burleigh's mind, the omission moved the couple up a few rungs on the ladder of suspicion.

This was followed by another surprising bit of information: an appraiser hired to evaluate antiques had stumbled upon what was probably the aforementioned object in an old desk in Karl Erikson's study. Ms. Erikson felt the information might be helpful and might explain why Brooke and this Ted Roslyn creep had been acting so mysteriously when Brett dropped by the house.

"Doesn't look too good for the Greenwoods," Jason Radley remarked once they were back in the car. "Funny they never mentioned that medallion thing."

Burleigh frowned. "Funny, to be sure, but there's something about this story that's even more perplexing."

"What's that?"

"Brooke never contacted us to say she'd found what I'm supposing is the occult ritual object at the heart of this case. Why the devil didn't she call?"

"Good question," Radley agreed. "She called about every other spooky thing that crossed her path. You'd think she would have been on the phone the moment the appraiser found this whatever it is."

Burleigh started the car and eased out into traffic. "I'll follow up with the Greenwoods," he said. "You can head to the city for a chat with Mordecai and Ezra Simmons. Find out everything they know about this medallion and call me the moment the interview's over."

"You got it, Boss."

The senior detective drove along in silence. Why hadn't Brooke called him? Given the circumstances of the case, the omission made no sense.

▾ ▾ ▾

"What do you mean you told Stephi about the medallion? I told you not to utter a word to anyone!"

Janine cowered before her husband's angry outburst. Greg claimed to be a master of serenity. Yoda the Second, people often called him. But today, Yoda the Second was pacing back and forth like a raging lion. Like a bull ready to charge, his face red, his nostrils flaring.

"You promised you wouldn't mention it," he roared, "but the minute my back was turned, you blabbed the story to

Stephanie and she turned around and blabbed it to the cops."

He pointed at the door through which Burleigh had just exited. "Did you see how he looked at us? Did you? He thinks we broke into Karl's house looking for that piece of junk—whatever it is. And now it's just a matter of time before he returns with a warrant and starts snooping through our things and blaming us for Karl's death. I warned you this would happen. When the energy around this place takes a nose dive and the good name we've built for ourselves gets trampled in the mud, we'll know who's to blame, won't we?"

Janine watched Greg pace the floor and all of a sudden she didn't think he looked like either a lion or a raging bull. He looked like a rooster. An arrogant little bird marching back and forth, crowing and flapping its wings. He looked ridiculous, and she had to try hard to keep from laughing. The fact remained that she had an alibi for the Sunday of the retrospective, but Greg? A spontaneous outbreak of bird watching? Was that the best he could do?

"You're making something out of nothing," she said calmly. "If you've done nothing wrong, you've got nothing to fear. I suggest you calm down and pull yourself together."

Her words were like fuel thrown on the flames. Greg's face grew even redder, and she braced herself for the verbal darts that were soon to fly her way. And then she relaxed, because, honestly, it didn't matter. Stephi's words earlier in the day had rung true. Greg was always talking down to her and she was tired of it.

"I think I'll take a bubble bath," she announced. "I'll light a candle and read some poetry. Rumi perhaps, or William Blake. Once you've got yourself under control, we'll figure out where to go from here."

She walked away, and she could sense that he was still fuming but it felt good to not care.

▼ ▼ ▼

Brooke looked out at the coffee shop from beneath the brim of her baseball cap. Had anyone followed her from the train station? Were those two guys from the city in a vehicle waiting outside? If so, how did Ted propose to get her out of this place without being seen?

Her phone vibrated and Ted's number appeared on the screen.

"Where are you?" she whispered.

"Around back. Leave your drink on the table and go to the ladies' room."

She did as instructed.

"Are you alone in there?" he asked when she confirmed that she'd arrived at her destination.

"Yeah, it's a one-seater."

"Okay then. I'm behind the coffee shop looking at a window—the bumpy kind that lets in light but you can't see in or out."

"That's the one."

"Perfect. See if you can open it."

It slid up without much effort but when she looked out, the pavement was at least seven feet below the sill.

Ted looked up at her, grinning. "Shimmy out backwards and let go. Be careful—it's a bit of a drop."

"Wonderful. What if I break a leg? Or both legs?"

"Trust me, you'll be fine."

Ted was as good as his word. And more robust than he looked, a fact Brooke realized once she let go and dropped to the ground. Strong arms softened her descent, turning a crash landing into something more graceful, like a ballerina being lowered to the stage.

Within seconds they were in his Jeep.

"Nice bruise," he remarked as they pulled out of the lot and into the alley behind the coffee shop. "You got that today?"

She nodded. "You should have seen the other guy."

"I'll bet. And the hat—I didn't know you were a sports fan."

She didn't bother responding. Her reservoir of small talk had just run dry.

"We've got two options," Ted continued. "I can take you straight to the police or we can head out tonight and meet up with my friend at noon tomorrow."

"This friend of yours—does he have a name?"

"Of course. Jackson Steele."

She tossed the name around in her mind. Jackson Steele. J. S. The same initials as Jeremy Stokes who was presumed dead.

"How exactly did Jackson Steele become an expert on the medallion?" she asked

Ted explained that his friend had been a media tech guy who'd risen to prominence in several esoteric societies, including a cult related to the medallion. Out of the blue, he experienced a road-to-Damascus religious conversion that caused him to sever ties with the circles in which he'd formerly traveled. He'd sought isolation in the Endless Mountains so he could think and get his life together.

That too, dovetailed with Mordecai's story.

"And how did you and this Jackson Steele get to be friends?"

Ted explained that Steele had watched some of Ted's videos and reached out to him through a network of contacts. Soon Ted was acting as Steele's spiritual mentor while Steel provided material for Ted's lectures and videos.

"But back to the subject at hand," he said, as though reluctant to say anymore about his friend. "Should we take the medallion to the cops or are you still up for a trip to Steele's hideout?"

Hideout. Brooke found that an interesting choice of words.

She felt for the medallion in her pocket. The sensible thing would be to go to the police and let them decide the next move. But the police wouldn't be able to tell her a thing about the object or its history or its purpose. This friend of Ted's—whoever he was—might be the only person who could answer her questions. She wanted answers, and if she didn't follow through as planned, she'd never get them. She told Ted as much. And that's why she didn't voice her suspicions. If she were right, the whole venture might be scrapped out of concern for this person's privacy.

"Let's meet with your friend. Once he's answered my questions, we'll be on our way."

"That settles it then. We'll meet with Steele and then we'll hightail it to the cops. In the meantime, we'll avoid the turnpike. No need to leave an EZ pass trail. I doubt the turnpike authorities are looking for my Jeep, but that could change."

She glanced over at him. Was he serious or just clowning around?

"You don't know what this thing is," he said, "and neither do I. We've got no idea who's looking for it or what connections they might have or how big this could get before it's finished."

He was right. After what she'd endured that day, she preferred that no one had the slightest clue where to find her.

She ran her fingers over the carvings on the back of the medallion. Why had Jackson Steele insisted on seeing the medallion for himself—weren't the pictures Ted had sent him sufficient to render a verdict? If he was such an expert, couldn't he have discussed the medallion on the phone and been done with it?

A chill shuddered up her spine and spread through her body. She'd been so freaked out by her ordeal in the city that she'd jumped at the first solution that had presented itself. But she knew next to nothing about Ted and nothing at all about his friend. Were they on the up and up, or had they concocted a scheme to steal the medallion and leave her in the Endless Mountains to fend for herself? Or worse, were they among the many individuals Mordecai had mentioned who'd be willing to kill to possess the medallion and its power?

Twenty-two

Detective James Burleigh knocked on the door, and when there was no answer, he went to the kitchen window and looked inside. The house was dark except for a single night light that burned dimly, illuminating the counter near the sink. He went back to the door and knocked again. No response, but he wasn't surprised. Brooke's SUV wasn't in the driveway.

He dialed her number for the third time. And for the third time, the call went to voicemail.

He heard a rumble of tires in the driveway and turned to watch headlights making their way down the gravel lane. Excellent. This might be easier than he'd expected.

But it wasn't Brooke who pulled up. The window of the white Lexus slid down and Brett Erikson looked out at him.

"Evening, Detective. My stepmom's not at home?"

"She doesn't appear to be. Any idea where I might find her?"

"She crashes at her uncle's now and then. But there's another place you might check." A sly smile crept over Erikson's lips. "You might find her at Ted Roslyn's dump in Allentown."

"And why do you think she'd be there?"

Brett Erikson laughed—a thoroughly dark and unpleasant laugh. "She got her hands on a valuable medallion that belonged to my dad, and just like that she's nowhere to be found. Find lover boy, and you'll find Brooke. I'd put money on it."

Burleigh watched the younger man turn his car around and disappear down the drive. This was the same story he'd heard from Stephanie Erikson, namely that Brooke and Roslyn were a couple and they'd probably been a couple before Erikson's death. The innuendos had ranged from adultery to theft to murder and back to adultery and theft. It appeared that Stephanie's brother had drawn the same conclusions.

Burleigh had no reason to doubt Brooke's story about having met Roslyn for the first time just a few days earlier. Ted Roslyn had a stellar reputation, but so did lots of people who strayed from the straight and narrow. And while Burleigh's gut told him that Brooke and Roslyn were right as rain, his gut didn't count as evidence, especially now that both of them were missing. He supposed he should follow up on Brett Erikson's remark and check out the place in Allentown.

Half-way there his phone rang.

"You won't believe this, boss," Jason Radley said breathlessly. "I mean seriously—you won't believe it."

"Calm down, son. What's on your mind?"

And then Radley told him.

A violent incident earlier in the day at Mordecai's Antiques and Oddities. The store in shambles. The owner and his son being treated for injuries at Jefferson Hospital. Their condition unknown.

Brooke Roberts had been at the store earlier in the day and was wanted for questioning in the matter. An all points bulletin had been issued for her vehicle.

Burleigh was dumbfounded by the news. The case had begun with an accidental death followed two months later by a break-in. It had been a local matter for local cops—nothing more. But just like that it was no longer local and just like that city cops were involved, and just like that, Brooke was at the center of something bigger than she'd dreamed and there was no telling how any of this would end.

▾ ▾ ▾

The wind whistled through the trees and tore at the fringes of the shawl that had once belonged to Elena's mother. She closed her eyes and imagined the campfires, the fiddle music, the tambourines and the wild, frenzied dancing that were part of her Romany heritage. Generations had come and gone, but this paisley shawl with its threads of violet and indigo brought the ancestral memories alive as surely as if she'd experienced that wild, nomadic existence for herself.

She thought of the stories her mother used to tell, tales woven from magic and moon glow. One story in particular lingered in her mind: a tale of twelve brave sailors who'd journeyed to uncharted lands, each of them bearing a treasure. Seek one of those treasures for yourself, her mother used to whisper. *Seek it with all your heart, and when you find it, it will make you a princess in an age that is yet to come.*

To Elena those words had been more than a bedtime story. They'd been a prophecy spelling out her destiny.

Tonight she'd chosen a different location for her ritual—not in front of her home altar or near the fireplace in the library as was her custom, but out here on the patio with the wind teasing at her hair and the moon weaving ribbons of light across the lawn. She'd already bathed in herbs and anointed her body with fragrant oils as her mother had taught her. Now, cleansed and purified, she'd chosen a black dress accented with onyx, the gem of Saturn that would allow her to see her tasks through to completion and overcome the obstacles in her way.

She raised an onyx ring toward the smiling moon and allowed its beams to ignite the energy of the stone. After that, she placed an image of a pentagram on the patio table, positioned a black candle at each point and invoked the sacred elements of air, fire, earth, and water.

Tonight would be a different sort of ceremony. Tonight she would chant the words her mother had taught her. A nursery rhyme? Not exactly. More of a poem or a charm to usher in all that she desired.

She closed her eyes and spoke the words into the darkness:

"From a distant ancient shore,
Phoenix rise and phoenix soar.
From your nest of fiery light
Spread your wings into the night.
Feathered serpent, bird of prey
Strike down those who block the way.
Bring the magic. Bring the power.
Bring the long awaited hour.
Phoenix fly o'er land and sea
And thus fulfill my destiny."

She opened her eyes and gazed at the five flames burning before her. There. The spell was cast, the spirits were set in motion, and even now they were speeding to do her bidding. Before long the medallion would be hers and she would speak the secret language of angels and welcome them into her life.

The wind roared through the night like the breath of a mighty dragon. The trees bent and moaned beneath the blast, and the candles flickered wildly, causing her shadow to leap and dance like a gypsy princess around a blazing fire.

The wind blew again and one-by-one the candles flickered and died. At the same moment a cloud passed over the moon, bringing with it deep darkness and a weight of despair that bore down on her with crushing force. Still the wind blew, but colder this time, so cold that her mother's shawl was unable to block the chill that held her in a breathless embrace.

Something had gone wrong—but what? Her spirits should be soaring, but instead they bent earthward beneath a burden of gloom. What was the source of this dark foreboding? Had she been trying too hard? Yes—that had to be it. Instead of fretting, she should have trusted her instincts and trusted the foot soldiers she'd hired to do her bidding.

She rebuked her negative thoughts and breathed an incantation to drive away the malaise that had overtaken her.

A sound splintered the night.

Her phone.

Her contacts.

Would they bring good news or bad?

Her hands trembled as she answered.

A few words and she collapsed into a chair. "Your quarry was well within your grasp. You had her in your sights. How could you let her slip away?"

She listened to a litany of excuses, each one more pathetic than the next. "She was yours for the taking, and you let her disappear. How is that possible?"

She listened to the rest of the story. "So, you've made Ezra Simmons pay for his betrayal. At least you've done something right." She listened again with growing impatience. "Of course you'll be remunerated. I keep my word which is more than I can say for those I've hired."

She was about to end the conversation when her contact mentioned something the old man had muttered in his confusion and pain. She rose to her feet, reinvigorated and flushed with hope. She understood now how things had been playing out and as clarity dawned, the moonlight escaped the clouds that held it captive and spilled its silver glow upon the earth.

There was a chance—a slim one, but a chance nonetheless—that Jeremy Stokes was still alive.

▼ ▼ ▼

Ted cast a glance at his passenger. He'd hated to lie to her, but it had been necessary to protect his friend's cover, a cover that had been skillfully maintained in the three years since Jeremy Stokes was spirited out of California. His isolated property in the Endless Mountains served as a base of operations from

which he interacted with law enforcement, independent journalists and people like Ted who sought to expose the depraved
actions of those who'd embraced the darkness. Some of these
people were deeply steeped in Satanic lore; others were self-
serving individuals whose greed had entangled them in a web
of bribes and blackmail from which they couldn't escape. But
all of them possessed a ruthless determination to honor their
blood oaths and the secrets that went with them.

And that's why Ted had been surprised when Stokes insisted on seeing the medallion for himself. It was a risky propo-
sition since it involved bringing an outsider into his world, but
Stokes seemed to think that handling the thing was the only
way to verify its authenticity. He'd been willing to take the risk,
but things had grown more complicated in the last few hours
thanks to Brooke's spontaneous trip to the city. People were on
the lookout for them, and that's why they'd had to flee, but they
weren't expected at Stokes's place until noon the following day
and that meant finding a place to crash for the night.

On other trips to the area, Ted had passed a 1950's era
motor lodge that consisted of a bunch of dumpy little cabins
surrounded by towering pines. Not exactly quality lodgings, but
it beat sleeping in the Jeep.

Ted wondered how things might look to the average Joe.
A woman jumps out of a restroom window and hops into his
Jeep. They speed off into the night, just the two of them—a
divorced guy and a widow whose husband was only two
months in the grave. The scenario would do wonders for Ted's
reputation—and hence his ministry and livelihood—if word
got out.

He looked over at Brooke. Her face was turned away, her
gaze focused on the passing scenery. Scenery—that was a laugh.
There were trees and lots of them, their branches reaching out
like arms, their fingers extended and grasping at the Jeep. The
better to strangle you with, my dear.

Finally he broke the silence of the last half hour. "You realize we've got to spend the night somewhere."

There was no answer.

"There's a motel thirty miles from our destination. It's not the greatest spot in the world, but it's cheap."

Brooke responded without looking at him. "Cheap isn't an issue. Find a decent place and I'll put it on my credit card."

"There aren't decent places to choose from out here. And even if there were, credit cards are risky since we're trying to maintain a low profile. I've got some cash, but not enough for luxury accommodations, assuming there were luxury accommodations which there aren't. What I'm trying to say is that credit cards leave a trail. We don't want to be found out, do we?"

"I'm not so sure about that. Maybe it's time for people to find me. Maybe I don't like the situation I let you get me into, and maybe I'm having second thoughts and I'd rather be in the hands of the police than in the hands of someone I know almost nothing about."

"You' don't have to worry about me," he said, "not with all the other stuff there is to worry about."

She leaned back in the seat, her eyes closed. "Do you have any idea how this looks?"

He shrugged. Of course he had an idea, but there wasn't much he could do about it.

"Let me share my thoughts," she said wearily, "I've been thinking that you might have dragged me out here in the middle of nowhere because you know the medallion's valuable and you'd like to get your hands on it. Perhaps you intend to kill me. It would be easy to dispose of my body out here among the trees with vultures waiting to clean up the mess. Meanwhile, you and your mysterious friend could cash in on the medallion and no one would be the wiser."

He couldn't believe his ears. Being worried about spending the night with some guy she'd just met was one thing, but treachery and murder? That was way too much, and he intended to let her know it.

"You've got a lot of nerve," he said angrily. "Here I am, risking my life to help you and you think I want to kill you?"

"Do you?"

"Don't be ridiculous. Do I seem like a murderer?"

She gave him a sort of once over. "Maybe not, but I haven't met enough murderers to say. Either way, I want a private room with clean sheets, a hot shower and room service. And triple locks on the door."

"I'm afraid that's impossible. The room service part at least."

"Okay then. I'm calling the police."

She reached for her cell, looked at the screen and put the phone back in her bag. He already knew there'd be no signal because there never was out here where they were.

Ten miles later a sign appeared in the darkness. *Happy Campers Motor Lodge.*

Ted pulled into the parking lot in front of a dozen fake-looking log cabins. A neon sign on the center unit read, *Office. Vacancy.*

He parked next to the only other car in the lot which probably belonged to the poor sap manning the desk in the office. He hoped Brooke wouldn't freak out when he made his next announcement, but he was pretty sure she would.

"Under normal circumstances," he began, "we'd get separate cabins. But people are looking for you, and I think it would be a whole lot safer if we stayed in the same unit."

She looked at him, wide-eyed in spite of her earlier signs of exhaustion and misery. "If you think I went through everything I went through in the city today and if you think I jumped out a bathroom window and came all this distance so I could shack up with a lunatic who believes in demons and devils and magic medallions and whose mentor is a former wizard who all the other wizards think is dead when he's really alive, then you are sadly mistaken. None of this is normal. None! What if you try to kill me in the night? What if you're a…"

He stopped her before she could say *rapist*. "It's not that way at all," he insisted. "We'll get a cabin with two double beds. You'll have one to yourself and I'll take the one next to the door."

"And at two in the morning when I feel someone slither between the sheets?"

"It won't happen. But if someone should break in…"

She cut him off. "If someone should break in, you'll do what? Leap out of bed and beat him to a pulp? Rip him limb from limb and feed him to the wolves?"

Ted reached into his jacket pocket and withdrew a handgun. A Glock 26, commonly referred to as a Baby Glock. Compact. Lightweight. Easy to conceal.

He held it out for her to see. "I've got a concealed carry permit, so there's nothing to worry about."

But she was worrying. He could see it on her face. No, it was way stronger than worry. She was terrified. Certain she was being kidnapped and held hostage at gunpoint by a rapist and a murderer.

He returned the weapon to his pocket. "You wait here while I check in."

Just to be safe, he took the keys with him. The last thing he needed was for her to speed off and leave him stranded.

Twenty-three

Brett inched along the block in Allentown. The neighborhood was nothing to brag about, but on closer scrutiny, it wasn't quite the disaster it had seemed when he'd followed Ted Roslyn home the night before. It was bleak, to be sure, with row houses sporting satellite dishes on the roofs and air conditioners in the windows, but most of the places showed a modicum of care. It was a neighborhood that could go either way depending on the influx of drugs, guns, and pimps.

He scrutinized the cars on either side of the narrow street. Brooke's Sportage wasn't among them, but neither was Roslyn's beat-up Renegade. He parked his Lexus along the curb, and on a whim he looked up Roslyn's name on his phone.

Well, how do you like that? Ted Roslyn. *Dispelling the Darkness Ministries.* What in the world was this?

He scanned the home page. The guy was an exorcist or something. Well, maybe not an exorcist, but a fanatic who lectured about demons and deception and a coming Great Tribulation.

A light went on in Brett's head. This explained everything. His dad must have found out that Brooke was tangled up with this weirdo, and that was the reason the old man got all religious at the end.

Brett sat for a couple of minutes, staring out the window

and trying to piece the story together. He couldn't quite work it out, but he knew there had to be a connection there somewhere.

He let out a laugh when he noticed a white sedan cruising by. Good old Detective James Burleigh, following up on the tip Brett had so generously given him.

Burleigh parked his car, and when he approached the house, Brett emerged from his Lexus. If the detective was surprised to see him, he didn't let on.

"Anybody home?" he asked.

"Doesn't look like it. Neither car's parked anywhere I can see."

Even so, Burleigh went up on the porch and knocked. When there was no answer, he knocked again. After a few seconds, he repeated the action.

Brett shook his head. The man obviously didn't have a clue. "Looks like you let the love birds slip through your fingers," he observed as the detective came down the stairs.

"Any idea where I might find them?"

"Seriously—you're asking me that question? Seems to me it's your job to figure that out—not mine. And by the way, it's funny you never mentioned that this Roslyn guy is a religious fanatic."

The detective didn't answer and it was obvious why he didn't. The jerk probably hadn't even bothered to figure out who or what Ted Roslyn was.

Brett thrust his phone under the detective's nose and showed him Roslyn's home page. "This is what I'm talking about. The guy's an exorcist or something like that. Who knows what kind of crap he's capable of?"

The detective ignored the remark. "Let me know if you hear from Brooke. And rest assured, we're following up on every lead."

"Oh yeah? And were you following up on every lead when my dad died last summer? Your people said it was an accident, and now that you've changed your mind, any evidence that might have existed is long gone, and the case will go nowhere. It's pathetic and so are you and so are the people you work with. You wouldn't have even known about the shenanigans of this Roslyn creep if I hadn't tipped you off."

"Your comments have been helpful," the detective said. And just like that he turned and walked away.

Brett stared after him. Burleigh thought he was smart, but he was really an imbecile, and his smug attitude ticked Brett off.

"Someone killed my dad," he shouted after the retreating figure. "You morons called it an accident and you did nothing about it. And now you're dragging your heels and you let Brooke run off with this Roslyn creep, and they've taken a valuable medallion that belongs to me and my sister. You're useless—do you hear me? Useless! Every last one of you!"

A porch light went on across the street. A door opened a few doors away. Neighbors peeked out, curious about the racket. Brett was about to tell them where to go, but instead he got in his Lexus and sped away.

▾ ▾ ▾

Ted held the door while Brooke flicked on the light.

He glanced warily at the cobwebby corners, the tacky pine paneling and the shabby carpet.

"I'm not sure which is scarier," Brooke said. "The thought of rodents and bedbugs crawling on me while I sleep, or the thought of being trapped in a room with a gun-toting religious fanatic who believes in demons."

"I assure you—I'm the least terrifying of those options."

"So that leaves rodents and bedbugs. I feel better already."

He tossed his duffel bag on the bed closest to the door. "I threw in an extra toothbrush and a tee-shirt and sweats for you to sleep in."

"Nice to know my abduction has been so well planned."

She eyed the second of two double beds. "I'm afraid to pull back the covers. What if something jumps out at me?"

"Don't be silly. Nothing's going to jump out."

"It's obvious you've never lived in the woods. Stand by with your gun just in case."

She peeled back the covers, a little bit at first and then completely. "Not exactly Egyptian cotton," she said, running her hands over the fabric. "But clean. Surprisingly so. I wonder what shape the mattress is in."

"Don't press your luck. Just be glad the sheets are okay."

She seemed a tad more relaxed as she sat down on the bed. Or maybe she'd just resigned herself to the situation. Or maybe she was exhausted, and being freaked out required too much energy.

"What's next?" she asked.

"We'll talk. Watch TV."

"No. I mean what happens next? How far are we from Jackson Steele's place?"

"He's about thirty miles north of here near a town called Dushore."

"Never heard of it."

"Its claim to fame is that it has the only traffic light in the county. Or at least that was the case a few years ago."

"So we really are in the middle of nowhere."

"Pretty much. But given the precautions we've taken, it's safe to assume that nobody has a clue where we are."

Or so he hoped.

▾ ▾ ▾

It was nearly midnight and Greg still wasn't home. This wasn't like him. Other than those mysterious meetings, he always told Janine where he was going. Coffee with a friend. A meeting with a client. A walk along the canal to calm his mind.

Tonight, he'd stormed out the door without a word.

She hugged her pillow and squinched her eyes. *Sleep!* She told her brain. *Go to sleep!*

Her brain did not obey.

She tried again with no success. Finally she rolled out of bed and without putting on a robe or slippers, went down to the study in her nightgown to look for something to read. Something comforting. Something to quiet the thoughts that refused to settle themselves.

She flicked on the light and surveyed the library she and Greg had amassed over the years. Books on aromatherapy. Crystals. Mythologies from around the world. Precognition and astral projection. Remote viewing, hypnosis and the Akashic records.

At the moment, none of those topics struck her fancy. She wanted a purely sacred text. A touch of divinity to send her to her dreams. Her eyes flitted over the titles. *The Bhagavad Gita. The Koran. The Tao Te Ching. The Bible.*

Strangely, she chose the latter. Something different and perhaps a tribute to Karl. She placed it on the desk, spine down, and let it fall open. The passage in front of her was from the book of Isaiah:

...All we like sheep have gone astray, we have turned, every one, to his own way; and the Lord has laid on him the iniquity of us all.

The words evoked an eerie feeling of déjà vu and a barely remembered moment from her past. It came gradually into focus. She'd been twenty-years-old that night on the beach near Costa Mesa. She'd smoked something crazy that had made the stars seem way closer than they were—like she could pluck them from the sky and string them together in a necklace. Mesmerized by the thought, she'd wandered away from her friends, her hands raised above her head to grab at the specks of light as she danced at the water's edge.

She'd heard the soft strumming of guitars from somewhere

nearby, and turning, saw people seated around a fire. She drifted over to join them, charmed by the songs and the discussion that followed.

When she realized they were Jesus freaks, she rose to her feet.

I believe in reincarnation she'd announced. *After thousands of lifetimes, we work off our karmic debt and attain Nirvana.*

With that, she'd wandered off to resume her free flowing dance beneath the stars.

She hadn't noticed a girl rise from the sand to follow her. Suddenly the girl was beside her, walking in the shallow surf, her long white skirt trailing in the water, the hem sopping up salt and sand.

"I need to tell you something," the girl said, her face glowing in the moonlight. "The karmic debt you mentioned back there—the one that takes all those lifetimes to work off. It's already been paid."

Janine felt confused. What was this person talking about? Karmic debts took hundreds of thousands of years—maybe millions—to settle.

The girl tried again. "Jesus lived a sinless life—no bad karma at all. His death on the cross canceled our debt—all of it, if we're willing to believe."

She took Janine's hands in hers, like they were two little girls about to play ring-a-round the rosie and fall down laughing in the sea. But they didn't fall down laughing in the sea. Instead she prayed, and while Janine couldn't remember the exact words, they'd sounded beautiful out there in the starry night with the waves rolling in around their ankles and the guitars strumming gently in the background.

They were interrupted by Janine's friends.

There you are, you crazy freak. We didn't know what happened to you.

Later, back at the beach house, she told them what happened.

And then they laughed. Christians. How corny.

She laughed too, and soon the magic of the moment was gone.

Until now. All these years later, it came back to her. The stars. The ocean. The guitars. And the girl—dressed in white.

Paid in full, she'd said.

Your karmic debt is paid in full.

And the words from the prophet: *the Lord has laid on him the iniquity of us all.*

▼ ▼ ▼

Greg Greenwood took a sip of beer and glanced at the clock. He didn't feel like going home. At least not to Janine and the police investigation that threatened to expose his secrets and blow the cover he'd struggled for years to maintain.

He tried to imagine how Janine would handle the truth. What would she say when she realized there'd been no important meetings like the ones he'd hinted at? No esoteric teachings or secret rituals or sacred ceremonies with advanced practitioners presiding over Delphic oracles.

There'd just been Nicole.

Greg had met her nearly two decades ago in the dunes in Cape May with the late afternoon sun lingering lazily over the bay and long shadows painting stripes across the sand. She'd been barefoot in white shorts and a denim shirt, her curly blond hair tangled from salt spray and wind. She'd stood silhouetted against the sky with a pair of binoculars trained at orange-billed birds skittering at the water's edge.

"American oystercatchers," Greg had observed.

She'd looked at him as though surprised that she wasn't alone. A smile lit her face as though she was glad to see him even though they'd never set eyes on each other until that moment.

"I've been told that oysters are aphrodisiacs," she said. "Do you think our fine-feathered friends are onto something?"

They spent two nights together in a cottage she'd rented for the weekend. After that she returned to Washington D.C. with its cocktail parties, charity balls, and the congressman husband who made that life possible. But each September, and sometimes on other occasions as well, they returned to Cape May to seek out oystercatchers—and each other—in the dunes.

He downed his beer and wiped his mouth with his sleeve. That was the story of his secret meetings, and that was what he didn't want Janine to know, and that was what he wanted to keep from the cops.

Was that too much to ask?

▾ ▾ ▾

Brooke had been asleep for awhile now, but Ted was wide awake. Not that he wasn't tired. He was beat. Worn to a frazzle even. But his brain was on high alert, his ears attuned to noises in the night.

He heard an owl hooting in the distance and the scurrying of something small and four-footed overhead. But mostly he heard Brooke's rhythmic breathing in the darkness.

It had been two years since his divorce and he hadn't been with a woman since. At least not in that way, and he was painfully aware of Brooke's proximity. Too close for comfort as they say. Way too close.

He tried to think of other things. Like the stuff he and Brooke had talked about earlier. Pillow talk on separate pillows in separate beds.

She'd gone to college. Taught English for a few years. Became an editor. Studied painting and became an artist. Married an artist 24 years her senior.

Before that?

She was an only child and an orphan—sort of.

Her dad had walked out on her and her mom when Brooke

was ten. To this day, she didn't know if he was dead or alive. Her mom had taken her own life when Brooke was in her early twenties. Their relationship had been a rocky one based on role-reversal. Brooke the sane, sensible adult. Her mother the confused, needy child.

And now, on top of all that, she was a widow with no one to anchor her to this world. No one except an 82-year-old great-uncle she adored. They shared a love of Bach and Shakespeare. Of mint tea and chocolate truffles and book stores on rainy Sunday afternoons.

Ted glanced over at her as she slept, her hair a cloud of chestnut on the pillow.

He'd hoped that in getting to know each other, he'd have found a reason not to be attracted.

Instead...

He looked at his cell. Two-thirty. Only four hours until dawn but it seemed like an eternity.

Twenty-four

Wednesday morning Burleigh and Radley entered the foyer of the seven-story retirement center. They pushed a buzzer and waited until a man's voice came over the intercom. "This is Nelson Roberts."

The senior detective explained their mission. He and his colleague were there to discuss the man's niece.

Those words were followed by a long silence.

"Can you buzz us in?" Burleigh asked.

"Forgive me," Nelson Roberts responded. "You took me off guard. I'm on the third floor, five doors from the elevator on the left."

A buzzer sounded followed by a loud click. The door swung open, allowing the detectives to enter a tastefully appointed lobby. They signed in at the desk, boarded the elevator and made their way to Nelson Robert's apartment.

He opened the door when they knocked. It appeared that he'd dressed hurriedly: his shirt was barely tucked in, he wore slippers instead of shoes and there was a bit of shaving cream next to his right ear that he'd failed to wipe off.

"Is Brooke all right?" he asked, his eyes scanning first Burleigh's face and then Radley's. "She didn't return my calls yesterday. It's not like her. Not like her at all."

"She didn't stay here last night?"

"Stay here? She has a home security system. The best money can buy. I made sure of that, so why would she be staying here?"

"That's what we're trying to find out," Burleigh said. "Brooke wasn't home last evening and she wasn't there this morning when we stopped by, She didn't answer the phone or return our calls."

He could tell from the expression on the old man's face that he was worried about his niece. Their visit was exacerbating his fears.

Jason Radley held out a picture of Ted Roslyn. "Have you ever met this individual?"

The man looked at the face and nodded. "He was at the Hewitt Gallery on Sunday afternoon. We came upon him studying Brooke's portrait. She introduced us, but I can't recall his name."

"Ted Roslyn," Radley said. "He recently spoke to your niece about an object her husband owned. A medallion supposedly linked to occult rituals."

Nelson Roberts scoffed at the suggestion. "My niece isn't interested in such things and neither was her late husband."

"So she never mentioned a medallion that was hidden in her house?"

"Never. But this Roslyn fellow. Is he a threat? Should I be worried?"

"Worry never does much good, does it?" Radley remarked off-handedly

The elderly gentleman bristled at the words. "That was an evasive answer, young man. I repeat, should I be worried?"

Burleigh took control of the situation. "All we know is that Brooke and Ted Roslyn have gone missing. We'd like to speak to them."

"Gone missing? What's this all about?"

"That's what we're trying to find out. Until we've located them, that's all we know."

The old man's shoulders sagged beneath the weight of that

announcement. "She's in danger, isn't she?"

"We don't know. But if you hear from her, call us right away."

They said their goodbyes and left Nelson Roberts alone with his fears.

▾ ▾ ▾

Autumn was well underway in the Endless Mountains. The leaves were tinged with coral and gold, and the sky was a crazy turquoise blue. It was a day for picnics. For savoring God's creation. For driving on back country roads with a beautiful woman and forgetting that the world is populated with dark beings who wish us harm.

He was struck by how much more relaxed Brooke appeared in the light of day. And no wonder. She seemed grateful that he hadn't raped her or killed her or stolen the medallion and left her at the cabin to fend for herself. She'd had a good night's sleep, the first in days, or so she said. But more than that, even a sad-eyed woman of mystery couldn't be a basket case on a day like this.

She seemed upbeat while they ate breakfast at a mom and pop diner, but as they drove around, enjoying the morning sunshine before their appointment at noon, Brooke's silent edginess made a reappearance. Ted wished she would talk more, like she'd done last night in the cabin when her words rolled forth in slow drowsy waves, but the mellow mood seemed to have vanished with the clouds gathering in the west.

By the time Ted turned onto the bumpy lane leading to Stokes/Steele's property, the sky had turned a sinister gray and the wind had gathered steam. After a mile or so, he pulled up at an iron gate set in an eight-foot stone wall. He rolled down the window and punched a series of numbers into a metal panel mounted in a stone kiosk. A green light flashed and the gate slid open. In front of them was a stone house that might have appeared welcoming were it not for iron bars mounted in the windows. The surrounding property was nothing to boast about either, given the dense undergrowth dotted with scrappy seedlings and rotting, tangled vines.

"The bars at the windows are a nice touch," Brooke remarked. "From what I've heard, the medieval torture chamber look is big these days."

"Wait until you see the inside." He thought of the Gothic stage-set in which Stokes lived. Massive high-backed chairs that looked like thrones. A marble baptismal font shaped like a sea serpent. Icons of saints. Cement statues of angels like those that presided over cemeteries. Battleaxes and swords mounted on the walls.

He parked near the house and a gust of wind greeted them as they got out of the Jeep. At the doorway Ted entered some numbers into a keypad, and once again a welcoming green light flashed. The front door swung open, and a bunch of cats came scurrying into the dimly lit foyer, mewing curious hellos as they greeted their visitors. Brooke bent down to pet a friendly gray tabby and laughed as Ted confronted a hostile orange creature who hissed and scurried away.

He heard footsteps on the second floor, and suddenly Stokes appeared at the top of the staircase. He wore red and black plaid pajama bottoms and a floor-length black robe that hung open, revealing a muscular chest covered in black and gray hair that matched his shoulder-length mane and beard.

"You're early. I told you not to bother me before noon."

Ted smiled up at his friend. "It's twelve on the dot. We're right on time."

"If I say noon, I mean one. You should know that by now." The man lumbered down the stairs and stopped at the bottom to clasp his friend's hand in a hearty shake. He didn't wait for introductions and in fact, he didn't even seem to notice Brooke. Instead, he turned and strode down the hall toward the rear of the house, his long robe billowing out around his pajama bottoms as the cats raced along at his feet.

"Don't just stand there," he called over his shoulder. "We've got things to discuss."

▾ ▾ ▾

Elena stood at the window and gazed out at the gathering gloom. She'd had her revenge on Ezra Simmons and the pathetic loser was lucky to be alive. He and his dad would be banged up for a while, but Ezra would live to serve her another day, and by then he'd have learned his lesson and there'd be no more shenanigans.

But at the moment she couldn't waste time and energy thinking about lowly peons like Ezra. Not now when a pattern was unfolding before her eyes. That trip to Mordecai's and the rough treatment Elena's lackey's had meted out had yielded fruit she'd never anticipated. How else would the words have been forced from the old man's lips: *Jeremy Stokes is still alive.*

The thought filled her with unspeakable elation. No one had been more powerful or more knowledgeable or more eccentric or more difficult or more charmingly unpredictable than Jeremy. And out of all those who'd desired him, Elena had been the only woman to command his love. She'd heard stories about his alleged conversion experience, but once she reminded him of all he was missing, his capitulation would be rapid and complete.

She closed her eyes and called out to him. As usual, she saw only trees. Miles and endless miles of trees. She'd assumed that this was a vision of Jeremy's final resting place, but perhaps she'd misinterpreted the message.

She looked again at the vista spread out before her mind and a thought occurred to her. One she hadn't considered in her hundreds of remote viewing sessions. *Miles and endless miles of trees.* That was it. Not the trees so much, but the word *endless.*

As if confirming her discovery, the scene shifted, and she waited, breathless, as a second vision came into focus. A number was barely visible in the swirling mist and soon another emerged to stand next to it. She saw a four and a one. They were followed by a dot and a five: 41.5. She jotted them down before they could melt into nothingness, and as soon as they'd been committed to paper, other numbers arose from the shadows. A seven followed by a six followed by a dot and another six: 76.6. She quickly wrote them down and then stared at the paper in front of her. The numbers were clearly important, but she had no idea what they meant.

On a whim, she entered them into her computer, only to find that each response was more ridiculous than the last. Fuel consumption conversions. EPA System of Registries. Daily treasury yield curves. Machine embroidery designs.

None of these responses meant anything to her.

She sat at her desk, fretting and mindlessly spinning a small globe that served as a paperweight. Around and around it went, cities, states, nations, oceans spinning past her and blurring into one another.

And then it came to her, and she nearly laughed at the obviousness of the answer.

A map.

The numbers were lines of latitude and longitude.

She turned back to the computer monitor and this time when she entered the numbers she included those words. Within seconds, the name of a town in Pennsylvania appeared in front of her. She clicked on the link and discovered that it was situated in an area known as the Endless Mountains.

She stared at the words in amazement. The Endless Mountains and her vision of endless trees. So that's where Stokes had been hiding—somewhere in those mountains near the intersection of the numbers that had just been revealed.

She placed a hurried call, threw a few things into an overnight bag and thirty minutes later she stood waiting on the porch. An SUV pulled up and a chauffeur got out. He opened the back door and as she slid inside, she gave him an address.

Soon she was on her way, speeding to a reunion that was long overdue.

▼ ▼ ▼

Brooke followed Ted and his friend into a kitchen at the rear of the house. It was a mess—much like Brooke's kitchen had been after it was ransacked, but this was apparently the way Jackson Steele lived. The table was piled with books, dishes and unexpected odds and ends like dirty socks and electronic gadgets. The counters were stacked with jars of this and bottles of that, and the sink was full of dirty pots and pans. Brooke watched the cats make acrobatic leaps and land gracefully on stacks of books and papers that threatened to tumble to the floor.

Their host brushed a cat off a counter and revealed a grungy coffee maker. "Java?" he asked.

"That'd be great," Ted said. Brooke wasn't so sure.

He set about making coffee and once it started dripping he turned and stared at Brooke. "I assume you're the person with the phoenix medallion?"

She returned the stare. The man in front of her was wild and unkempt, but brutishly attractive, like a Viking or a Scottish warlord. But more importantly, he was a perfect match for Mordecai Simmons' description of Jeremy Stokes. Six-foot three or better. Robust. Imposing physique. Wild black hair and a beard to match. Eyes that breathed threats. A perpetual scowl.

Should she ask him about his true identity? No—doing so might put her in danger. Better to wait and see how things played out.

"I'm Brooke Roberts," she said.

"So I've heard. I'm Jackson Steele, but I guess you figured that out." He picked up a pair of hand weights from the counter and lifted them in the air, at the same time gesturing with his chin toward a chair. "Clear the crap away and make yourself at home."

He hoisted the weights and after a few reps he set them down and picked up a remote control device. He took aim at a box on the counter and a moment later a brass fanfare exploded from tiny speakers mounted on the walls. The opening salvo was followed by a barrage of strings and the soaring voice of a soprano.

"Some folks wake up to the morning paper," he explained, "but I seem to require opera to get the juices flowing. This afternoon's offering is Monteverdi's *L'Orfeo*, an oldie but goodie for your listening pleasure."

Opera. Mordecai Simmons had told her that Jeremy Stokes had a passion for opera. This was too significant a detail to be a mere coincidence, especially when considered in light of the man's physical description. She had no doubt whom she was dealing with—not Jackson Steele but Jeremy Stokes.

He launched into a description of the myth on which the opera was based. It was a familiar story about Orpheus's marriage to Eurydice who died shortly after the wedding when she was bitten by a serpent. Grief-stricken, Orpheus made a journey to the Land of the Dead to do some wheeling and dealing with Lord Hades, the ruler of the underworld. Hades agreed to permit Eurydice to venture back to the Land of the Living under one condition: Orpheus must not look back to verify that his young bride was following him, and if he did, Eurydice would be trapped forever in the shadow land of death. Orpheus agreed and the couple began their journey with Eurydice bringing up the rear. All was well until Orpheus failed to hear her footsteps and in a moment of panic, he turned and looked back. As promised, Eurydice vanished before his eyes, and death had the final word.

"The symbolism's fairly obvious," the man opined. "The story begins with a serpent and it ends with a simple command that when disobeyed, brings death. The tale is one of many mythic echoes of the true narrative. The serpent enticing Adam and Eve, our primordial parents, in the Garden of Eden."

He closed his eyes as the tenor began a lamentation and he stayed that way until the chorus joined in. By then the coffee had finished brewing so he gathered the necessary paraphernalia and took it to the table.

He sat down and stared at Brooke, his eyes dark and penetrating as they bored into hers. "Enough frivolity," he announced. "The thing you brought here today. Let's have a look at it."

▾ ▾ ▾

A bell rang from the hallway, and on cue, teachers at the alternative school collected their things and rushed out of the faculty lounge and off to class. Alone at last, Stephi Erikson poured a cup of coffee and sank down in a chair. She had three back-to-back therapy sessions to get through before she could pack up and go home. She thought of the activities she'd be overseeing and the preparation that had gone into each one. *Draw what sadness looks like. Create a collage that expresses your rage. Paint your greatest fear.*

Ironically, she was the one who could use some art therapy. What could be more satisfying than making pictures of your feelings and splashing them with gobs of angry red paint? But instead of getting to work through her own issues, she'd be forced to pull herself together and focus on a bunch of mixed-up kids. Normally she was up to the task, but not at the moment. Not when her own world was crumbling all around her.

She thought back to yesterday's conversation with the cops. She'd given them an earful about Brooke and lover-boy, Ted Roslyn, but things hadn't unfolded as she'd hoped. At their first meeting, Jason Radley had seemed kind and understanding, but yesterday he'd sat slumped in the futon, his eyes glued to his notepad while he took down her remarks. Every time she tried to make eye contact, he looked away, and once the conversation was over, he'd bolted out of his seat and raced out the door like he couldn't wait to escape.

So much for her daydreams of a few days ago. She recalled her fantasies. A shared drink followed by a movie or a walk in the park. What a laugh.

Well, she'd show him. She'd met his type before. Guys like Jason Radley were egomaniacs who got their kicks out of building women up so they could let them down and she wasn't about to become his latest victim. If he and his dopey boss thought they'd get any more information out of Stephanie Erikson, they were sadly mistaken.

She stared out the window at the dark clouds moving in from the west. So much for the sunshine and so much for any chance of being in a better mood once she'd put this chamber-of-horrors school behind her.

She took a sip of coffee and pictured Radley's face in her mind. She wished she had a photo of him so she could make discrete changes to reveal the person he actually was. Amused by the thought, she scribbled a drawing of a long-faced guy with big mopey eyes. Not bad for a quick sketch. She got a marker from her bag and colored his face red and then she drew devil's horns and gave him two long, pointy fangs. She held the finished product out at arm's length to study it. Amazing. It actually looked like him.

She laughed and felt better. For all of five seconds.

Quickly the misery was back. She was beginning to think she'd never meet a decent man. Her father had been a decent man, or so she'd always thought. But maybe he wasn't all that decent. He'd robbed the cradle when he married Brooke, and Stephi had always thought there was something kinky and weird about that.

Her phone rang and she glanced at the screen. Could it be Jason Radley calling to apologize for his rudeness the day before? Of course not. It was Brett.

"I had an interesting conversation with Detective Burleigh last night," her brother began. "The idiot actually let Brooke and Lover Boy slip away. They're missing in action, and the cops don't have a clue where they might be."

Stephi sprang to her feet and paced back and forth, stunned by what she'd just heard. "I spent half-an-hour yesterday telling those cops everything they needed to know about Brooke and this horrible person she's taken up with. And the cops let them disappear? How is that possible?"

"My thoughts exactly," her brother said. "And who knows? They could have left the country by now."

Stephi stared at the drawing of Jason Radley with devil horns and thought of what a despicable loser and a stupid detective he was. It would be up to her and Brett to sort all this out and get the justice their father deserved.

An idea came to her. "Here's what we should do. Let's call the detectives' superior officer and tell him what a mess the dynamic duo are making of everything."

Brett chuckled at the remark. "As it turns out, I've already done just that. The chief happens to be a Lodge brother, and as the saying goes, it's not so much what you know as who you know."

Stephi smiled at the news. "You've got it covered, so I guess there's no need for me to place a call."

"*Au contraire,* Little Sis. I need you to confirm the things I already said. Namely that the detectives are a pair of lazy and completely clueless morons."

Stephi felt her spirits lifting. "I'm with you, Bro. There's no way I'm going to stand by and let Brooke and that creep get away with this."

"Terrific. We'll do this for Dad."

The words brought tears to Stephi's eyes. "That's right. We'll do it for Dad."

Twenty-five

The medallion was just as he remembered it. A circle of rubies with a single ruby marking the eye of the phoenix. He reached for it, hungry for even a touch. But how could a mere touch satisfy when it was possession he craved?

He pulled back his hand, mindful of his manners. "May I?" he asked Brooke.

"Of course."

Fingers quivering, he took the golden object and rested it in his palm. The mythological creature staring up at him was an ancient alchemical symbol. It had many meanings but one in particular stood out. The phoenix stood for apotheosis, the merging of the human and the divine, or to put it another way, the phoenix represented man's ultimate evolution from mortal to god.

Stokes turned it over and gazed at the carvings. Yes—there it was, the secret language of angels that he'd spent years mastering.

But was the medallion authentic?

His answer came quickly. It began with a tingling at the base of the spine, weak at first but gaining force as it sped upward. A fire erupted in his brain, bringing with it a surge of electricity that reverberated through his entire being.

The awakening of the Kundalini serpent.

Suddenly fearful, he let the object fall from his fingers and land with a thud on a stack of printouts, while in the background Orpheus and Eurydice raced through the underworld, desperate to escape the clutches of death.

Trembling, he rose to his feet and staggered out the back door. Slate gray clouds swirled overhead, obliterating the sun and bringing with them a chill wind that set the leaves tumbling.

"*It could all be yours,*" voices seemed to whisper from the roiling skies. *The power that transcends all earthly powers is yours for the taking.*"

He recalled that night ten years earlier. The Long Island mansion. The altar ablaze with candles. The chalice. The invocation. The robes, the ceremonial rites and the whispered incantations. And after that, the anointing as the master who possessed the phoenix medallion held it above his head, chanting in the secret language of angels.

Elena, the beautiful enchantress who'd initiated Stokes into the mysteries, had been by his side. He recalled her words in his ears and her stories of past ages when they'd stood together as priest and priestess to watch the sun rise above the Nile. In yet another lifetime they'd served the Pythia as she breathed her oracles from within the smoky mists of Delphi. And in a much earlier time, they'd served before the great God Poseidon, initiating his followers into the mystery cults of Atlantis.

Every story and every fantasy Elena had spoken had been a lie. But he'd believed her stories then, and he'd found power in believing them just as he'd found power in the obsessive love they'd shared.

He'd given her up three years ago, and yet he knew he could have her back if he chose, and he knew she'd rejoice at finding him alive. And with the medallion in their possession, their power would be unstoppable. Until the very end, that is.

It could all be yours, voices once again seemed to whisper in the wind. *It was promised to you that night in Long Island. You are the chosen one and it is yours to claim.*

He recalled the power that had surged through him the night of his initiation and on nights thereafter. Followers had come to him. The rich. The celebrated. The famous and the infamous.

See how they bend to your will, Elena had observed, pleased with the way he'd assumed the mantle or power. He could almost hear her now, her voice whispering to him in the language of the fallen ones who in antediluvian days had descended upon Israel's Mount Hermon to seduce the daughters of men.

He could sense the spirits all around him. Principalities. Powers. The rulers of the darkness of this world. They were calling him. Asking him to return. Asking him to put on the robes he'd discarded when he put on the armor of God.

He knew what he should do—knew what he must do—but the yearning was strong and he felt no hunger for the words that would set him free and render him just a man. Just a sinner and not a ruler of the dark realms he'd once inhabited.

He looked up at the sky, and as he looked a single ray of light broke through the clouds. This was his choice. The narrow path that leads to life or the path of darkness that leads to death and Hades.

"Help me," he whispered. "I can't do this on my own."

He felt battles rage within him and in his mind he saw kingdoms rise and fall.

The single ray of light grew brighter, and as it broke forth, the words tumbled from his lips: *Get thee behind me Satan in the name of Jesus Christ."*

He sagged to his knees, drained of strength.

It was over.

The spell was broken.

He'd stared down the devil. At least for now.

▾ ▾ ▾

"Okay, so he's impulsive," Ted agreed. "And a little crazy. But he knows what he's talking about and that's why we're here."

Brooke stared at the cats grooming themselves on the table. At the dirty dishes in the sink. At the books and papers and assorted junk stacked precariously on every surface. At the tiny speakers that spewed forth choruses in frenzied Italian.

"We got here at noon," she reminded Ted. "He was still in his pajamas and he still hasn't bothered to get dressed. And this kitchen—who would invite people into a mess like this?"

"Put up with him until you hear what he has to say. If anyone can unravel the mystery of the medallion, he can."

"Is that so? Well, here's a mystery for you to unravel. The mystery of your friend's identity."

There was a moment's hesitation. "I don't know what you're talking about."

"No? Then let me jog your memory. A wildfire in California. Dangerous persons who wished your friend harm. So much so that he faked his own death and is living here under an assumed identity. His name isn't Jackson Steele, is it? It's Jeremy Stokes and he's on the run from a bunch of nasty people who want to kill him."

She heard a noise behind her, and when she turned, the man she'd recognized as Jeremy Stokes stood in the doorway, looking frightful in his pajama bottoms, floor-length robe, and the rat's nests that passed for his hair and beard.

"Who told you that?" he demanded, his voice constrained but barely so, as though he were trying to hold back a volcano boiling just beneath the surface.

"I learned your story from a man named Mordecai Simmons." Brooke explained.

From there the words spilled out of her. Her decision to go to the city. Mordecai's description of a deceased individual who'd been the foremost expert on the subject of the phoenix medallion. Mordecai's warnings as he sent Brooke out the rear exit.

The thugs who chased her through the streets. Her mad dash to the train and her escape later through a bathroom window.

Through it all, Stokes stood in silence, his fingers clutching the back of a chair. "Did you give Mordecai Simmons an idea of where you'd be today?"

She shook her head. "I was about to mention the Endless Mountains, but I held back."

"Well done!" he said, his expression brightening. "At least when pressed, Mordecai won't be able to provide his assailants with that bit of information." His expression darkened again. "He will be pressed to provide information, make no mistake about it, and I'm afraid the experience won't be a pleasant one."

He raked his fingers through his tangled hair, sank into a chair and gazed into space. When he turned to Brooke, he seemed surprisingly calm.

"I won't lie about my identity," he said. "You've already figured it out, so there'd be no point in trying to maintain a story you wouldn't accept. I'm asking, however, that you keep this information to yourself. No threats or coercion involved. Just a simple request that you respect my circumstances."

He didn't wait for a response. Instead he turned his attention to Ted. "I trust that you took precautions traveling here."

Ted nodded. "Cell phones off—for the most part. No EZ-pass routes. We used cash, no credit cards. I can't see how anyone would know where we are."

Stokes let out a laugh. "You have no idea who you're dealing with and no idea how high up the ladder their connections go."

He pivoted back to Brooke. "Do you have family, my dear?"

"A stepdaughter and stepson. We rarely see each other. My only blood relative is my 82-year-old Uncle Nelson."

"You and this uncle are close?"

"He means the world to me."

"I see. Well, I don't want to alarm you, but there's every reason to believe that the individuals responsible for yesterday's drama will attempt to use your uncle to get to you."

Brooke was a step ahead of him. "I thought of that, and that's why I didn't go to his apartment last night. I didn't want to place him in danger."

Stokes laughed at her words. Not a nice laugh, but a dark laugh that suggested he had knowledge of things she knew nothing about. "Believe me, the people you're dealing with already know who your uncle is. What's more, they know where he lives, they're aware of his habits, and by now they've concocted a scheme to trade his safety for the medallion. You'll need to get him relocated immediately."

Brooke was stunned. More than stunned. Stokes's words were ridiculous. "Where's he supposed to go? He's an old man. He lives alone in a retirement community. He stopped driving a year ago."

"Call someone you can trust to get your uncle out of harm's way. Go light on the details and make the call brief. Until we've disposed of the medallion in a very public manner, you and your uncle are in grave danger. Do I make myself clear?"

Brooke stared at the phoenix and the circle of rubies and the ouroboros surrounding the perimeter. Her own danger was one thing, but Uncle Nelson? The old man deserved pleasant days and peaceful nights with Bach playing in the background and *The New York Times* Crossword Puzzle to keep him entertained.

Stokes pointed toward a phone. "Use the landline. No doubt your cell's being monitored."

"I don't know who to call."

"Think of someone and be quick about it. The danger increases with each second you waste."

▾ ▾ ▾

David Price was disappointed in the outcome of this morning's meeting. The couple who'd expressed an interest in conserving the family farm had taken packets of information with them and they'd promised to discuss the matter and get back to him. But he wasn't going to hold his breath. A developer was wooing them, and the scent of money had hung heavily in the air.

His cell phone rang and he glanced at the screen. Unknown name. Unknown number. In other words, spam.

He was about to let it go to voicemail, but he didn't, in the off chance that it might be the couple calling with a decision. Hopefully a positive one.

He answered and suddenly his world brightened and preserving farmland no longer struck him as important.

"This is a pleasant surprise. What can I do for you?"

The brightness faded as he listened to Brooke's request. Her words struck him as absurd, and yet her message, confusing as it was, seemed urgent.

That quickly the call came to an end.

He sank back in his chair, a single word playing over and over in his mind.

Danger.

Brooke's Uncle Nelson was in danger, and she'd called to ask David for help. She'd made it clear that by rushing to the old man's aid, David would be putting himself in danger as well. Was he willing to run the risk?

He'd said yes, but he'd done so without having a clear understanding of what he might be walking into, and now that he'd hung up, he was beginning to regret his hasty words.

He glanced toward the window. A storm was brewing, a big nasty blow that had the weather forecasters in a dither.

Better to make a move now before the rain arrived.

He picked up the phone and after two rings, Nelson Roberts answered.

"Sorry to bother you, sir," he began. "I just had a call from your niece and…"

The old man cut him off. "My niece? How is she? Where

is she? Is she all right?"

"Yes. She sounded fine."

"Why would she call you instead of me? It makes no sense."

"It's confusing to me as well," David said. "She asked me to tell you that she's gone into hiding for reasons she wasn't free to discuss over the phone. She's been warned that some not-so-nice persons might use you as a way to get to her. Kidnap. Ransom. That sort of thing. I'm to tell you to gather up your overnight things and meet me outside your building at the rear of the parking lot and out of sight of the security cameras."

"I don't enjoy foolish stunts," the old man said firmly. "Explain what's going on."

"I wish I could, but I've told you all I know. Hurry, sir. She said the situation is desperate."

They wrapped up the conversation, and David buzzed the receptionist. "I'm leaving for the day. You can send my calls to voicemail."

Twenty-six

B rooke looked across the table at Ted. "I can't stay here. Not when my uncle's in danger. You'll have take me home."

Stokes understood Brooke's fears but he knew she had only the vaguest sense of the powers they were dealing with. He laid a hand on her shoulder. The gesture was meant to be comforting but she pulled away as though cringing at his touch. He didn't take it personally. This was all a bit much for her to absorb.

"You'd feel a lot worse if something happened to your uncle," he reminded her. "And think how he'd feel if you met with some terrible fate because you decided to run back and protect him. Do you want him to spend his final days in heartache, grief, and loneliness?"

When she didn't answer, he kept going. "The stakes are that high. Until those pursuing you are convinced that the medallion is out of your hands, you're not safe and neither is he. Having said all that, I believe you came here because you wanted answers about this thing that's been dumped in your lap, so let's get to it."

She nodded but he could tell her thoughts were elsewhere.

"Assuming the medallion's authentic," he began, "and I have every reason to believe it is, it's one of twelve crafted in the Elizabethan Renaissance by famed occultist and navigation expert, John Dee. Legend said they're made from alchemical gold—lead transmuted into gold—but I think we can dismiss that idea out of hand. At any rate, the objects were given as talismans—good luck charms and a bit more as I'll explain—to each of twelve mariners embarking on voyages of discovery.

"Its rarity makes it valuable, but its monetary value pales in comparison to the promise of power that comes with it, and that's what those pursuing you are most interested in. Over the centuries the medallions have rarely come to market. Occasionally they've been passed down upon an owner's death, but more often they're stolen, in which case they leave a trail of blood in their wake. But I digress."

"I want you to imagine that it's the Renaissance—the Age of Discovery—with European monarchs in a frenzy to dispatch explorers to the New World in search of gold, fur, lumber, tobacco, cotton, and untold treasure. While the New World represented material wealth to those in command of the high seas, to those of an esoteric or alchemical bent, the New World offered an unfettered atmosphere where esoteric teachings could take root free from the constraints of the church and its inquisitors, whether Protestant or Catholic."

Stokes drew their attention to the carved phoenix on the medallion. He reminded them that the phoenix was a mythological creature reputed to die in flames every 500 years only to be reborn from the ashes. The word phoenix was associated with the land of Phoenicia, the home of the ancient Canaanite religion which in turn was based on the even more ancient Babylonian mysteries.

"The Phoenicians were renowned for their maritime exploits," he said. "Over time the symbol of the phoenix was adopted by sailors and mariners. Thus, alchemist John Dee, the leading navigation expert of his day, saw the phoenix as both a sea-faring and an alchemical symbol and that's why you see it depicted on all twelve medallions.

"Each of the twelve English sea captains who received a medallion were tasked—knowingly or unknowingly—with transporting the esoteric doctrines of the mystery cults to the New World just as the ancient Phoenicians sailors had carried variations of those beliefs and practices throughout the Mediterranean world."

He paused in his narrative to rummage through the clutter on the kitchen table. There was a digital tablet buried somewhere in this jumbled mess. He rooted through papers and books, inadvertently dislodging a gray tabby that awoke with a hiss and leaped from the table. Ta-da—she'd been sleeping on the tablet and keeping it warm. He scooped it up, turned it on and scrolled around.

"Ted tells me you're an artist," he said to Brooke. "I'd like to hear what you think of this painting."

He placed the tablet in front of her on the table and waited for an answer.

She looked at it briefly. "It's *The Rainbow Portrait*, of Queen Elizabeth I."

Stokes nodded approvingly. "Very good. What else do you know about it?"

"Not much. She's holding a clear tube-like thing in her right hand and while the colors have faded, it was once a rainbow, hence the name: *Rainbow Portrait.*"

"Excellent. Other than the faded rainbow," Stokes continued, "is there anything else that strikes you as unusual about the image?"

Ted moved behind Brooke and looked over her shoulder. "Her robe is covered with pictures of eyes and ears."

"Don't forget the mouths." Brooke pointed to a third design element. "At first they look like folds in the fabric, but when you look closer, you can tell that they're actually mouths."

Stokes nodded. "Curious markings for a royal robe, don't you think? That's because they're a coded message for those willing to understand. They remind the viewer of the all-seeing eyes and all-hearing ears that surround the throne. The mouths are a warning: be careful what you say because you never knew who might be watching and listening. Elizabeth's spy network wasn't as all-encompassing as our modern day surveillance state, but it was pretty impressive for the time period.

"But there are other anomalies in the painting," he said. "See if you can find them."

Ted leaned in to take a closer look. "Something's not right about the hat or crown or whatever it is the queen's wearing. It sits slightly above her head and slightly in back, like someone's standing behind her, but doesn't want to be seen."

"An interesting observation," Stokes agreed," and one that raises important questions. All-seeing eyes. All-hearing ears. Mouths that whisper secrets. And a hidden power behind the throne. What could it mean?"

He didn't wait for an answer. Instead, he picked up the tablet and enlarged the image to focus on the left sleeve of the queen's gown. He placed it on the table and pointed to an appliquéd snake slithering up Elizabeth's arm.

"As far as I know," he said, "slithering serpents aren't exactly popular motifs in women's fashion—even in the Renaissance. So why was Good Queen Bess wearing a snake on her sleeve?"

Brooke brought the image closer to study the details. "There's a heart-shaped ruby in the snake's mouth. And something resting on its head. An orb of some sort."

Stokes nodded in agreement. "Now you're onto something. Scholars say that the orb symbolizes the queen's intellect while the ruby heart signifies her emotions, particularly in regard to romantic love. The idea, in other words, is that the wise Virgin Queen was ruled by her head rather than by her heart. A valid explanation, I suppose, but it leaves a few questions unanswered."

He brought up a picture of a golden ball with a cross

mounted on it.

"This familiar image is called the *Globus Cruciger*; it represents the world ruled by Christ. Since the Renaissance, the Globus Cruciger has appeared in countless portraits of kings, queens, and emperors to remind them that God is the final authority, not the crown. But in *The Rainbow Portrait*, there's no cross on top of the orb. An interesting omission, wouldn't you say?"

He pointed to the red jewel dangling from the serpent's mouth. "Scholars interpret the jewel as a ruby heart, but perhaps our friendly serpent has come bearing something else."

Brooke looked up at him. "Forbidden fruit?"

"A possibility. Consider a passage from the early pages of Genesis: *And the serpent said to the woman, Ye shall not surely die: For God doth know that in the day ye eat thereof, your eyes shall be opened, and ye shall be as gods, knowing good and evil.*

"This verse summarizes the core doctrines of every occult society and mystery religion throughout the ages, namely that the serpent, i.e. Lucifer, brings enlightenment to mankind in the form of forbidden knowledge. That forbidden knowledge can be summarized in three basic teachings cited in the passage I just quoted. First: death is an illusion. Second: by following the hidden teachings, mortals may transcend their earthly limitations to become gods. Third: The knowledge that liberates requires an intimate knowledge of both good and evil.

"That," he said, "is the crux of the Luciferian lie that has manifested itself in countless ways through the millennia from primitive mythologies to complex metaphysical constructs to the fringes of science and technology."

He paused to let that sink in. There was much he could tell his guests about his own pursuit of the serpent's knowledge. Memories flashed through his mind of visits to Himalayan caves in search of lost wisdom. Journeys deep within the Amazon Rain Forest in pursuit of shaman's secrets. Nights beneath the stars in the Arizona desert with drums beating and voices chanting and pipes of peyote unleashing visions of other realms. Travels to the world's mystic sites. Add to that, hours of study and practice and discipline and meditation and ritual and surrender to beings beyond the realm of human sight. And then, add to all of that, Elena Voss and the medallion and the power that could be his if he chose to seize it.

He forced himself back to the present moment.

"Let's take another look at the Rainbow Portrait," he said, struggling against the memories crowding his mind. "As we noted, there's no cross on the orb. None at all. And the orb, instead of resting in the monarch's hand as is typical, rests above the head of the serpent who offers the gift of forbidden fruit."

He glanced at Ted. "You raised a question about a hidden power behind the throne. Is the *Rainbow Portrait* raising that same question while simultaneously providing the answer? In other words, is the portrait telling us that the serpent is the true power behind the throne, and in fact, the true power behind the world's systems of government?"

He didn't wait for a response. "To answer that question," he said "and to understand how the question relates to the medallion, we'll need to take a look at another painting."

▾ ▾ ▾

Elena Voss gazed out the window as the black SUV sped toward a small regional airport. A helicopter waited for her, ready to speed her to her destination. Hopefully the approaching storm would contain its fury until her mission was complete.

She thought of the lines of latitude and longitude that had appeared to her in a vision. They weren't precise enough to pinpoint Jeremy's hiding place with absolute certainly, but at least they'd provided an area for Elena's henchmen to search. What they couldn't see from the ground, she'd discover from a higher vantage point.

If Mordecai's hunch was correct, Brooke Roberts was already meeting with Jeremy. But Elena suspected there was a third party involved, and it irritated her that she had no idea who this person might be. Her minions had followed Brooke to the train station in Philadelphia. When she'd eluded them, they'd dispatched others to await her arrival at the train station nearest to her home. From there, they'd followed her to a coffee shop and waited outside for her to exit. She never exited, and that meant someone else had met up with her and spirited her away.

Elena had tried to visualize this person in her mind, but nothing had come to her. She hated setting out without a clear picture of her quarry, and the lack of information made her feel ill at ease. But how could she feel otherwise, given the abysmal job her recruits had done so far at carrying out their mission?

But all would be forgiven, she reminded herself, if their apparent failures were part of a master plan to lead her to Jeremy.

She ran an index finger over the bracelet he'd purchased for her years earlier in the days following his initiation into the secrets of the phoenix medallion. He'd had the item custom made by a London jeweler who specialized in the exotic and the esoteric. This piece, the jeweler had claimed, was among his finest creations. He'd crafted it to resemble a serpent depicted in a famous portrait of Elizabeth I. Like the snake appliquéd to the queen's gown, this one was studded with diamonds. Like the shining one. Like Lucifer himself. Above the serpent's head was a golden orb signifying world dominion, and in its mouth, a sparkling ruby. The forbidden fruit of esoteric knowledge.

She recalled the serpent's whispered promise: *Ye shall be as gods.*

Jeremy Stokes had believed that once, and before long, he would believe it again.

▾ ▾ ▾

Stokes held out a second portrait of the queen for his guests to consider. In it she wore a white gown studded with jewels, and she held what appeared to be a faded flower in her right hand.

"Same question," he said. "What strikes you as odd about the painting?"

Ted took a quick look. "That's the lousiest excuse for a flower I've ever seen."

"I totally agree," Stokes concurred. "The image has faded over time, but if you look closely, you can see a hint of what was painted underneath. There's a term for this artistic phenomenon, but it slips my mind."

"Pentimento," Brooke said. "From the Italian word for repentance. The artist repents of his first attempt and atones by painting something over it."

"And that begs the question," Stokes continued, "what was the artist trying to hide? For decades scholars fretted over what might be hidden beneath the flower, but in recent years, infrared technology has given us the answer."

He brought up a second version of the portrait and held it out for inspection.

Brooke looked at it and frowned. "Why is the queen holding a snake?"

"An important question, indeed. Art historians have suggested that the unknown artist covered up the snake out of fear of offending Her Majesty, but I find the hypotheses doubtful. Why paint a snake in the first place and risk creating an offense? A better answer is that the snake was purposely painted and purposely hidden beneath what appears to have been a Tudor rose. And that begs the question—why go to all this trouble? Is there a hidden message painted in oil on canvas?"

Brooke gave him a puzzled look. "I'm not sure I'm following you."

"Then allow me to explain. In Medieval churches, a rose carved above the door to the confessional assured the penitent, who was typically illiterate, that the sins confessed *beneath the rose* would remain a secret. The same symbolism was used by members of trade guilds and city councils. A rose hung from the ceiling prior to a meeting indicated that the information discussed in that meeting was for their ears only.

"From this we get the term, *sub rosa: beneath the rose.* The term denotes secrecy. Confidentiality. You get the picture. In this painting, the serpent is hidden *sub rosa,* and it's once again linked to Queen Elizabeth. What, I ask you, are the paintings telling us?

Brooke's look of bewilderment deepened. "Are you suggesting that Elizabeth I was a practicing occultist? How is that possible when history tells us she was a staunch defender of the Protestant faith?"

"Consider the options open to her," Stokes responded. "Catholics sought to have her deposed on charges of heresy and treason. If she intended to keep her throne—and her head—she had to hold back the Catholic opposition while at the same time placating the Protestant factions whose support she relied upon to keep her crown. In public she faithfully executed her role as leader of the Church of England, but I would argue that in private, she was a devotee of the occult teachings circulating through the secret societies of her day."

Stokes motioned for Brooke to turn the medallion over. After his earlier experience, he knew better than to touch it again.

"And that brings us back to John Dee, the astrologer the queen publically endorsed until his many scandals made a public endorsement impossible."

He pointed to the carvings on the back of the medallion. "These words are written in a language allegedly given by angels to John Dee and his colleague, a man named Edward Kelley. They say: *'Open the mystery of your creation.'*"

"That's it?" Brooke asked. "All this fuss over something that innocuous?"

"The words may appear innocuous in and of themselves, but when joined with those on the other eleven medallions, they form a longer incantation designed to summon celestial beings. The legends surrounding the medallion suggest that when all twelve are reunited, their combined energy will open a portal through which spirit beings may freely enter the world to usher in the next phase of human evolution, the *Novus ordo seclorum*, the New Order of the Ages. Check the back of a dollar bill if you're unfamiliar with the term."

Brooke frowned at those words. Stokes wasn't surprised by her reaction. This was a lot to swallow in one gulp.

"You believe all this?" she asked.

"What I believe is immaterial. What matters is the beliefs that drive those who seek to possess the object."

"In other words, confirmation bias," Brooke responded. "A person's beliefs shape the outcome of a situation to match his or her expectations."

"In part," Stokes agreed. "A person's beliefs exert tremendous influence over his actions. But I assure you, there's more going on behind the scenes than just that."

Brooke let out a sigh. "Well, if nothing else, I'll have some interesting material to contribute to the Art of Living Network's *Unveiling* series."

The remark took Stokes off guard. He was intimately familiar with the series, having helped Elena Voss develop the content in the months before his conversion. "I'm familiar with the series," he said, eyeing Brooke curiously. "Why did you mention it?"

"I'm doing some editing for the producer, a woman named Elena Voss."

Had he heard correctly? Brooke was working for Elena? How was that possible? He turned away, trying to hide his reaction as he struggled to bring his thoughts under control.

"Is something wrong?" she asked.

He didn't answer. How could he when her words had

upended everything he thought he understood about the current situation? Somehow he had to figure out if Brooke was what she claimed to be or if she was an operative dispatched by Elena Voss to ferret him out.

He turned around and forced himself to appear calm. "How do you know Elena Voss?"

"We met just last week after she took an interest in two of my husband's paintings. She asked the gallery owner to invite me to join them so we could help her decide which painting would look best in her home. She ended up buying both."

"Of course she did. That meant twice as much of your energy to work her spells."

Brooke was about to speak but he held up a hand to silence her. "Allow me to finish your story. Feel free to stop me if I get something wrong. Elena welcomed you to her home. She made you feel comfortable. She seemed to know the right things to say. She expressed empathy—not too much, just enough to establish a connection. When she sensed you were distressed, she backed off and changed the subject. She found things the two of you had in common, and she centered the conversation around you and your interests. She made amusing comments. She found out you were an editor as well as an artist and made an offer of an assignment. Out of kindness. Out of an appreciation for your gifts. Out of concern for your circumstances. You left feeling surprised at the pleasant time you'd had."

Brooke nodded. "How did you know?"

"It doesn't matter how I know. I just do." He let out a sigh. "If you'll excuse me, I need to retire to my study to seek higher guidance. I trust that a solution to our present circumstances will be forthcoming."

Twenty-seven

The rain began as a light drizzle, and in no time at all, foot traffic disappeared from the streets. Business was dead, but that gave Madeleine Hewitt an opportunity to dive back into the suspense thriller she'd started earlier in the week.

At this point in the narrative, three cardinals lay dead beneath the dome of St. Peter's and the Pope had fled to an obscure monastery in the Caucasus Mountains. The suspense was building to a dizzying crescendo and then the buzzer sounded from the front of the store.

She threw the book on the desk and glanced at the monitor. To her surprise, Janine Greenwood, Karl Erikson's first wife, stood in the doorway, an umbrella in her hand.

Madeleine experienced a pang of nostalgia at the sight of her old friend. Back in the day the two couples, she and Sid, and Janine and Karl, had been nearly inseparable. Together they'd logged in countless hours of cookouts, movie nights and concerts, not to mention shared vacations and camping trips. They'd raised their kids together, and Madeleine had vivid memories of Brett and Stephi and her own two boys romping in the woods behind Karl's house while the moms fretted over ticks and poison ivy and the dads drank beer and told the moms they worried too much.

All that had ground to a halt when Janine and Karl split up and Greg Greenwood took Karl's place. Not long after that, Janine and Greg launched their hocus-pocus, metaphysical business, and the women seemed to have less and less in common with each passing year.

So how long had it been since they'd seen each other? Three years? Four? It didn't seem possible that so much time had elapsed.

She took a moment to touch up her lipstick before stepping into the gallery.

"Janine," she began. "What a nice surprise. It's been ages."

The two women shared a heartfelt embrace and then stood looking into each other's faces. Madeleine noticed lines around Janine's eyes that hadn't been there the last time they'd been together and more than a touch of sadness in her smile.

"It didn't seem right not having you with us at the retrospective," Madeleine said. "I thought of you all afternoon."

"The kids convinced me it would be awkward," Janine said with a sigh. "You know—the ex-wife crashing the party. I didn't want to upset Brooke."

"It was sweet of you to put others before yourself. But then you've always been thoughtful."

Madeleine watched Janine's eyes sweep over the paintings. How many did she remember? Years of Janine's life hung on these walls and it had to be difficult having so many memories rush over her at once.

"Shall I leave you to yourself for a bit?" Madeleine asked.

Janine nodded. "That would be sweet. I'm feeling a tad overwhelmed."

"Of course you are. Just promise you won't leave without saying goodbye. Better, yet, why don't I order coffee and pastry? When you've had your fill of paintings, we'll enjoy a treat in my office. It'll be just like old times."

Janine shook her head. "The old times ended long ago. But it'll be nice to catch up."

Madeleine turned toward her office and was surprised when Janine stopped her.

"Have you heard from Brooke?" she asked.

"Not since Sunday when she stopped in with her uncle. Why do you ask?"

"It's probably nothing, but it appears she's gone missing."

"Missing? How's that possible? She never leaves the house."

"That's what everyone thought," Janine said, lowering her voice as though the walls had ears. "The police need to speak to her, but nobody seems to know where she is. Two nights ago Brett stopped by the house and found a man there with her. He's gone missing too."

"A man? With Brooke? I find that hard to believe."

Janine nodded. "I was surprised as well. Brett said Brooke seemed embarrassed at being discovered, and the guy acted shifty, like he had something to hide. Brett wanted to keep an eye on things, so he parked his car behind some trees and kept watch. He said the man was there until two in the morning—just him and Brooke all alone in the house."

Madeleine was stunned. "There has to be a misunderstanding. Brooke's done nothing but grieve and mope, and mope and grieve ever since Karl died. And now this?"

"I know it's hard to swallow, but it gets even worse. That same day an antiques appraiser was at the house, and she found a valuable medallion in an old slant-top desk. Within hours of finding it, Brooke and the man disappeared. Brett and Stephi think they took the medallion with them."

"A medallion?" The thought triggered an alarm. "Could this be what the thief was looking for the day of the retrospective?"

"It's possible. Apparently the medallion is some kind of occult ritual object. A charm or an amulet or something like that. At any rate, the kids are drawing the worst possible conclusions. They think Brooke stole the medallion out from under them and worse, they think she'd been cheating on Karl long before he died."

Madeleine found the suggestion ridiculous. "Brooke and Karl were fabulously happy together. At least until he found religion and started telling everyone to repent."

Janine nodded. "It got morbid, didn't it?"

"Indeed. So let's not talk about it. Spend some time with the paintings," she told Janine, "and when you're done, we'll enjoy a treat in my office."

Half an hour later the two women sat in the back room, nibbling pumpkin scones and sipping coffee.

"This man Brooke supposedly ran off with," Madeleine said as she wiped a crumb from her lower lip. "Do you know anything about him?"

"Only a few superficial details. Brett said he was tallish— six foot or thereabouts. Dark eyes and scruffy dark hair. Not bad looking but not particularly handsome either."

Madeleine sat up straighter. "He was in the gallery on Sunday."

"What?"

"That's right. He was looking at Brooke's portrait. She came in a few minutes later with her uncle, and I couldn't help but notice that there was something strange about the way she and this fellow looked at each other—like a secret had passed between them."

Janine wrapped her arms around herself as though warding off a chill. "Something strange is going on here. Something to do with the medallion the appraiser found in the desk. I wish I knew what it all meant."

She sat in silence for a moment and then raised a hand to a purple crystal that hung from a chain at her throat. "Remember when we used to hold up a pendulum and ask it for guidance?"

Madeleine certainly did remember. In the early days of Janine's New Age journey, Madeleine had helped her practice her emerging skills. They'd spent countless hours at Janine's kitchen table, watching in amazement as the pendulum answered their yes and no questions.

"I still use it now and then," Janine said, "and I got to wondering if you and I could give it a whirl."

"I'm surprised you haven't consulted it already."

"When I'm alone, nothing seems to happen. I thought that here in the gallery surrounded by Karl's paintings, I'd get a better response. Shall we try it?"

"I suppose it can't hurt."

Janine reached to the back of her neck and unhooked the chain. "You remember how it works. A circular motion means yes. Back and forth means no. I'll ask the first question."

She held the chain so that the tip of the pendulum pointed at the desk and then she closed her eyes. "Did Brooke run off with the person Madeleine met on Sunday?"

A circular motion—yes.

Madeleine grabbed Janine's arm. "That confirms my suspicions. I knew there was something funny going on."

Janine focused her gaze on the pendulum and again closed her eyes. "Did they take the medallion with them?"

Another yes.

After that the answers came fast and furious.

Is the medallion valuable?

Yes.

Is it old?

Yes.

More than one-hundred years old?

Yes.

More than one-hundred-fifty?

Yes.

And so on.

At four-hundred fifty they hit their first *no*.

Madeleine felt suddenly breathless. The medallion was created sometime in the late fifteen-hundreds—at the height of the English Renaissance.

She chimed in with a question. "Does the medallion have connections to royalty?"

Yes.

She drew in her breath at the thought. This thing, whatever it was, might be worth a fortune.

She followed with a bold question, one that got straight to the heart of the matter. "Was Karl's death linked to the medallion?"

She sat spellbound, her gaze fixed on the pendulum. Seconds ticked by, but it didn't budge.

"It doesn't seem to like that question," she remarked impatiently. "Let's move on to another."

Janine let out a weary sigh. "When it stops moving, the session's over."

Madeleine was dismayed by the news. "You can't be serious. We were just beginning."

"I know. But it's refusing to answer. If I force a response, we won't know if it's accurate, so there's no point in proceeding."

That was it then. The moment of magic and nostalgia was over. Madeleine walked Janine to the front of the gallery. They said a few words in parting, exchanged hugs, and promised to let each other know if they heard from Brooke. After that, Madeleine stood in the doorway, watching Janine put up her umbrella against the downpour.

Back in her office she berated herself for being carried away by the pendulum exercise. No sensible adult would put stock in such nonsense. In reality, it was a kind of Rorschach test that revealed what was already inside the mind of the person controlling the pendulum. Janine believed that Brooke ran off with a secret lover, and so she transmitted that message to her brain, and her brain gave off electrical impulses that caused her fingers to move the pendulum and give the answer she anticipated. It was that simple.

Madeleine picked up her novel and laid it down again. She couldn't concentrate on the Pope in his mountain hideout. Not when she was fretting over Brooke. She took her phone from her bag, dialed Brooke's number and listened as the call went to voice mail.

Again she picked up the book, but after three pages, she hadn't absorbed a word. How could she when she was being tortured by thoughts of the grief-stricken creature she'd comforted in the days following Karl's death. Overwhelmed by a mother's instinct to nurture and protect, Madeleine tossed her book aside and pulled on her raincoat. Once she'd locked up for the night, she raised her umbrella and turned her face toward the storm.

▾ ▾ ▾

Ted adjusted the earplug on the tablet Stokes had left behind. He listened for the tenth time as a male voice recited the words John Dee had downloaded from spiritual beings he'd envisioned as angels. Dee's followers in the modern era—notorious figures like Aleister Crowley and rocket scientist Jack Parsons—had shared Dee's obsession with this secret language of angels. As they'd found out, conjuring, in all its many forms, brings forth not angels, but more sinister beings. And yet occultists continued to use these incantations in the hopes that they'd get it right where so many others had failed.

By now Ted was feeling the effects of having not slept much the night before. To make matters worse, the voice chanting in Dee's secret language was lulling him into a sleepy stupor. He pulled the plug from his ear. The last thing he needed was Luciferian incantations subliminally controlling his thoughts.

He glanced at the time and was surprised to see that Stokes had been gone for nearly an hour. How long did he intend to stay locked away in his study? Once he disappeared into that rabbit hole, there was no telling when he'd emerge.

"What's taking him so long?" Brooke asked for what seemed like the hundredth time. She too appeared drowsy as she mechanically dragged a piece of string along the floor so a cat could swipe at it.

"Trust him," Ted said. "Stokes knows what he's doing."

"Oh, really? That romp through history was entertaining, but it didn't help us figure out how to get rid of the medallion or how to get my uncle back to safety."

Ted frowned. He wasn't in the mood for whining, even from the Sad-Eyed Woman of Mystery who under other circumstances had seemed so enchanting. "You wanted to know about the medallion—remember? Now you know about it. It wouldn't hurt to be grateful."

She let out a sigh. "Sorry. I'm upset about my uncle. At this point, nothing else matters."

He met her sigh with a sleepy sigh of his own. Once again he picked up the tablet and reinserted the earpiece. The voice droned on, its nonsensical syllables like a lullaby in his ears. He was just nodding off when footsteps thudded in the hall outside the kitchen.

Stokes appeared in the doorway, his lips drawn in a frown, his eyes dark with suspicion. He placed something on the counter and pointed to Ted. "In my study. We need to talk."

He turned a hostile gaze toward Brooke. "Give me your phone. You'll get it back as soon as we're done."

Ted didn't expect her to cooperate, and true to expectation, she didn't. She looked startled at the request and he didn't blame her—it had come out of the blue and sounded more than a little threatening. Stokes must have decided the battle wasn't worth fighting because he turned and waited in the hall for Ted to follow him.

▾ ▾ ▾

The rain was falling in earnest and the wind seemed to drive the dampness right through the walls of the two-hundred-fifty year old stone house. "I think I'll light a fire," David announced. "That should cozy things up a bit."

The offer fell flat. Feeling cozy didn't seem to be high on Nelson Roberts' list of priorities. The old man stood at the window, staring blankly at the lawn stretching east toward the river. He paid no attention to the grilled cheese sandwich his host had prepared for him and he certainly expressed no interest in a fire.

David could empathize with the man's somber mood. Doctor Roberts been routed out of his routine by his niece's strange request, and if that wasn't bad enough, he had no idea where she was. All he knew was that she was in danger and the security system he'd purchased to provide safety and peace of mind had provided neither.

He turned to his host with a bewildered expression. "Other than the few nights she stayed at my apartment, Brooke hasn't been away overnight since Karl died. Why now?"

"I'm sure there's a good explanation."

"Is that so?" he snapped. "Then I wish you'd tell me what it is." His angry expression quickly faded. "Forgive me. I'm not handling this very well. My nerves are on edge."

David nodded toward the grilled cheese cooling on the coffee table. "Sit down and eat something. You need to keep up your strength."

"I have no appetite."

"I get that. But give it a try anyway."

Nelson Roberts shrugged and went back to the sofa where he sat staring at the sandwich as though trying to convince himself to eat. Finally he took a bite of melted cheddar and apple slices encased in toasted bread. He swallowed hard and put the plate back on the table as though the food held no interest.

"The detective showed me a photo of a man they're searching for," he told his host. "The fellow looked familiar and then I remembered that I'd met him on Sunday at the Hewitt Gallery before Brooke and I went to the concert. We found him standing in front of her portrait."

David perked up at the comment. "I know the painting. The one of Brooke in a canoe. It's stunning isn't it?"

He nodded. "It was strange the way Brooke reacted when she saw this Roslyn fellow. There was an awkward silence followed by some hasty introductions. He said a word or two about the exhibition and then he hightailed it out of there. I didn't mention the encounter afterward, and neither did Brooke, but now I regret not asking a few questions because it seems the man is somehow involved in her disappearance."

"Did the detectives say why they'd concluded that?"

"No. And when I asked if Brooke was in danger, they gave an evasive answer that did nothing to put my mind at ease." He reached into his pocket for his phone. "Perhaps I should contact them for an update."

David shook his head. "You can't do that, sir. Brooke was quite adamant about it. She said that no one—including the police—can know where you are. Not until she gives the word." He nodded at the sandwich. "I'd encourage you to eat a bit more. If she should call—if she needs your help—you'll want to be ready to do as she asks."

Dr. Roberts let out a sigh and caved to the pressure by taking another bite.

"Well then," David said, "I guess I'll get back to making a fire. It'll drive away the chill."

He left Dr. Roberts to his grilled cheese and went back to the fireplace to arrange the logs and kindling. He tossed in a match and watched the flames licking at the twigs and bits of old newspaper as the fire took hold. Satisfied with his efforts, he crossed the room to a cabinet, got out a bottle of cognac and poured some into each of two snifters.

"Something to calm our nerves," he said.

Nelson Roberts took the glass but put it down without taking a sip. Instead he stared blankly at the flames and David had no trouble reading his thoughts. Until he heard from his niece, grilled cheese, cozy fires and calming glasses of cognac would have little effect.

Hoping to distract him, David picked up the TV remote and turned on the news. There was a story about a pile-up on Route 80 followed by another about a fire that burned four row houses in Allentown. Next was a tribute to a local scout troupe, and the fourth story described a break-in in at a senior apartment complex on the outskirts of Bethlehem.

The old man's mouth dropped open. "That's my building!"

The anchor filled in the details. *Suspicious noises. A phone call to the police. The door jimmied and the place ransacked. And a final detail: The resident's whereabouts are currently unknown.*

Nelson Roberts pointed at the image on the screen. "That's my apartment they're talking about. I have to speak to the police."

That quick David was out of his chair. "No," he said firmly. "Brooke insisted that I keep your whereabouts a secret. She said it's a matter of life or death. Not just yours, but hers as well."

At those words, the color drained from Professor Robert's face. He sank back in the sofa, his head in his hands, and David had a feeling it would take something stronger than cognac to soothe the old man's nerves. And his own as well.

Twenty-eight

E lena stood with her cell to her ear, her gaze fixed on the rain pummeling the narrow strip of pavement that passed for a runway. Until the precipitation slacked off, she'd be stuck in this pre-fab building that served as the nerve center of the pathetic little airport where her helicopter had been forced to land. At least she had a signal out here in no-man's land, and that allowed her to take advantage of the delay so she could attend to business.

A stocky guy in jeans and a flannel shirt offered her a cup of coffee and a packaged snack cake. She turned up her nose at both. She had more important things to do than sip bad coffee and eat toxic junk food. She had contacts to update. Details to iron out. Coordinates to double check. And idiots to rebuke for failing to locate their quarry.

She listened, appalled by the sniveling excuses being dished out in bucketsful. Dirt roads leading nowhere. Miles of nothing but trees. Few gas stations, stores or restaurants where a person could stop and ask questions. And now the rain.

"You're hopeless," she snarled into the phone. "I pay you a fortune, and this is the service you provide?"

She hung up and stared out the window. She needed to access her powers of remote viewing, but in order to make that happen, she needed privacy.

The helicopter sat on the runway like a wounded bird. The pilot had stayed in the cabin, monitoring the weather and biding his time. She'd find no privacy there.

And in here?

She glanced at the guy at the desk and caught him leering at her. He quickly turned his gaze away, but she knew what he'd been thinking. He was wondering how a hot babe like her had managed to drop in on him from the clouds. He was thinking that this was his lucky day, and all he needed was a sexy pickup line to convince her that he was her man.

The lecherous energy the guy exuded was powerful enough to neutralize any and all attempts at remote viewing. If Elena expected to isolate her quarry, she'd have to put some distance between herself and Don Juan at the desk. The restroom was her only hope for a moment of undistracted contact. As she walked in that direction, she could feel the man's eyes all over her, but it didn't matter. Let the moron enjoy his fantasies. Life couldn't get any duller than the one he was living.

The restroom turned out to be a dingy little space that looked like it hadn't been cleaned in years. Rust and who-knows-what-else stained the toilet bowl and the faucet had a slow and annoying drip. This was so not the refined atmosphere she was accustomed to, but it would have to do.

She leaned against the wall, closed her eyes, and drew in her breath. At first all she could visualize were the germs and bacteria presently entering her nasal passages and lungs, but eventually she moved past that and into the shadowy world inhabited by her spirit guide. But this time, instead of focusing on Jeremy Stokes, she focused on Brooke Roberts. In no time at all, her face emerged from the mist, and pity, pity, pity, the poor thing looked scared and lonely.

Perfect. Those negative emotions made her vulnerable, and Elena was more than ready to take advantage of the woman's vulnerability if it meant bending Brooke to her will and bringing Elena that much closer to the medallion and to Jeremy Stokes as well.

▾ ▾ ▾

Madeleine turned into the long gravel driveway. Brooke wasn't answering her phone and there was no reason to expect her to be at the house, but she had to check nonetheless. She was fond of Brooke and stopping by the house felt better than doing nothing.

To her surprise there was a black pick-up truck parked near the door. She drew closer and when she saw Rob Tate on the porch, she rolled down the window. "What brings you out on an afternoon like this?"

"I was about to ask you the same thing," he shouted back. The rest of his words were drowned out by the wind.

Madeleine got out of her car and dashed over to the porch.

"When I was here the other day," Rob said, his back to Madeleine as he looked through the kitchen window, "Brooke and this antiques appraiser had just found a medallion thing in an old desk. Brooke stuck it behind her back like she didn't want me to see it, but ever since I've been thinking that it must have been what the intruder was looking for when he broke in. I keep thinking she's in danger."

Madeleine's interest was immediately aroused. "I just heard about the medallion from Karl's ex-wife. She says it has ties to Renaissance royalty and is incredibly valuable."

"That would explain the robbery, wouldn't it?" Rob squinted through the window like he was trying to see beyond the kitchen and into the rest of the house. "I hope everything's alright in there."

Fear gripped Madeleine's heart. She pictured Brooke prostrate on the floor, knocked unconscious by the intruder who'd returned for this strange medallion that seemed to be at the center of all this upset. She looked at the shiny blue sticker on the door. *Stay Safe Security Systems.* Attempts to enter would have alerted the authorities, and within minutes the driveway would have been full of cop cars.

Unless the intruder had known how to disable the alarms. She thought of the novel she was reading. Art thieves had out-smarted the Vatican's security system—the best system in the world, bar none. Perhaps someone of equal skill had set his or her mind on breaking into Brooke's house in order to obtain the medallion.

"We need to go inside," she announced. "This is no time to worry about the security system alerting the police. Not if Brooke's been harmed in some way."

"Don't sweat the security system," Rob said with a smile. "I've got it covered." He bent over and touched a spot on the base of a massive potted plant. A section slid out and a key pad appeared. He entered some numbers and at the sound of a click, he opened the door and held it so Madeleine could go in first.

They emerged ten minutes later, relieved on the one hand that they hadn't found Brooke—unconscious, or worse—but still concerned that her whereabouts remained a mystery. Instead of going their separate ways, Rob suggested they meet for coffee to discuss the matter. The idea appealed to Madeleine. She could pick his brain about the medallion while at the same time hinting at the possibility of showing his work in her gallery sometime in the future.

The location Rob recommended was unfamiliar to her. When she arrived, she found that the place appeared to cater to a youngish crowd. There was a lot of multi-colored hair as well as a wide variety of tattoos and piercings. With only a few exceptions, everyone sipped their coffee in silence, their eyes glued to phones and other mobile devices. Not Madeleine's idea of coffee with a friend, but it didn't matter. The place was a convenient spot to enjoy a warm drink while she and Rob ana-lyzed the situation.

She gazed out the window at a couple laughing in the rain as they dashed from their car to the coffee shop. Toward the rear of the parking lot, a female cop in a black slicker talked into a phone. Madeleine didn't envy her—it was a miserable day to be on duty.

Rob arrived at the table with his coffee and Madeleine wasted no time filling him in on all she'd learned about Brooke, Ted Roslyn, and the medallion.

"Karl's kids think Brooke is in a relationship with this Roslyn fellow," she confided. "They've even suggested that something might have been going on before Karl's death."

Rob frowned but said nothing. He didn't have to. She could tell what he was thinking. His first loyalty was to the man whose work had inspired his own. But perhaps there was something else there as well. He'd spent a lot of time with Karl and Brooke, and Madeleine had wondered on more than one occasion if there was an attraction there. Not that Rob would have acted on it then, but now that Karl was out of the picture?

She put the thought out of her mind and instead asked him about his latest work. He was just getting his phone out of his pocket to show her some photos when she noticed flashing lights out in the parking lot. Two cop cars glided up to the officer in the black rain slicker, and were joined seconds later by a white sedan. The door opened, and a short stocky man in a trench coat got out.

Madeleine grabbed Rob's arm. "It's that detective fellow," she said breathlessly. "Hurley. Murleigh. I can't quite remember his name, but it's the guy who's been handling the break-in at Brooke's house. I'm sure of it."

Rob turned to take a look. "You're right. I wonder what he's doing here."

Madeleine pulled on her raincoat and fumbled with her umbrella. "I have no idea, but I intend to find out."

▾ ▾ ▾

It had been awhile since Ted had been inside Stokes's inner sanctum and it felt good to be back. The walls were lined with books and journals, many of them old and musty and collected from sources around the world. The rest of the room was a techie's dream come true with a bunch of computers that provided access to complex networks of intelligence agents, independent journalists, law enforcement, and experts in a variety of disciplines.

"I took some time to look into Brooke's background," Stokes began. "I should have done so earlier but it wouldn't have mattered because the pertinent details have only emerged in the last several hours."

He went on to explain that he'd been in touch with discrete contacts in law enforcement who'd informed him that Mordecai's Antiques and Oddities had been ransacked yesterday sometime after Brooke had left. The owner and his son had both pretty roughed up and were presently in the hospital with injuries sustained in the attack. Brooke was wanted for questioning in regard to the incident and Ted was wanted for questioning in regard to Brooke's disappearance. There were APBs out for both of them, not just in regard to the above but also in regard to the circumstances of the late Karl Erikson's death, given the disappearance of a valuable item thought to be connected with his demise.

"The rumors," Stokes explained to Ted, "have been exacerbated by the knowledge that you were the last person known to have spoken to Brooke's late husband on the day of his death."

"I thought I'd set the detectives straight on all of that."

"Apparently not. But don't worry—it will sort itself out once this is over with. What concerns me more is Brooke's mention of a woman named Elena Voss, writer and producer of *The Unveiling* documentary series. We spent a good deal of time together back in the day, and I happen to know that she's coveted the Phoenix Medallion since childhood and will stop at nothing to possess it. The fact that Elena has taken Brooke under her wing is intensely alarming."

He picked up a fountain pen from his desk and rolled it back and forth between his thumb and index finger, gazing at it in the lights from half-a-dozen large screen monitors. "Elena Voss and I were lovers," he said, "and ironically, I helped her with the original plans for the series, a fact I regret every time I hear it mentioned. But more to our point, Elena was with me when I was initiated into the cult of the medallion. She knew that its owner intended to bequeath it to me upon his death, and she fully expected that she and I would share the prize and the power it bestows. She scoffed when I turned to the light, and while I indeed fled the West Coast to escape those who wished me harm, I also took that drastic action to escape Elena's bewitching charms. I suspect she's heard rumors that I'm alive, and if so, she's been using her considerable powers of remote viewing to find me. Only the grace of God has prevented her from doing so, and only the grace of God has kept me from returning to her. That's how powerfully we were drawn to each other."

Ted hadn't known this part of his friend's story, but he saw no reason to question it. Once a powerful woman sank her claws into a man, it was tough to break free. Throw money and magic and mayhem into the mix and things could get complicated.

"Sometime last spring," Stokes continued, "my sources informed me that the Phoenix Medallion had been stolen from the Long Island mansion where it had been kept under lock and key for nearly four generations. I of course suspected that Elena was behind the theft, but I heard no more about it until you texted me two nights ago with pictures. I was unwilling to discuss the matter over unsecured lines, and that's why I asked you to bring the medallion here in person.

"And that brings us to Brooke. Years of tangling with Elena Voss have made me skeptical of any story in which Elena plays a part. I'm left wondering if Brooke is an innocent victim who stumbled into a web of intrigue, or is she's a paid operative dispatched to lure me back into Elena's clutches."

Ted spoke up quickly. "Brooke's totally legit. If you could have seen her the morning I first met her at that coffee shop…"

Stokes cut him off before he could finish. "Trained operatives are trained to appear genuine. That's the whole point."

"So what are you suggesting?"

"I'm suggesting that we can't risk being deceived by a show of pathos. From now on, we'll need to keep Brooke on a short leash which is why I asked her to hand over her phone. As upset as she appears to be, she might attempt to contact her uncle on the one hand and Elena on the other, assuming she and Elena are working together. If my cover's going to be blown, I'd rather it be on my own terms than on someone else's. By the way, you may have noticed that I placed something on the kitchen counter."

Ted had noticed, but he'd paid it little attention.

"A recording device. If Brooke made a call, I'll soon know about it.

"And that brings me to the final point I need to make. I fully anticipate that my identity and my whereabouts will be exposed before this whole ordeal is over. I'd love to familiarize you with the things I do in here, but it would take weeks and months and is obviously impossible. Elena's people will be closing in soon, and we'll need to get on the road before we're trapped like rats.

"So here's the plan. Brooke will call her detective buddies and offer to turn herself in. In a second call, she'll provide information about a rendezvous location where she can turn over the medallion. I'll explain the details once we get moving."

He rose from his seat. "Let me handle Brooke from this point forward. Your feelings for her will only complicate things."

"My feelings?" Ted sputtered. "What would you know about my feelings?"

"You're an open book, my friend."

He was surprised to hear it. He hadn't realized he'd been so transparent. "And what about your feelings for Elena?" he countered. "Won't that complicate things?"

Stokes gave his friend an ironic smile. "Remember how Odysseus made his fellow sailors chain him to the mast so he wouldn't succumb to the Sirens' song?"

Ted nodded.

"Keep me chained to the mast and we should be all right."

Twenty-nine

Burleigh glanced at the incident report. Two hours ago the owner of a coffee shop near Allentown had phoned to report an abandoned SUV in the parking lot. The responding officer had looked up the license number and realized that the car belonged to a fugitive who was wanted, not because she was a suspect in a crime, but because the authorities had questions to which she alone had answers. Two cars had been dispatched to the parking lot, and minutes later Burleigh cancelled the APB on Brooke's Sportage but not on Brooke herself. Meanwhile, the location of Ted Roslyn's Jeep Renegade and its passengers remained unknown.

Somehow Madeleine Hewitt had shown up in the middle of this chaotic scene with Rob Tate trailing behind her. Burleigh couldn't very well question them in the downpour, and the coffee shop had been far too crowded to allow for privacy, so they'd agreed to meet at the station. Burleigh had just concluded an interview with Tate in which he'd informed him that he was being detained for further questioning and might want to contact a lawyer.

It was time now to hear Madeleine Hewitt's side of the story. He recognized most of the details she related from the story he'd been told by the Erikson kids, a now-familiar narrative of Brooke and Ted Roslyn being lovers who'd run off with a valuable heirloom. Mrs. Hewitt added emotion and drama to the story but little substance. He was just about to let her go when she chimed in with a curious detail. The medallion at the heart of the matter had once belonged to Renaissance royalty.

"Renaissance royalty?" he echoed. "Who told you that?"

She hemmed and hawed, but eventually she described an exercise that involved a pendulum and a series of yes and no answers. She insisted that while she didn't take the activity seriously—it was all in fun—she couldn't help but wonder if the answers might be true.

"And that's why I insisted Rob and I enter the house," she said as though the logic of the decision was inescapable. "Security system or no security system, with a valuable object from the Renaissance inside the house, Brooke's safety was at stake. I was concerned that we'd trigger the alarm, but as it turned out, Rob pushed a few buttons and just like that, we were in."

The detective stared at her in something like amazement. "Did it ever occur to you, Mrs. Hewitt, that breaking and entering is a crime?"

She seemed surprised to hear it. "Breaking and entering? The thought never crossed our minds. We were concerned for Brooke's safety." She drew back as though offended. "Are you impugning Rob's motives? Or mine?"

"I'm just stating the law so you're clear what we're talking about."

She made a snorting sound that suggested that the law was of little relevance in this instance. "Go inspect the house for yourself if you think we were up to no good. We didn't ransack the place. We didn't rip through drawers and closets. We made a quick inspection and once we were sure Brooke wasn't there, we locked up and left."

"How about Rob Tate? Did he appear to be searching for something?"

"Other than Brooke lying dead on the floor? No."

"Okay, so you checked out the house and then you ran-

domly decided to get coffee at the same coffee shop where
Brooke abandoned her car. What are the odds of that?"

"I told you earlier, that was just a coincidence," she said
impatiently. "We didn't know Brooke abandoned her car at the
coffee shop. We just needed a place to talk. What do you people
call it? Debriefing. That's right—we needed to debrief."

She sat back in her chair and glared at him, like she was
in charge of the interview and not the other way around. "Do
you think that if I broke into Brooke's house to steal a medallion, I'd have run out in the rain to say 'how do you do' to the
police?"

She was right. That wouldn't have made sense.

He felt a sudden throbbing in his temples. His blood pressure must be rising. Maybe it was time to go on meds, like his
doctor had been suggesting.

He wrapped up the interview and sent the gallery owner
on her way. After that, he returned to the evidence room and
stared at the whiteboard. The chart of relevant persons, places,
and things had grown exponentially in the last 24 hours. He
studied the details listed beneath Rob Tate's name. Tate had
learned to disable Brooke's home security system, but by entering the house, he'd shown his hand, and there was no way he
could pull that stunt a second time now that the police were
on to him. Kind of self-defeating if he was looking for an opportunity to break in and help himself to the medallion or whatever.

Burleigh rubbed the ridge of his nose. He hated to admit
that the case was spiraling out of control with so many factors
manifesting on all sides, but that was about the size of it.

He heard footsteps behind him. He turned and saw his superior, Captain Matt Feldman, looming like a gargoyle in the
open doorway.

"I've had a couple of phone calls today," Feldman announced. "Both calls were from the children of the late Karl
Erikson."

Burleigh chuckled. "I can only imagine what they told you."

He noticed that Feldman wasn't chuckling. His face was stern. More than stern. Hostile, like an ancient Roman general about to unleash the troops.

"The Eriksons are less than pleased with the way you're handling things," Feldman informed him. "After listening to their complaints, I've concluded that they have good reasons for their concerns."

"You can't be serious."

The captain raised an eyebrow. "Of course I'm serious. Look at the facts. Out of the blue, Ms. Roberts interrupted her months of isolation to make a trip to an antique store in Philadelphia. Following her visit, the store was ransacked and the owner and his son suffered a violent attack that left them both in the hospital. Later that day, Ms. Roberts vanished with Ted Roslyn, the man who, as far as we know, was the last person to see Karl Erikson alive. It's rumored that she and this man are lovers. What's more, they made off with a valuable heirloom that had surfaced the day before they disappeared."

He gave Burleigh an imperious stare. "The case is far bigger than it first appeared, but you failed to uncover the facts and left it to others to piece things together."

Burleigh fought back the irate words forming on his tongue. How dare Feldman say such a thing? Feldman was the one who'd wanted to dismiss Erikson's death as an accident unrelated to the break-in. And now he had the audacity to blame Burleigh's team for not taking matters seriously? It was outrageous.

The chief approached the white board and studied the details with his back to Burleigh. "As of this minute," he said tersely, "the case is reassigned. I'll expect your notes and any related material on my desk within the hour."

With that, he turned and left the room.

Burleigh stared at the whiteboard. Okay, so he hadn't

wrapped up the investigation and tied it with a bow, but he doubted Feldman would do much better. Not if he was relying on Brett and Stephanie Erikson as star witnesses.

His phone rang in his pocket. Must be Jason Radley asking for an update.

But it wasn't Radley. It was Brooke.

"Where the devil are you?" Burleigh hissed into the phone. "The whole state's been turned upside down trying to find you. And Roslyn—I'm assuming you know where he is? And why in the world didn't you tell me you'd found the medallion?"

He glanced out the window at his car. Nothing would make him happier than to hit the road and bring those two in for questioning. He'd be defying orders if he set out after them, but at least he'd put these cockamamie theories to rest once and for all and find out what was really going on.

He listened to her story. She was upset—that much was clear, and it was difficult to understand what she was saying.

The medallion showed up in an antique desk—he knew that.

She took it to Mordecai Simmons to have it evaluated—ditto that.

She slipped out of the store through a rear exit, and two guys followed her to the train station—one was the man she'd seen late at night on her home security video.

Okay, so this was new information.

Ted had suggested they meet at a coffee shop. They eluded the people following her and drove off to show the medallion to an expert who identified it and described its history.

Also new information.

She'd just learned about the incident at Mordecai's Antiques and Oddities and knew the police were looking for her in regard to the crime. In addition, she'd learned that Elena Voss, producer of a cable documentary series, had been using Brooke to get to the medallion. Elena was an elite occultist with powerful ties to East and West Coast media.

Burleigh frowned at this news. Suddenly the stakes were

sky high, and all bets were off as to where the investigation might lead.

Then Brooke made an odd proposal involving a rendezvous with Burleigh and Jason Radley at a site she'd specify in a later call. She'd hand over the medallion and they'd pretend to arrest her—or arrest it for real, it hardly mattered. Meanwhile, Roslyn would videotape the operation on his phone, send the video to certain individuals who would make sure it went viral, and then those interested in obtaining the medallion would know for certain that it was no longer in Brooke's possession.

Burleigh wondered how he should play this. There were two options. He could let Feldman handle it or he could defy orders and set off with Radley to meet the demands as given. He thought of his pension. His benefit package. The days ticking down to retirement.

Was he willing to take the risk?

Either way, he'd have to make her believe her demands were being met. Otherwise it would be game over and there was no way to predict what might happen.

"That can be arranged," he said.

He heard voices in the background.

A strident command to fill the cats' bowls with food and water.

Orders to hurry up and get moving, there was no time to waste.

And then the phone clicked and all was silent.

▾ ▾ ▾

"Come on," Stokes bellowed as Brooke placed the phone back in the charger. "We're getting out of here."

She pointed to his bare chest and the robe draped over his pajama bottoms. "Like that?"

He breathed an oath and tore up the stairs. He appeared a few minutes later in jeans, a flannel shirt, a hooded sweatshirt and a pair of work boots. The three of them raced into the rain and into Ted's Jeep. As they settled into their seats, Stokes explained that the plan was to swap the Jeep for a friend's van in hopes of evading the police and anyone else who was looking out for Ted's license plate. He told them that he hadn't phoned ahead to alert his friends to the plan—it was bad enough that they'd risked exposure when Brooke called Detective Burleigh.

Instead of exiting through the front gate, Stokes directed them to the rear of the property. The tires spun wildly in the mud, but the Jeep pressed forward, and as they approached the rear wall, Stokes aimed a remote control device. A section slid open, revealing a narrow road that seemed to disappear into the surrounding forest.

The overhanging branches acted as a massive umbrella, but even so, Ted's wipers could barely keep up with the torrential downpour and the mud that splattered up from the rutted lane. Two miles later they emerged from the trees and soon the scruffy undergrowth on their left yielded to cultivated fields.

"The farmhouse is just over that ridge," Stokes shouted from the backseat. A blur appeared on the horizon and after a few hundred yards the blur became a barn. He directed Ted up a long gravel driveway and as they approached the barn, Stokes bolted from the Jeep and opened the double doors. He gestured for Ted to pull in next to a minivan and then he dashed through the rain toward the house.

Brooke was reluctant to follow him. For all she knew, Stokes had cooked up something ahead of time with whoever waited inside the farmhouse.

"Let's get moving," Ted said to her.

"I have no idea what I'm walking into."

His gaze seemed sympathetic but he quickly turned his face away. There was a distance between them that hadn't been there before his private meeting with Stokes. What had he said that changed Ted's attitude toward her?

Not knowing what else to do, she reluctantly got out of

the Jeep and followed him to the back porch where Stokes stood pounding on the door. When there was no answer, he crossed to a window and looked inside.

"There's a kerosene lantern burning on the table. Somebody must be home. And by the way, Jenny and Adam know my name and my story, but the kids know me as Uncle Jack."

He tried the door, and finding it unlocked, he stepped inside and beckoned for Brooke and Ted to follow. The kitchen was fragrant with the scent of something hot and spicy on the stove. The aroma reminded Brooke that she hadn't eaten since breakfast.

"Hands in the air," a voice roared out, and a petite blond with a shotgun braced against her shoulder emerged from an adjacent hallway.

All three pairs of hands flew into the air and that quickly a grin broke out on the woman's face. She lowered the shotgun and let out a laugh. "What are you doing here, you crazy lunatic?" she asked Stokes. "I was just about to blow your head off."

"I'm glad you didn't. You'd have had a nasty mess to clean up."

"You're not kidding. And I'd have some explaining to do when Adam gets back. But I suspect he'd have understood once he's heard what's being going on around here all day."

Stokes raised an eyebrow. "And what would that be?"

"A helicopter flew over earlier," she told him. "I didn't pay much attention until it circled back a few times. It seemed strange, so I kept a lookout and after a bit, I noticed a black SUV cruising back and forth in front of the house. It struck me as odd since hardly anybody ventures down this road, especially in a rainstorm like this one. It's just me and the kids here at the moment, so when I saw a Jeep barreling down the drive, I grabbed the gun and shooed the kids to the front room."

Stokes took a moment to explain their situation and then he introduced the woman as Jenny Myers. Jenny gave Brooke and Ted a friendly smile and an apology for her less than cordial

greeting. She explained that her husband, Adam, was out rescuing folks caught in flash floods and she'd been holding down
the fort all afternoon.

Once the introductions were out of the way she turned toward the hallway. "It's all right, kids. It's just Uncle Jack. You
can come out now."

At the sound of her voice, three children emerged from
the shadows, a boy of about six and a girl of nine or ten who
toted a baby on her hip. When they saw Stokes, they came running. He welcomed them with hugs and laughter before turning
his attention back to Jenny.

"The police are keeping an eye out for Ted's Jeep," he explained. "At the moment, he and Brooke are fugitives. It sounds
pretty bad, but I assure you they're harmless."

"I've never met anyone who was harmless," Jenny said with
a laugh. "But your friends seem nice enough, so I'll take your
word for it."

"I have a huge favor to ask," Stokes told her. "More than
one favor, to tell you the truth. I'm wondering if you'd be willing
to temporarily swap vehicles so me and my friends can stay
under the radar. I'll take full responsibility for the van if anything happens to it."

She frowned as she considered the request. "So you're saying there'll be three fugitives—yourself included—out on the
road in a vehicle that doesn't belong to any of you?"

"You got any better suggestions?"

"Let's talk about it over dinner." She looked at Brooke and
Ted. "I'll bet this guy never bothered to feed you, is that right?"

They both nodded.

She pointed to the pot on the stove. "Let's have some chili
and cornbread while we work this out."

As they ate, Jenny explained that she and her husband
were researchers who funneled material from Stokes and other
sources to bloggers, authors, and speakers who exposed disturbing trends in contemporary culture. The channels, websites and

blog posts with which they worked were visited, not only by supporters of their cause, but by those they sought to expose.

She listened as Stokes described a plan to have Ted take footage of Brooke handing the medallion to the detective on the case and asked her if Ted could ship her and Adam the footage for distribution to their various contacts. Given the massive viewership involved, the story of a legendary occult medallion with connections to the English Renaissance would quickly go viral. Once Brooke's pursuers were convinced the medallion was out of her hands, they'd back off on their quest.

Jenny took a bite of cornbread and contemplated the scheme. "The way I see it, there's a couple of problems with your plan. The first one I already mentioned. You'll be three fugitives driving a van registered to none of you. The other problem," she said, looking at Stokes, "is that you're supposed to be dead which means you'll need to keep your ugly mug out of sight. So if the cops get it in their heads to arrest both of your friends, there'll be no one on standby to shoot the footage. I guess I'll have to tag along and lend a hand. Designated driver and designated camera person all in one."

"And the kids?" Stokes asked with a nod in their direction. "This could get dangerous."

Jenny smiled at the kids who'd finished eating and were laughing as they entertained the baby in her highchair. "How'd you guys like to spend the night at Grammy's?"

Twenty minutes later, Brooke and Ted cleaned up the dishes while Jenny grabbed some overnight things for the kids. After that they trooped out to the van, and within minutes, Brooke and Ted were sequestered beneath tarps in the back— they were fugitives, after all. Jenny strapped the kids into the backseat while Stokes pulled his hair back in a pony tail that he tucked beneath a loose-fitting knitted cap.

And then they set out into the storm.

Thirty

David flopped down on the sofa. There'd be no sleep for him tonight. Not when he needed to remain vigilant.

He reflected on the events of the day. Although he'd found Brooke's phone call bewildering, he was flattered that she'd chosen him for this important mission, and he wondered how it might affect their relationship going forward. It sounded crass, but there was no denying that she was in his debt.

As was Dr. Nelson Roberts. The elderly gentleman sat on the board of the Tri-County Historical Conservancy. He'd in all likelihood insist on recognizing David for his heroic efforts on his behalf. David envisioned a banquet with distinguished guests and photographers hired to publicize the event. He pictured the look in Brooke's eyes as a speaker described how he'd rescued her uncle from certain death at the hands of the violent intruders who'd ransacked his apartment. It would be a grand moment, to be sure.

He stifled a yawn. There was nothing to do now but wait for morning and an update from Brooke. Although it was still early, he switched off the light, kicked off his shoes and tossed his cell phone on the coffee table. He lay back against the sofa pillows and listened to the steady drumbeat of the rain against the windows. punctuated every now and then by the crackle and sputter of dying embers on the grate.

Nelson Roberts had taken an over-the-counter sleep aide before retiring, and there was no doubt the old man was grabbing some much-needed shut-eye. With things quieted down, David felt his own tension abate, and for the first time since Brooke's phone call earlier in the day, he began to unwind.

He closed his eyes. He wasn't going to sleep. He just needed to savor a moment or two of relaxation. The rain had assumed a rhythmic kind of tempo as it battered the house. One-two-three-four; one-two-three-four. Or was it one-two-three; one-two three? A march or a waltz? It didn't matter. Whatever the time signature, it was hypnotic.

And just the thing to lull a person to sleep.

▼ ▼ ▼

Burleigh's phone jangled in his pocket. "This is it," he told the six other officers gathered in the evidence room.

He answered the call and nodded to his colleagues. Yes, it was Brooke.

He listened to her instructions. A truck stop off of I-80. Well-lit and busy. Just him and Radley—no other police. Ted Roslyn would shoot footage on his cell as Brooke handed over the medallion. The footage would be posted on various sites as described in her earlier call.

"Roger that," he said when she finished.

He hung up and waited for Matt Feldman to take control of the meeting. What else could he do? This was no longer Burleigh's case.

A hush fell over the room as Feldman went to the white board and made a show of studying the notes scribbled in blue marker. Finally he turned and faced Burleigh.

"Act cordial and nonchalant as you approach our fugitives," he instructed. "Put them at ease in your presence. Give them time to look around to make sure you're alone. Once you and Radley have your hands on the medallion, State Police in plain clothes will move in with a warrant to seize Roslyn's phone and take him and Ms. Roberts into custody.

"Excuse me, sir," Burleigh spoke up, "Seizing the phone negates the whole purpose of the operation. The idea is to broadcast the footage and let people know the medallion's safely out of her hands."

"Yes," Feldman agreed, "but until the medallion is verified by the antiques appraiser who found it, there's no way of determining if it's truly the item in question. As to the footage, Roslyn may be planning to send a message to some as yet unidentified individuals with a stake in this scheme. I trust that you've checked out his website?"

"Of course."

"The man's a fanatic," Feldman insisted. "There's no telling who he's teamed up with. His texts and emails could be crucial in determining that." He nodded at an officer. "I want a rundown on all information exchanged between Roslyn and the late Karl Erikson, and between Roslyn and Brooke Roberts as well."

Burleigh stifled the sarcastic remarks that rose to his lips. Feldman was still running with Stephanie and Brett Erikson's asinine version of events based on their absurd speculations.

"One last detail I'd like clarified," Burleigh said, hoping he sounded cooperative and compliant when he felt just the opposite. "As I informed you earlier, Ms. Roberts mentioned a woman name Elena Voss who has an interest in the medallion. I looked into her background and discovered that she owns a residence in Manhattan and another in the Lehigh Valley. She's been known to socialize with highly questionable..."

Feldman cut him off. "You are no longer running this investigation. I've already asked another officer to look into Ms. Voss's background."

A cute little rookie gave Burleigh a condescending smile. Darla Phillips had been given the assignment and that was that.

As his boss left the room, Burleigh noticed a lodge ring on his little finger. Who or what was guiding Feldman's interest in this case? Loyalty to Brett Erikson, a junior lodge brother, or loyalty to someone higher up the ladder who was in turn loyal to Elena Voss?

▾ ▾ ▾

Brooke shifted her weight and tried to get comfortable. She didn't know how much longer she could tolerate being scrunched up on the floor of Jenny's van. She and Ted lay next to each other, so close that she could feel his breath on the back of her neck. She thought of how sweet it used to be to wake up and sense Karl's warm presence beside her in the night. But Karl was gone and she was too close for comfort to this bizarre human being whose ideas about God and the devil had thrown her life into chaos. Last night in that dank, musty cabin she'd told herself that things couldn't possibly get any worse. But they had.

She listened to the chatter from the front seat. Stokes seemed to think that in spite of instructions to the contrary, the police would show up in force simply because the case had grown too big for Burleigh and Radley to handle on their own. They'd probably attempt to confiscate Ted's cell, hoping to discover what secrets might be hidden there. And that's why Jenny's role was vitally important. While the cops were crowing over having seized Ted's phone, Jenny would blend in with the crowd, grab the footage and upload it without the cops being the wiser.

Brooke might have shared their optimism about the mission if it weren't for the lack of information about her uncle. Had she made a mistake when she'd asked David Price to intervene? Under the time constraints, he'd been the first person she'd thought of, but she knew little about him and had no idea if he was trustworthy. Given his bumbling behavior at the retrospective, could he be expected to handle a life-and-death matter such as this?

For a moment she thought about praying, but she quickly banished the thought. Prayer had done nothing for Karl. If it had, he'd still be alive and she wouldn't be in the back of a van hoping to awaken from the nightmare that her entire life had become. But once the medallion was delivered, once the video was posted, the nightmare would end and things would be normal again.

No. Without Karl, nothing would ever be normal.

She reached into her pocket and ran her fingers over the surface of the medallion. Once she was rid of it, she'd shut the door on fanatics and crazies, and life would be safe and sane. Sad and lonely perhaps, but at least safe and sane, and she'd be free to turn her attention to things that needed to get done, like shipping the appraised items off to auction and getting the house ready to sell in the spring.

She thought of the antique desk with its secret nooks and crannies, and she recalled the breathless moment when she'd found the medallion wrapped in tissue paper—and with it, a worthless anti-war button. Odd that those two items had been hidden together, and odd too that a duplicate of the button had shown up in the grave where Sid Hewitt's dog had been buried.

She puzzled over the matter for a moment or two, but by then the hum of tires on the pavement had become a sort of lullaby, beckoning her closer and closer to sleep. She dozed off only to be startled to her senses by a dull thud. She awoke to find the van careening spastically on the road.

"A flat!" Jenny shouted from the driver's seat.

"No problem," Stokes answered. "We'll have it changed in no time."

"Don't count on it," Jenny shot back. "The spare's in the shop being fixed. Unless you've got an extra tire in your back pocket, we're sunk."

Thirty-one

Like many riverfront properties, David Price's was located on a swath of land between the Delaware Canal and the Delaware River and was accessible only by a wooden bridge that spanned the canal. He'd been startled out of his slumbers by the sound of tires clattering over that bridge.

He bounded to his feet and raced to the window. An SUV was stealing up the driveway with its lights off. Someone must have followed him earlier in the day after he'd picked up Nelson Roberts at his apartment building.

He thought of his handgun upstairs in the bedroom. He'd purchased it for a moment like this, never dreaming that a moment like this would ever arrive, and that's why he'd never gone to the shooting range to figure out how to use the thing. He raced up the stairs, two at a time, hoping he'd be able to hit his target if it came to a choice between life and death.

He stopped near the top step when he heard the sound of breaking glass coming from the garage directly adjacent to the guestroom where Dr. Roberts slept. It was followed by the rumble of tires on the bridge. Were reinforcements joining the first vehicle?

He raced down the stairs and across the room to the window in time to see the solitary SUV turn out of the driveway and disappear down the road. Could someone have made a mistake?

Had a drunk made a wrong turn while looking for a different house? And the garage window—why would someone break it? Should he call the police? No, he couldn't do so until he'd heard from Brooke. But if their cover was already blown, what did it matter?

An acrid fragrance teased at his nostrils.

He glanced at the fireplace. The fire was long gone, so why did he smell smoke?

The answer hit him like a punch in the gut. Whoever smashed the window had set the garage on fire.

He raced to the guest room and pounded his fists against the door. No response. He jiggled the knob. The door was locked from inside.

"Dr. Roberts! Wake up!" he shouted, but there was no answer.

He stared at the doorknob. It was relatively new and could be opened by inserting something small and pointed. He dashed to the kitchen, clawed through a cluttered drawer, and fished out a paper clip that he unbent. In seconds he was back at the door, poking and prodding.

The lock yielded, and he threw the door open and bounded across the room. "Fire!" he shouted as he shook the slumbering man's shoulders. "We have to get out! Now!"

His guest stirred and emitted a low moan.

David tried again, and this time Dr. Roberts raised himself on one elbow.

"Fire! Hurry. Get moving."

The old gentleman fumbled for his glasses. "Hand me my trousers," he muttered groggily. "And a shirt."

"Pull your pants over your pajama bottoms and put on your slippers. There's no time for anymore than that."

In the foyer David grabbed a water-proof jacket from the closet. He helped Dr. Nelson into it but stopped cold at the front door. What if the arsonists had parked their SUV farther down the road and returned on foot, waiting to flush them out and nab them as they exited?

He steered Dr. Nelson to the kitchen and stopped again. Somebody could be waiting at the back exit as well. That left the root cellar that was connected to the basement.

He grabbed a flashlight from a drawer and guided his guest down a flight of rough wooden stairs. They rushed through the basement to the low-ceilinged passageway leading to the root cellar. A stream several inches deep flooded the narrow tunnel, but there was no option other than to splash through it to safety.

He urged Dr. Roberts toward the mossy stone steps leading to the outside. He opened the overhead trap door and helped the old man up the slippery stairs and out into the rain-drenched night.

Behind them flames erupted from a first floor window. David fumbled in his pocket for his phone and when he didn't find it, he checked the other pocket. And then he remembered. He'd laid it on the coffee table before he fell asleep. Soon it would be just a mess of melted plastic and sizzled circuits.

"The fire department," he blurted out to his guest. "Do you have your phone?"

The answer was a terse no.

He forced himself to sound confident. "No need to worry. My neighbors to the south will give us shelter."

Or so he hoped. Earl Martin's place was half-a-mile away. He split his time between the house and an apartment in Manhattan. What if he weren't home?

No problem. If he were away, they'd have to break in. The security system would alert the police and the police would cart them off to jail. Jail was warm and safe and a lot better than rain and mud and abject terror.

They headed in that direction with roots and rocks threatening to trip them with each step they took. All at once Dr. Roberts let out a cry and clutched at David's arm.

"Steady," David said, but it was too late. Both men lost

their balance and came down with a splash. David spit mud from his mouth and struggled clumsily to his feet, but it took several tries before his guest regained his footing.

By now they were soaking wet and muddy and shivering from the cold. David wondered who might be out there, watching as they made their way through the trees. The thought propelled him forward, but Dr. Nelson was having trouble keeping up. A few more yards and he bent forward with his hands resting on his thighs.

"I can't go any farther," he gasped.

"You've got to try. The river's already breached its banks."

"I said, I can't go on. You go ahead. I'll wait here."

"I can't leave you, sir."

"You can, and you will."

David noticed a downed tree that could serve as a bench. He got Dr. Nelson situated, instructed him to stay put, and left him shivering in the dark.

He made his way forward, and when a clearing loomed ahead, he broke into a run. All at once his foot caught on a root and he was airborne. He came down hard, and suddenly the night that had been so dark and rainy was full of stars.

▾ ▾ ▾

The van came to a stop amid shouts about a flat tire. Ted stretched to get the kinks out of his back and struggled to a sitting position. His whole body was tied up in knots, and danger or no danger, he needed to get out and move around.

He could feel Brooke watching him as he threw off the tarp and opened the rear hatch. They'd said very little to each other since leaving Stokes's place and the silence had worn on him. But it was probably for the best. In a few hours the mission would end—one way or another—and they'd probably never see each other again. He glanced at her with a smile and she returned it. He wondered if he'd always remember her that way with her eyes drowsy with sleep and a wistful smile stealing over her lips.

He slithered out of the van and stretched his limbs. The rain had dwindled to a bone-chilling mist, and the dampness bit through his hooded gray sweatshirt, but it felt good to be on his feet again.

They'd come to a stop in the parking lot of an abandoned bar and grill. *Devil's Inn*, the place was called. With a name like that, what could possibly go wrong? Other than everything.

He took a look at the tire. Flat as a pancake and not a spare in sight. He walked to the front passenger's side door and Stokes rolled down the window.

"Time to recalibrate," Ted said.

"Indeed."

Stokes turned toward the rear of the van and looked at Brooke. "Call your detective buddies and tell them the plans have changed. They'll be meeting us here, wherever we are."

"We're at a place called The Devil's Inn," Ted informed him.

Stokes raised an eyebrow. "Seriously?"

"I couldn't make it up if I tried."

Stokes turned his attention back to Brooke. "Use your own phone. We can't risk them tracing Jenny's."

Brooke got out of the van and came around to the passenger side while Jenny checked the GPS to pinpoint their location. Brooke placed the call and walked slowly back and forth as she spoke. She hung up and informed her friends that Burleigh and Radley had just arrived at the truck stop and thought they'd be able to make it to the new rendezvous spot in about twenty-five minutes.

Ted wondered how things would play out. They'd planned to leave the van in the parking lot of a busy truck stop. That way, Stokes could remain safely out of sight and anonymous while Brooke and Ted met the detectives. Instead they were in the middle of nowhere next to a vacant field that stretched several hundred yards to the surrounding woods. And instead of the van being one vehicle among many, it sat all alone on the macadam, a prime target for a search. And that meant Stokes's cover would be blown as he'd feared and it was anyone's guess what complications might ensue.

A thrumming sound in the distance interrupted Ted's thoughts. At first it sounded like a swarm of approaching locusts, but the sound soon grew deafening. A bright light pierced the roiling clouds, casting its beams in all directions in the misty dampness.

A helicopter, of course. Dispatched by the cops? Probably not. In all likelihood, it was the same one Jenny had observed earlier in the day.

"It's Elena," Stokes said through clenched teeth. "It has to be. " He gazed at the helicopter hovering overhead, his eyes dark and haunted in a way that Ted had never seen before.

"I have to see her," Stokes said. "Just a glimpse. It's been more than three years."

He opened the door, but Ted forced him back inside. "The mast," he said, reminding Stokes of his earlier words. "Consider yourself tied to it."

Stokes looked at the light descending from the sky. He let out a tortured sigh and turned his face away, his fists clenched. "Pray for me," he said.

"I've already got you covered."

With that, Stokes scrambled into the back of the van and burrowed down beneath the tarp. Ted wondered how long he'd be able to hold himself back once the helicopter landed. Would the police arrive before Elena had a chance to lure him into her clutches?

Brooke took the seat Stokes vacated. Ted could see the fear in her eyes as she watched the helicopter make its way earthward. Jenny, on the other hand, seemed upbeat and animated as she shot footage of the behemoth nestling down into the field, its lights illuminating the dreary landscape.

For a breathless few seconds nothing happened, and then the door to the cabin opened and the steps unfolded. A man appeared, silhouetted in the open doorway. He carried an AR-15, and he was followed by an African American who wielded a similar weapon.

Brooke grabbed Ted's arm through the open window. "They're the guys who chased me through the city," she told him, although he'd already figured as much.

They descended the stairs and stood guard at the bottom as a dark-haired woman appeared in the doorway. Her features could barely be distinguished, but apparently Brooke had no troubled recognizing her.

"It's Elena," she announced.

Ted's eyes drifted from Elena to the AR-15s her minions carried. Those suckers made Jenny's shotgun and his Baby Glock seem like pea shooters in comparison. A wave of despair washed over him at the sight of so much firepower. Barring a miracle, he and his friends were doomed.

The Devil's Inn lay behind them blanketed in shadow. If Ted could make it over there without being seen, he might be able to sneak around the building and surprise the thugs from the rear.

"See if there's a flashlight in the glove compartment," he told Brooke. "I've got a plan." He didn't really, but he was hoping one would occur to him. Otherwise, they might soon be dead. Except for Stokes. Elena Voss would spare him, and once she possessed the medallion, the two of them would disappear together into the sky.

Ted took the flashlight Brooke handed him and then he crouched down beside the van and darted into the shadows blanketing the deserted tavern. He arrived safely at the front and stared through plate glass windows that provided an unbroken view of the building's interior. Much of the space had been stripped down to studs and wiring while a smaller section appeared to be newly dry-walled and painted. It looked like someone was actually planning to reopen this dump. He made a silent promise to return for a burger and fries if he survived.

A dumpster full of construction debris stood just to the side of the building. He took a look inside and an idea began to form in his mind.

Would it work?

No. It wouldn't.

Not in a hundred years.

And yet, nothing else was coming to him.

He pulled a white canvas drop cloth out of the dumpster and noticed an empty paint can labeled *alabaster white*. He fished out the can and when he pried it open, he discovered a bit of paint at the bottom. Another look inside the dumpster revealed a metal thing shaped like a T-square with an unusually wide cross member. He wasn't sure of its purpose, but it might just do the trick.

Or not.

He stared at the junk he'd assembled.

The idea was absurd and not worth a second thought.

Do it, a voice seemed to whisper.

No way, he whispered back.

He continued toward the rear of the building but stopped to look back at the dumpster.

What other option did he have?

He returned for the paint can, the drop cloth and the T-shaped thing and carried them to the front of the building. Using the window as a mirror, he ripped off his hoodie and tee-shirt and smeared alabaster white across his chest, arms, and face.

This had to work. There was no time to cook up another plan.

He stuck the T-shaped thing in the back of his jeans and positioned it so the cross beam came just to his shoulders. It was tricky to arrange the white drop cloth over the T-square and secure it at his neck, but somehow he managed. That left his arms free while the canvas remained stretched out like wings.

Sort of.

As a final touch, he stuck the flashlight in the front of his pants with the light aimed beneath his chin.

He gazed at his image in the window.

Not exactly the Archangel Gabriel. More like a zombie or a kid in a cheesy, homemade Halloween costume.

His heart sank. This stunt would get them all killed.

But he had no other plan, so he'd have to see this one through. It would either succeed spectacularly or he'd soon be dead.

Thirty-two

David spit out something that tasted like blood. He opened his eyes and looked at his surroundings. What was he doing lying in the mud and muck? He'd been going somewhere, but he couldn't remember where. And then it came back to him. Dr. Roberts was waiting to be rescued.

He moved his arms one at a time. After that he tried his legs. Everything seemed to be working, but it was a few seconds before he could coordinate his limbs and struggle to his feet. A dizzy spell washed over him, and he braced himself against a tree until his equilibrium returned.

He chastised himself for his weakness and staggered forward, slowly this time to avoid another tumble. And then he heard footsteps off in the night. Had Brooke's uncle regained his strength and come to join him?

A light flashed through the darkness and a man's voice splintered the silence. "Hands above your head and no funny business."

He felt his knees go weak. The thugs had found him and all his efforts had been for nothing. Had they found Nelson Roberts as well? And if so, what were they going to do with him? Would they use him to lure Brooke out of hiding, as she'd feared.

"Hands up," the strident voice repeated. "I haven't got

all night."

He raised his hands in the air and turned around, ready to stare down the devil. But it wasn't a devil who greeted him. It was a couple of cops.

"That's my house back there," he told them, pointing toward the flames. "And over there.." he gestured in the direction of the spot where he'd left Nelson Roberts, "there's an old man out there among the trees. I was going for help."

One of the cops flashed his light in the direction David had indicated. "Show us where you last saw him."

They trudged off together into the gloom, but when they arrived at the fallen tree, Nelson Roberts was nowhere to be seen. David looked around, dismayed. "He was right here. He must have wandered off."

The cops swept the area with their lights, and as the river came into view, David was overcome by a fresh wave of despair. There was no way the old man could survive an encounter with those raging waters.

"We'll call for backup," one of the officers shouted over the roar of the current. "If he's in these woods, we'll find him."

The strength seemed to drain from David's body. Brooke had trusted him with her uncle, and he'd failed. He thought of the weary hours that lay ahead. Dawn would bring gray, somber skies and a lifeless body washing up downstream from where they now stood. How would he ever face her again?

He accompanied the officers on their search, paying little attention to the icy chill that numbed his bones. They trudged through the mud and muck and finally came to a stop at the river's edge where they were joined by a third officer.

"We've just called off the search," the officer announced somberly.

David's heart sank. It was too late. Someone had found the body.

The officer gestured for them to follow, and after what seemed like an eternity, the lights of the neighbor's house blazed into view. The sight of Earl Martin standing on the rear deck with his dog told David all he needed to know. Earl had stumbled upon Nelson Robert's body while walking his dog. He called the police who were waiting for David to identify the remains.

They climbed the steps to the deck and entered the house by way of the kitchen. Once inside, David's knees buckled and he braced himself against a counter, watching in dismay as muddy puddles formed on the floor around his feet.

"I'm a mess," he apologized.

His neighbor clapped him on the shoulder. "Don't give it a thought. We've got hardwood floors throughout, and they're easy to mop up. Having said that, I'd appreciate it if you'd avoid the rugs if at all possible. Now, if you'll follow me..."

Earl escorted them down a corridor to the front of the house. Ahead of them a female officer stood guard at a door on their left. David turned his face away. He didn't know if he could go through with this.

"Are you okay?" Earl asked.

He nodded. But he wasn't okay, and he was pretty sure he'd never be okay again.

Even so, he summoned whatever was left of his strength and entered the room.

There by the fire was the body of Nelson Roberts, the man David had left to fend for himself in the cold and dark.

But the body was sitting up and smiling. And fully clothed in clean pants, a shirt and a sweater, all of which seemed a bit too large for his spare frame. On his feet were thick, dry socks.

For a moment, David was speechless. "I thought that...I mean, the police said...that is, they didn't exactly say, but I assumed..."

He crossed the room in long strides, and without considering his muddy clothes, dropped to the rug beside the old man's chair.

"We have Gretchen to thank for finding him," Earl Martin

said. He nodded toward the Golden Retriever whose eyes gleamed at the sight of so many friendly faces. "I took her outside to do her business, but when I tried to bring her back to the house, it was clear she had something else in mind. I followed her lead, and that's when we came upon Dr. Roberts."

Nelson Roberts cast a warm smile at the individuals gathered around him. "It's been a hellish ordeal, but here I am among a host of angels, including a four-legged one who came to my rescue."

At that, the dog wagged her tail as though acknowledging her role in the evening's drama.

The charming moment was interrupted by the sound of fists beating on the front door, followed a second later by EMT's barreling into the room. They checked Nelson Roberts' vital signs, and in spite of his insistence that he was perfectly comfortable by the fire, they strapped him onto a stretcher. As they wheeled him out of the room, he placed a hand on David's arm. "My niece," he said softly. "Have you heard from her?"

"No, but that doesn't mean anything. I left my phone in the house—remember?"

Once Nelson Roberts was deposited in the ambulance, a second wave of EMTs invaded the room. This time they closed in on David.

He didn't argue with them. Now that his house was in ruins he needed a safe haven for the night. The hospital ER wasn't exactly a luxury hotel, but it would do in a pinch.

▼ ▼ ▼

Ted inched toward the rear of the deserted tavern. A quick glance showed him that things had changed dramatically since he'd made his mad dash to the Devil's Inn. Brooke and Jenny stood next to the van with their hands in the air, listening to whatever Elena Voss was telling them. Meanwhile, Jenny's shotgun lay useless on the ground while the two thugs stood guard, their weapons raised and ready to fire. The sight filled Ted with a helpless rage. He should be doing something. Something meaningful instead of this crazy stunt he was about to pull.

He breathed a prayer into the night, but there was no response. Not audibly anyway. Instead a verse came back to him.

No greater love has any man than that he lay down his life for his friends. The Savior had laid down his life, and so had countless martyrs in countless arenas over twenty centuries. Maybe it was Ted's turn to step up to the plate.

He emerged from the shadows, raised his arms, and with the flashlight triggered on his face, he spoke the words in the secret language he'd listened to earlier in the day: John Dee's message carved on the back of the phoenix medallion: *I have come to open the mysteries of creation.*

▾ ▾ ▾

Elena spun around. What was that chanting sound?

The creature she beheld was male with unnaturally white skin. His torso was illuminated by an otherworldly glow that seemed to begin in his abdomen and travel upward, spiraling through his chakras and escaping at the top of his head.

It was him.

The angel John Dee and countless others had tried to conjure.

She took a few steps back and turned to look at the others. Yes. They saw it too. It wasn't just a vision within her mind but an actual celestial being who'd slipped through the veil to enter the earthly realms She'd beheld countless entities in her hypnotic trances. Slippery, ethereal things made of moonlight and mist, but never this. Never before had she witnessed something of substance descending from the higher realms to manifest in physical reality.

The creature in front of her was glowing.

Translucent.

Brilliant.

She now understood the reason for the many detours that had dogged her steps in the last few months. It was all for this moment. She'd been directed here to experience an encounter with an angelic being, Surely this meant she'd been chosen to possess the medallion.

She moved toward it, and when she spoke in John Dee's secret language, the creature called back in the same tongue: *I have come to open the mysteries of creation.*

She approached worshipfully, awestruck and ready to pay homage.

"Come no closer," the angel commanded. "Fall to your knees in reverence."

And so she did. Head bowed. Eyes closed.

She heard a noise behind her. Shouts. Groans. Her eyes flew open and when she looked back, she saw her guards on the ground, writhing in agony. What was going on?

She looked, perplexed, at her angelic visitor. What was he holding in his hands? Why in the world would an angel be wielding a gun?

▾ ▾ ▾

Burleigh stuck the taser back in his belt. He and Radley had left their car on the side of the road and approached the abandoned tavern on foot. Meanwhile, officers waited just out of sight, ready to respond when needed.

He looked at the scene spread out before him. Who these people were and how this mess with the helicopter and the strange looking guy in white had come to be was beyond him, but he'd figure it out later. What mattered now was disarming the creeps with the heavy artillery.

In seconds he and Radley had the men in cuffs. Once they were secured, Burleigh phoned for back-up, and in no time at all, state and local squad cars came roaring into the parking lot, their lights flashing in the murky darkness.

His attention was diverted by a shaft of light as the helicopter began a turbulent ascent. At the same moment, the odd-looking creature in white stepped out of the shadows and fired a shot that connected with the rotor on the chopper's tail. A second shot to the rotor sent the craft into a tailspin. The helicopter lurched spastically about ten feet from the ground and dropped to earth—not with a crash but with a dull thud.

"Go get him, cowboy," Burleigh told his sidekick. In less than a minute, Radley had the pilot in cuffs.

Meanwhile, a state cop dragged a tall guy with a beard out of the back of the van. The man's eyes met those of the woman who'd just been taken into custody, and for a brief moment, something seemed to pass between them. Then the man looked away, and the spell or whatever it had been, was broken.

▾ ▾ ▾

Ted watched the cops load Elena and her cohorts into their vehicles. "Confirmation bias," he explained. "Elena Voss expected an angel. I gave her an angel."

He listened to the expressions of approval. "An answer to prayer," he informed the others. "I can't take credit for Divine intervention."

Brooke glanced at Detective Burleigh. "I believe you're here to arrest me?"

He smiled. "Something like that. And I believe you have a medallion you'd like to give me."

Within minutes, the transaction was complete. But more than that, it was recorded and uploaded, and in a matter of minutes, it was making its way around the world.

Thirty-three

Detective Burleigh's white sedan rumbled to a stop in front of the house. Brooke was looking forward to his visit—there were still questions that needed to be answered.

A lot had happened in the two weeks since the night at the Devil's Inn. After spending exhausting hours with state and local authorities, she'd retrieved her impounded vehicle and headed to the hospital to be with her uncle. Following his discharge she'd rolled up her sleeves and helped put his apartment in order. Their time together had done them both good. They'd had the opportunity to tell their respective stories—many times over. David Price had joined them for dinner one evening, and his rendition of events had added dramatic embellishments to a narrative that was already dramatic. His historic home had been rendered uninhabitable, but at least it wasn't a total loss. Rebuilding would take time, and in the interim, he was staying with a friend while he sought temporary living quarters.

A few days ago Brooke had met Ted for coffee. Apparently Stokes was in big trouble with the Feds about tax evasion, but things were expected to be settled amicably. He'd already disappeared into the FBI's witness protection program, and Ted expected that he'd soon hear from him via the complex web of contacts through which Stokes operated. The conversation had ended on a pleasant note, and while Brooke saw the meeting as closure, she suspected that Ted hoped it might be more of a beginning rather than an ending. He'd told her to stay in touch, but she'd made no promises.

Somehow she'd found time during those two weeks to replace the sofa and chairs that had been slashed during the break-in. She'd sent some of the antiques off to auction, and the living room had a clean, spacious feeling that suited her as she prepared for putting the house on the market in the spring.

"The place looks great," Jason Radley said when Brooke showed him and Detective Burleigh inside. "A big difference from the first time I was here."

They availed themselves of the new seating and once the small talk was out of the way, Burleigh provided a brief rundown of what he'd learned about the phoenix medallion. It had been stolen in 1914 from a museum in Prague, a city where John Dee and his colleague had spent a good deal of time in the late fifteen-hundreds. The curators were looking forward to welcoming it home.

As far as recent history was concerned, late last winter Elena Voss had hired a female proxy to steal the medallion from the mansion of a grand master of an occult fraternity. When the proxy failed to deliver, Ms Voss retaliated by arranging the woman's death. Her body had turned up late last March in a dumpster in Newark. She must have slipped the medallion into a Salvation Army drop box and that's how it ended up in the thrift shop where Karl Erikson had purchased it. After Karl showed it to Mordecai Simmons, Ezra Simmons alerted Ms. Voss to its whereabouts, thus setting off the chain of events with which Brooke was familiar.

"So the case is closed?" she asked. "Elena and her people will be going to jail?"

Burleigh cast a sideways glance at his colleague. "Ms. Voss and her lackeys have been charged with numerous crimes, among them the murder I just alluded to. There is, however, insufficient evidence to link her or her people to either your husband's death or the break-in. We know that they surveilled your property with the intent of stealing the medallion, but the plan was never executed because someone apparently beat them to it."

"Someone beat them to it?" Brooke echoed. "Who?"

"That's what we'd like to find out."

She found the answer unacceptable. "So you're telling me we're back to square one?"

"Not entirely. The medallion is no longer an issue, but to your point, the central questions remain unanswered."

Brooke turned her face away. How was such a thing possible? She still didn't know if Karl's death was accidental or if he'd been murdered. And the break-in—was it related to his death or had the timing been purely coincidental?

The detectives departed, leaving her with an uneasiness she'd hoped was a thing of the past. Her apprehension increased as the hours passed. She checked the video monitor several times and made an inspection of the house to make sure the doors and windows were locked. In her office she noticed the antiwar buttons lying in the wastebasket where she'd tossed them the day before. One had been entombed with Sid Hewitt's dog. The other had been stashed away in the antique desk. Why had such pains been taken to hide them?

She fished them out and laid them on her desk next to the computer keyboard. She had nothing better to do, so she began an online search for the image of a fist superimposed over a tank. At six that evening she still hadn't found a match. She made a sandwich and returned to her task—surely there had to have been an organization in the area that used the symbol. By ten o'clock she'd found none and was tired and cranky and had nothing to show for her hours in front of the screen.

She put on pajamas and settled down in bed with a book. Unable to concentrate, she laid it aside, but at one in the morning she was still awake and staring at the ceiling. Frustrated, she threw off the covers and went back to the computer to resume her search. Two hours later she stumbled on a decades-old newspaper article that described an antiwar button found near the scene of a fire. The story sounded familiar, and by the end of the piece, she recognized the narrative from David Price's account of the history of the Tudor Revival structure that housed the offices of the Tri-County Historical Conservancy.

The details were all there:

- A mansion owned by an entrepreneur with ties to the military-industrial complex.
- A late-night rendezvous between the man's daughter and her boyfriend in a garden shed.
- A fire that destroyed the shed and took both young lives.
- A single piece of evidence near the scene: an antiwar button with a fist superimposed upon a tank.

The authorities had never determined if the button belonged to the deceased young woman, her deceased male companion, or to radicals who might have set the shed on fire to make an antiwar statement. Interestingly, the tragedy had occurred the year Karl was a senior in high school. He and his friends had been pacifists. Retro hippies in an age of disco and mood rings, he used to say. Was it possible Karl had known something about this incident? Would his senior yearbook offer a clue?

Brooke left her office and crossed the living room to Karl's study, her hands trembling as reached for the door. The room was bathed in moonlight, its silvery glow illuminating the bookshelves and making the titles easy to read. After a bit of searching she found three yearbooks, but not the one from Karl's senior year. That was odd. He used to enjoy paging through it from time to time, and she couldn't imagine where he might have put it.

She searched again, starting on the top shelf, but by the time she arrived at the bottom, she still hadn't located it, so she repeated the process. After the third attempt, she accepted that it was missing.

At the same time a phrase crossed her mind, one that had become meaningful in the last few weeks.

Confirmation bias.

Everyone—the detectives included—had assumed that whoever had ransacked the house had been searching for the medallion. But what if confirmation had pointed them in the wrong direction? What if the object of the search had not been a priceless medallion but a high school yearbook and an antiwar button made of tin?

Ridiculous, she told herself. She was tired, it was late, and her imagination was working overtime. She went to the window, and gazed up at the laughing moon. As she did, a thought occurred to her. Jeremy Stokes had been forced to flee because of the secrets he possessed. Had Karl been in danger for a similar reason.

She went to the kitchen and made coffee. She'd get no sleep tonight.

▾ ▾ ▾

At a little after ten the next morning, Brooke left her car along the side of the road and headed through the trees on foot. It was 10:15, and according to the schedule posted online, Janine's therapeutic yoga class and Greg's past life regression session were well underway.

She entered The Center for the Mystic Healing Arts through the back door near the parking lot and glanced down the hallway toward the classrooms. The fragrance of incense hung heavily in the air, and she could hear Janine's voice over the ethereal music accompanying the yoga session. The door to Greg's office was closed.

She'd been to the Greenwood's home for Stephi and Brett's college and grad school graduation parties. On one of those occasions, Karl and Janine had gotten her year books out to reminisce about their glory days. The moment had been awkward for Brooke, but that didn't matter now. What mattered was that she knew where they were kept.

She tiptoed across the vestibule to the door separating the business from the residence. Finding it unlocked, she opened it and made her way down the carpeted hallway to the library with its walls of books. She scanned the contents of the shelves, conscious of the seconds ticking by. Mythology. Energetic healing. Ascended masters. Astral travel. And on the bottom shelf—four yearbooks. She pulled out the one she was interested in and placed it on the desk.

She glanced at Karl and Janine's senior portraits. Nothing there, so she turned to the activities section. Sports. Student council. Band. Debate society. Yes—there was Karl engaged in what looked to have been a heated debate. She found a picture of Janine as the editor of the literary magazine. Next to it was a shot of Karl painting sets for the spring musical. No buttons in any of those pictures. She turned the page and found a photo of Karl, Janine and Sid Hewitt as members of the newspaper staff. All three wore some kind of button, but only Janine's clearly was visible. Brooke made a quick comparison. Yes, it was identical.

So what did it mean? Sid buried a button with his dog. Karl buried one in the antique desk. And Janine?

There was no time to puzzle over it now. She'd show the picture and the antiwar buttons to Detective Burleigh and let him and his team sort things out. She picked up the yearbook and started for the door, but froze when she heard a door open and close out in the hall. She glanced around the room. There was nowhere to hide. Not a closet. Not even drapes to duck behind.

Janine appeared in the doorway and drew back, startled. Her eyes drifted to the yearbook tucked beneath Brooke's arm. "What in the world are you doing here?"

Brooke had to think fast to come up with a convincing story. "I wanted to look up something in Karl's yearbook at home. I couldn't find it and I wondered if you'd let me borrow yours. I was planning to wait here and ask you once your class was over."

"Surely you could have called."

"I was passing by and decided to stop in. An impulse, I suppose."

Janine shifted her gaze to Brooke's clenched fist.

"What's in your hand?"

"Nothing."

"Show me."

"It's nothing."

Janine lunged, her nails like claws prying Brooke's fingers apart. The buttons fell to the floor, and in an instant Janine scooped them up, her normally placid face filled with fury.

"How long have you known?"

"Known what?"

"Don't play Little Miss Innocent with me. I'll bet Karl laid it on thick, didn't he?"

"I don't know what you're talking about."

"The fire!" Janine blurted out. "Karl and Sid wanted to paint antiwar graffiti, but I told them graffiti wasn't enough—a fire would make a stronger statement. I didn't know those kids were in the shed. They were sophomores—their pictures are in the yearbook. The school was in mourning for weeks afterward. Do you have any idea what it was like going through all that knowing I killed them?"

Janine took a step closer, her eyes dark and threatening as she backed Brooke into the space between the bookshelves and the desk.

"We swore a blood oath to tell no one. For decades everything was fine until Karl started talking about repentance. 'Go ahead—repent', I told him. '*Just leave me out of it.*' But confessing his sins to God wasn't good enough for him. Oh no, he intended to confess the whole thing to the police.

"I had to stop him—you see that, don't you? I followed him after one Sunday to that spot in the woods he liked so much. I begged him to honor his pledge, but you know Karl. His mind was made up.

"Naturally I was upset," she continued, her voice petulant, like that of a whining child, "so I gave him a shove. A little shove—like people do when they're angry. I never intended for him to tumble down the embankment, and I never intended for him to die. None of that was my intention just like it wasn't my intention to harm anyone all those years ago and just like none of this is my intention now, but you showed up and drove me to it."

Her eyes darted wildly around the room and came to rest on a bronze Buddha squatting on the desk. She picked it up, but instead of channeling its serenity, she raised it above her head and brought it crashing down, missing Brooke's skull but striking her shoulder with sufficient force to throw her off balance. And then Janine came at her, using the Buddha as a battering ram. The impact knocked Brooke to the floor, and in an instant Janine was on top of her, holding a cord from an electronic device against her neck.

"When the police ask," she hissed, "I'll tell them I found an intruder crouched on the floor with her back toward me. I'll tell them I panicked and tried to defend myself. When I realized who it was, it was too late."

Brooke tried to voice her outrage, but with the cord pressed against her throat, breathing was difficult and words were impossible.

"After Karl was gone," Janine continued, "I started worrying that he'd left something in the house—the buttons, the yearbook, a letter of confession, a journal entry, something in writing that would reveal the secret. I waited for an opportunity to break in, but it wasn't until the retrospective that I had my chance. The trip to Philadelphia provided an alibi and the detectives never guessed that I'd left the city two hours earlier than what I told them. But after hours of searching, his year-book was the only thing I found. I burned it late that afternoon before Greg got home."

By now Janine's words seemed to be coming at Brooke from a distance. She needed air. Just a quick breath or two to clear her head. She tried to move, but was unable.

Faint sounds filtered through the mist.

"Where the devil are you?" a woman's voice trilled. "The class'll be over in five minutes."

"Go back!" Janine shouted. "This is a private residence."

"Oh, really? Well, I paid for this therapeutic yoga class and so did…"

The words were followed by a shriek. The ligature loos-ened, air flooded into Brooke's lungs and she watched as a large woman in yoga pants wrestled Janine for control of the cord. The woman was the stronger of the two, and within seconds she'd wrenched the cord away from Janine and was holding it out in front of her to keep her at bay.

Brooke reached for her phone, and within minutes the parking lot was aglow with red and blue flashing lights. A dozen therapeutic yoga students straggled out of their classroom, pointing and gasping at the sight of their instructor being es-corted from the building in cuffs. The students were joined by Greg Greenwood who shook his fist and shouted angry threats about attorneys, lawsuits and bad karma. Meanwhile, his past-life regressed client lingered on the sidelines, seemingly dis-oriented by his sudden return to the twenty-first century. Finally the cops hustled Janine into a waiting vehicle and spir-ited her away.

▾ ▾ ▾

Brooke listened as the ER physician explained that her shoulder was badly bruised but the x-rays had revealed no fractures. Thanks to the ligature, she'd have a sore throat for a week or so, and there was a high probability of nightmares and other adverse reactions to trauma. She didn't bother sharing the details of the last few weeks of trauma. It would have taken too long and she didn't have the time or the inclination.

Detective Burleigh put in an appearance, and his sidekick showed up a few minutes later. Burleigh had followed the ambulance to the ER while Jason Radley had kindly driven Brooke's car and left it in the hospital parking lot. They kept their questions brief out of regard for her ordeal. Mostly they wanted her to ID the evidence that consisted of two vintage antiwar buttons, a decades-old senior yearbook, a cord from an electronic charging device, and a blunt force object in the form of the Buddha.

Once the questioning was concluded, Brooke signed out of the ER and went to find her car. She'd promised Uncle Nelson that she'd meet him at his apartment for afternoon tea and she didn't want to keep him waiting.

Acknowledgements

I would like to thank Carol Billman, Jenny Fujita, Marielena Zuniga, David Kempf, Mike Gerow and Marlene's Thursday night group for their insightful comments at various stages of this project. Thanks also to Christie Distler for her professional critique and to Linda King and Sandra Carey Cody for their pep talks and encouragement over the years. Kudos to my son, Jon Labs, for developing my website, and special thanks to my husband, tech writer and editor, Wayne Labs, for his talent and endless patience in creating the cover and handling the layout, editing and numerous publishing details.

A final note of gratitude to "the Still Small Voice" that directed my research in ways I'd never anticipated. It's been quite a journey.

About the Author

Nancy Labs is an author, artist, editor and writing coach as well as a former English and theater teacher. She lives with her husband in Bucks County, PA. *Wishing You Harm* is the first novel in the Brooke Roberts mystery and suspense series. Visit her website: www.nancylabs.com

Author's Note:

The 12 phoenix medallions described in this story are entirely fictional. If such objects ever existed, I am unaware of it.

In the Summer

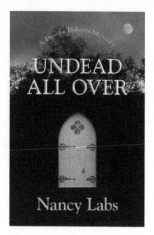

Undead All Over

The first rehearsal of Dracula goes off without a hitch—except for a corpse staring up at Brooke from a closet floor

It's not just any corpse. The victim is Nina Powell, a stunningly beautiful African American feminist and an art instructor at an elite academy for the progeny of the rich and powerful. The grief-stricken students thought Nina was amazing. Their parents, the school board and the cops—not so much.

Outraged by rumors that the police are intentionally bungling the investigation, Brooke decides to do some investigating of her own. Before long she's face-to-face with a white supremacist hate group, a bombastic radio talk show host and a vampire cult engaged in mysterious midnight rituals. Meanwhile, the killer is out there in the night, and like Dracula, he, she or it is thirsty for blood.

In the Fall!

Face Down in the Gene Pool

Brooke can think of lots of things she'd like to do on the first day of spring. Finding Jenna Henley's body in a fishpond isn't one of them.

At least the police have a suspect. Jenna left the genealogy conference with her ex-lover. Three hours later she's dead. Clearly, her ex-lover is the culprit.

Or is he?

Brooke has no desire to get mixed up in the police investigation, but her curiosity gets the better of her when certain themes keep rising to the surface: Ancestral secrets. Ancient bloodlines. Genetic modifications intended to reshape life on earth. The stream of evidence has more twists and turns than a strand of DNA. Before long, she's is in over her head and gasping for air in a gene pool that's deeper and murkier than she'd dared to imagine.